THE
BABYLON
AGENDA

Copyright © 2024 by Rob Jones

All rights reserved. No part of this publication may be used, reproduced, distributed or transmitted in any form or by any means, electronic, mechanical, photocopying, recording or otherwise, without the prior written permission of the author or publisher, except in the case of brief quotations embodied in critical reviews and certain other non-commercial uses permitted by copyright law.

THE BABYLON AGENDA is a work of fiction. All names, characters, places and occurrences are entirely fictional products of the author's imagination or are used fictitiously. Any resemblance to current events or locales, or to persons living or dead, is entirely coincidental.

This book is sold subject to the condition that it shall not, by way of trade or otherwise, be lent, re-sold, hired out or otherwise circulated in any form of binding or cover other than that in which it is published and without a similar condition including this condition being imposed on the subsequent purchaser.

ISBN: 9798332010224

Other Books by Rob Jones

The Joe Hawke Series
The Vault of Poseidon (Joe Hawke #1)
Thunder God (Joe Hawke #2)
The Tomb of Eternity (Joe Hawke #3)
The Curse of Medusa (Joe Hawke #4)
Valhalla Gold (Joe Hawke #5)
The Aztec Prophecy (Joe Hawke #6)
The Secret of Atlantis (Joe Hawke #7)
The Lost City (Joe Hawke #8)
The Sword of Fire (Joe Hawke #9)
The King's Tomb (Joe Hawke #10)
Land of the Gods (Joe Hawke #11)
The Orpheus Legacy (Joe Hawke #12)
Hell's Inferno (Joe Hawke #13)
Day of the Dead (Joe Hawke #14)
Shadow of the Apocalypse (Joe Hawke #15)
Gold Train (Joe Hawke #16)
The Last Warlord (Joe Hawke #17)
Scorpion Island (Joe Hawke #18)
The Midnight Syndicate (Joe Hawke #19)
The Poseidon Vendetta (Joe Hawke #20)

The Avalon Adventure Series
The Hunt for Shambhala (Avalon Adventure #1)
Treasure of Babylon (Avalon Adventure #2)
The Doomsday Cipher (Avalon Adventure #3)

The Hunter Files
The Atlantis Covenant (Hunter Files #1)
The Revelation Relic (Hunter Files #2)
The Titanic Legacy (Hunter Files #3)
The Excalibur Code (Hunter Files #4)
The Archangel's Sword (Hunter Files #5)

Standalone Fiction
Plagues of the Seven Angels (A Cairo Sloane Adventure)
The Armageddon Protocol (A Harry Bane Thriller)
The Raiders (A Jed Mason Adventure)

The Jed Mason Series
The Vatican Code (A Jed Mason Thriller)
The Illuminati Secret (A Jed Mason Thriller)
The Babylon Agenda (A Jed Mason thriller)

The Mason Files
The Alchemy Code (Mason Files #1)
The Inferno Sanction (Mason Files #2)
The Labyrinth Key (Mason Files #3)

The Bill Blake Series
The Operator (Bill Blake #1)
Against The Machine (Bill Blake #2)
Never Look Back (Bill Blake #3)

The DCI Jacob Mystery Series
The Fifth Grave (A DCI Jacob Mystery)
Angel of Death (A DCI Jacob Mystery)
The Ferryman (A DCI Jacob Mystery)

THE BABYLON AGENDA

JED MASON 3

ROB JONES

Dedication

For my family

"Three may keep a secret, if two of them are dead."
— **Benjamin Franklin**, *Poor Richard's Almanack.*

Chapter 1

Marcus Beausire lurched violently forward, only just stopping himself from tumbling over the stone parapet wall and falling to his death below. He paused in terror, drawing shallow, panicked breaths from the damp, stagnant air around him, and glanced up at his pursuers. He could not see them but heard the sound of their footsteps as they hurried down the spiral staircase towards him and it turned his blood to ice.

He was in the Masonic Initiation Well, in the Quinta da Regaleira, Sinta, Portugal, Midnight, just where the Conclave had asked to meet him, but the meeting had not gone well. Now, they meant to kill him. He went on down the steps, his left hand gripping the moss-streaked stone parapet wall to steady himself and reduce the risk of tripping and tumbling forward. His hunters would be on him before he could stagger up onto his old, aching knees. This much he knew was true, as was the fact of the brutal and bloody death he would suffer in their hands if they caught him. This was after all the price each one of the Fellowship knew he would pay for betraying the Conclave. He understood better than anyone else what befell those who broke their sacred vows and tried to bring light into the darkness.

He stopped for a moment and glanced over the balustrade, to see how far he was from the bottom. His lifelong vertigo now attacked him mercilessly, causing his heart to palpitate and sweat to bead on his forehead as he swayed back and forth, looking down at the floor which seemed almost to zoom up and down, as his panic-stricken mind played the most terrible of tricks on him. It was impossible to tell when running down the circular stairs but as he peered over the edge, he was able to see the ground was still so far away. He calculated that he would be lucky to reach the bottom before his pursuers caught up with him unless he speeded up, not easy for a man of his age and poor health. Continuing with his task of sprinting away from the men behind him, he concentrated hard not to take a tumble and gradually developed a rhythm where he was able to leap two steps at a time. For a moment, he thought he might make it and his heart felt a moment's flurry of relief, but it was not to be long-lived.

He reached for his chest and for one terrifying moment thought he had lost the tiny golden amulet that had hung around his neck for so many years. When he finally found it with his fingers, he gave a silent prayer of thanks as he continued to escape down the spiral stairs. The irony of his final journey was not lost on him. While the influence of Dante Alighieri on the Quinta da Regaleira was often overstated, he was still more than aware of the similarities to the great author's most famous work, *Divine Comedy*, particularly the symbolic descent into the depths as he continued running down the spiral stairs, also known to history as the famous Masonic Initiation Well. Designed by Carvalho Montero, the Initiation Well, like other parts of the estate, was a beautifully ornate and sublime example of the work of the period, and represented the concepts of transformation and rebirth. Beausire's descent into the bleak darkness at the bottom of the well symbolised the soul's journey; he would have managed a grim smile if the situation were not so dire.

When he finally reached the end of the steps and found himself at the very bottom of the famous well, he knew by the sound of the proximity of his pursuers' steps that he had only seconds to live. They had invited him here under the pretext of some kind of discussion – a negotiation perhaps in which they could discuss his terms of surrender. That was his fault too, because he had given them the impression that he might be willing to come back into the fold and give up what he knew, perhaps even betray the Fellowship. He knew as soon as he had floated even the vaguest notion of this that there was no way that he could go through with such a thing and the argument that had just broken out at the top of the Initiation Well had sealed his fate. He knew now that they meant to kill him and there would be no talking his way out of it.

Reaching up to his neck, he loosened his tie even further, then pulled it completely free before undoing the next two buttons on his shirt. Then he reached inside his shirt and released the strange golden amulet from around his neck. He brought it up to his eyes, staring at it in horror as he held it in his trembling hands. This was his only chance to fulfil his destiny but he had to act fast. While he had prayed this moment would never come, like the rest of the Fellowship, he knew there was always the possibility of this happening and with that in mind, each of them had agreed this course of action. He now dropped to his knees and with the amulet still held in his trembling hand, he got to work with seconds to spare.

As the men made the final few steps in their dogged pursuit of him, he staggered to his feet having fulfilled his duty, and turned to face them.

"I know you're going to kill me!" he said, his voice trembling.

"Then that makes what we must do much easier."

The man who had talked stepped forwards and pulled a dagger from a shoulder holster, hidden out of sight beneath his suit jacket. The other two men behind him were each aiming pistols at him, but Beausire knew it would be the dagger that dispatched him into the next world. Inside the Conclave some rules were more important than others, but this was the most important rule of all. Live by the sword, die by the sword – or in this case, an elaborate silver dagger, covered in Masonic symbols.

"You don't have to kill me," Beausire said. "I could make a vow of silence."

"Not this again, Marcus. We just went through it. You had your chance to come back into the Conclave, but the price was to betray the rest of the Fellowship, something which you are not willing to do. Now you will pay the price for your treachery."

"No, please! I mean it!" Beausire said. "I will renew all my vows and come back into the Conclave. I will start at the initiation again – right here in this sacred place!"

"I think not," the man said. "We know the value of your vows, Marcus. We know the value of all three of your so-called Fellowship of Light. All three of you are worthless traitors."

"We are not traitors! What we are doing is for the good of the Conclave. Can't you see that? We are fighting to ensure our survival and to bring light to the world!"

The man laughed, taking one step closer to Beausire – the silver dagger still gripped in his right hand. "We are not here to bring light to the world. We are here to protect the world from something which they will never understand. The attempt of you and your Fellowship to bring enlightenment to the world was a profound mistake. What you did was the most poisonous treachery imaginable and will never be forgiven by the Conclave."

"And that is why you killed Philippe Laroche?"

"Philippe Laroche was as much of a despicable traitor to the Conclave as the rest of your Fellowship. In fact, as your leader, his treachery was even more egregious. He was executed according to our law. He, like you and the rest of you, knew what he was getting into when he joined the Conclave, especially when he became such a senior member. Your breakaway group – your Fellowship – was completely unlawful in the first place, although the Grand Guardian probably would have tolerated it had you dissolved it when first asked."

"If that is how the Grand Guardian feels then let me go!"

"That is how the Grand Guardian felt about you forming a circle within a circle. Unfortunately, for you, it is not how he feels about the purpose of your Fellowship. Your desire to betray us in the most profound way possible and bring our greatest secret into the light of the world, under the scrutiny of every living soul in this world, was a profound betrayal. The Grand Guardian has therefore ordered the execution of all three of you. Laroche went first. That leaves you and your friend in California."

"Is there no way I can successfully plead for my life?"

"There is no way, Marcus. The secrets in the Tower will remain in the Tower. Make your peace and say your final prayers."

Beausire suddenly understood the profound grimness of this moment at the bottom of the Initiation Well. He knew his life had come to an end and he knew that Laroche had already been murdered – probably at his home in Paris. Now, he too was to be killed for what the Conclave called an act of treachery, but something of which he was extremely proud. He prayed these men did not know of the

Fellowship's final plan, because if they did not, there was a way that he could still defeat them from beyond the grave.

He now took a final step back until he felt the wall behind him brush up against his back. There was nowhere to run in this tiny space. As the man walked closer to him, still brandishing the dagger, Beausire looked up to the top of the well, nine storeys high, and saw the full moon gradually shifting into view. Its light glinted on the dagger in the man's hand as he drove it under his ribs. Beausire had felt nothing like this in his entire life and was horrified by the brutal ferociousness as the man continued to stab him over and over again. The man's fist, holding the dagger's handle, rammed up against his stomach and winded him as the blade deeply penetrated his insides. When the deed was done, the Conclave assassin stopped and stepped away, wiping the dagger on Beausire's suit as he slumped down to the floor, first on his hands and knees before rolling over onto his side and crashing down onto the tiles. They felt cool on his cheek and he felt his blood running out of him.

"You're a traitor, Beausire, but your treachery has ended here tonight."

Beausire was cradling his brutally slashed torso, now made sticky and slippery by the blood pumping out of him and spilling across the tiled floor at the bottom of the well. He felt his blood pressure dropping. He felt weak and dizziness began to overwhelm him. He prayed the senator would be able to evade these men better than he had, and then he closed his eyes and began to fade away. The last thing he heard was his killer performing the Conclave's ritual to the very end, just as they always did. Even a traitor received the Ave Maria.

"Ave Maria, gratia plena, Dominus tecum. Benedicta tu in mulieribus, et benedictus fructus ventris tui, Iesus. Sancta Maria, Mater Dei, ora pro nobis peccatoribus, nunc, et in hora mortis nostrae. Amen... Proditor!"

Proditor.

Traitor.

But then the traitor was no more.

Chapter 2

Wesley J. Baxter woke with a start.

Someone was calling his phone. He blinked, dazed and disoriented in the low morning light. Often when he woke, it was to find himself bathed in the neon blue glow of a large sign on the bar next door. He hated that light and the noise from the bar that sometimes kept him up until long past midnight, but he had nowhere else to go since he and his wife went their separate ways.

He reached for the phone, fumbled it and pushed it onto the floor. He cursed, pulled the blanket away and rolled off the old vinyl couch that had been his bed for longer than he cared to remember. He checked the time: nine in the morning. The phone was about to go to voicemail. He reached out and knocked it under the sofa. He cursed again.

A younger guy wouldn't have done that, man.

He picked up the phone.

"Baxter and Associates."

"Is that Mr Baxter?"

A woman's voice. She sounded like she was in her sixties and slightly nervous.

"Yes, this is Mr Baxter. How can I help?"

"My name is Charlotte Sullivan."

Baxter raised an eyebrow. "Senator Kent Sullivan's wife?"

"That is correct. I need your help."

"I'm listening."

"No, in person. I will only discuss this matter in person."

"I'm working in the office all day," he said. It was a lie, of sorts. The truth was work had grown extremely thin of late, but he wanted to give the impression of being in demand. "Shall we say, just after lunch?"

"I'll be there at one."

She hung up without another word. Baxter was intrigued, but he was also hungry, so he decided to take a short walk across the street and down the block to buy some chilli-crunch shrimp pasta and a strawberry lemonade from the Cheesecake Factory on North Beverly Drive. He'd worked his way down the menu a long time ago, and this was one of his favourites. Cooking was something Baxter had never ventured to learn and when he separated from his wife, the local food outlets all saw a substantial uptick in their quarterlies.

Baxter's office was situated in the heart of Beverly Hills, a stone's throw from the hustle and bustle of Rodeo Drive. It was a good place which was just as well, because for now at least he was also living there, out of a cheap suitcase resting on top of one of his filing cabinets in the back office, out of sight of the clients. *Gotta keep up appearances,* he always said.

When he turned the final corner he was surprised to see the woman he had presumably spoken to on the phone earlier already standing at his door. He walked over and greeted her.

"Hello, I'm Wesley Baxter."

"I'm Charlotte Sullivan. We spoke earlier about my husband."

Baxter didn't need a nudge to remember. Kent Sullivan was one of California's two serving senators. To say he was intrigued by why his wife had arranged a meeting with him today was the understatement of the century.

"Please, come in," he said.

He opened the lobby door and then led her up a flight of stairs to his office. He paused and hooked some keys from his suit pocket. "Just be a second."

The sign on the half-glass door read: BAXTER & ASSOCIATES – PRIVATE INVESTIGATORS. The 'associates' part, spelt out like the rest in gold-effect adhesive vinyl lettering, lent the impression to visitors, both casual and professional alike, that behind this well-worn door covered in scratches and scuffs, a team of battle-worn, experienced gumshoes could be found, busy working away in the fight against crime. This was more optimism than deceit on the part of Baxter, who for now, was running a one-man show. But these days, even optimism was in short supply.

Inside the suite, he walked her through to his private office and gestured for her to take a seat, then he padded around to his side of the desk and crashed down on his worn cloth swing chair.

"These days, I sigh more than the chair," he said with a smile. He opened up the carton of food and gestured at the pasta. "You want some?"

Mrs Sullivan never even looked at it. "No, thank you. I'd sooner get down to business."

Baxter sighed inwardly. He was hoping she might be hungry and that way they could have shared it. He didn't feel right eating it in front of her, so that meant no dinner. He pushed the box away and lightly mulled how well it would respond to microwaving. Not well, was his guess.

"Please, go ahead."

"This is delicate, Mr Baxter," she said. "My husband has disappeared and I'm very worried."

Baxter felt his pulse quicken. "Disappeared?"

"He went out last night and never returned. This is very unlike him, so I know something is wrong."

"All right, tell me more."

She paused. "I fear my husband may have become embroiled in something."

"Embroiled?"

"My husband serves on the Senate Appropriations Committee in Washington, specifically the Subcommittee on Defense. He is a very influential man, unfortunately, a little too influential if you understand me."

The Babylon Agenda

"I think I do," Baxter said. "Are you trying to tell me Senator Sullivan has been taking bribes?"

Mrs Sullivan went quiet for a moment and seemed to take some momentary solace by staring into her lap. When she surfaced, her face had hardened. "My husband is a good man, Mr Baxter, or at least he was. That damned city rotted his heart. Then there were the debts."

"Debts?"

"My husband ran on a platform of integrity and family values, but what the outside world never knew was he was greatly in debt. I'm concerned this might have something to do with his disappearance, but there was also his work. There was a new contract."

"Concerning?"

"I can't talk about it Mr Baxter – the contract that my husband was involved in is deep inside the realms of Top Secret."

"Then I'm not going to be able to help you," Baxter said. "When I leave this office on a case, I very often find myself in dangerous situations. Sometimes in life-threatening situations, Mrs Sullivan. That's because a private investigator's work can lead him into some pretty dark places. I won't be able to find your husband unless you are entirely honest with me from the very beginning. I hope you can understand that."

Mrs Sullivan took another moment down in her lap before looking back up and fixing her eyes on him. "Very well Mr Baxter, but I tell you this in the strictest confidence. First of all, let me make it clear that not even I am supposed to know about this. My husband told me when he was breaking down after a heavy drinking session, the same night he told me about the bribes."

"I understand, please continue – and rest assured that what you tell me in here will stay in here. I take confidences very seriously – they are my stock-in-trade, after all."

"My husband was dealing with a private defence contractor who has been working to create a state-of-the-art AI-guided unmanned aerial vehicle system which uses proprietary stealth technology to mask itself from various detection devices systems such as radar. Three companies are hoping to supply the US military with these vehicles. My husband has been receiving bribes from one of them to influence the decision of the Appropriations Committee. You'll understand that my husband is not only a very experienced and highly respected senator, Mr Baxter, but also served as a senior officer in the US Air Force. His views on the matter are central to the decision that the committee makes and that..."

"That is why he was approached in the first place."

"Evidently."

"And what's the cost of the contract, Mrs Sullivan?"

This time Mrs Sullivan got straight down to brass tacks with no demurring at all. "One billion dollars."

"One billion?" Baxter was quietly impressed with himself that he managed not to whistle.

The Babylon Agenda

"That is the total contract value," she continued, "but bear in mind the contract will cover nearly half a decade which would include the testing and production phases of the vehicle."

"And how much money was the bribe?"

"One per cent of the overall contract value."

Now he whistled. "Ten million dollars. That is a lot of money."

"They initially offered one million, but my husband pointed out the offer hardly reflected the risk he was taking with his career, not to mention the size of the profits the contractor would make supplying their vehicle to the military over who knows how many years."

"I'm glad your husband brought them up on their ethics."

"I don't need a morality lecture from you, Mr Baxter. I'm worried about my husband and I need someone whom I know is highly capable and also whom I can trust. Thanks to Sally Wilton you check both of those boxes."

Baxter was a little surprised to hear the Wilton name surface in this conversation, but on reflection, it was not so shocking. Sally Wilton had been married to one of the richest men in the world when she hired him to look into her husband's affair, and the Sullivans were the *crème de la crème* of Californian high society. That they knew each other was easy enough to accept. Now, he raised his palms in apology.

"I'm sorry, I shouldn't have said it. You've come here looking for help and you've been very honest about it as well. I apologise. But what I don't understand is why you think your husband's disappearance has anything to do with this bribe. What I mean to say is, Mrs Sullivan, the defence contractor is hardly going to make your husband disappear if they are relying on him to influence the Appropriations Committee and award the contract in their favour. To me, they're the very last people who would be responsible for anything happening to your husband."

Charlotte Sullivan let out a long, sad sigh. "That's because you still don't know all of the facts."

"I'm still listening."

"Kent's a good man. An honest man. He only started taking the bribes – they come in $100,000 increments – to pay off our debts, but he knew it was wrong. That was why he started drinking. He turned into a mess. Eventually, it broke him, and only then did some light break through the darkness. Then he knew what to do. He confronted the contractor and told them he was going to the authorities. He wanted to come clean, Mr Baxter. He wasn't afraid of going down and he was damn sure going to take the defence contractor down with him."

"Now I get it. You think they decided to silence him somehow?"

"I think so, yes." Tears rolled down her cheek, and Baxter opened his top drawer, pulled out a box of tissues and pushed them across the desk to her.

"Thank you," she managed. "I see you must do this a lot."

"Sadly, yes. Why have you come to me, Mrs Sullivan? You said your husband wanted to come clean. Why not go to the police and make it official?"

"Because I want to convince my husband to walk away with his dignity. He can tell the contractor he'll keep quiet about the bribe and everyone can go home happy. I know I can trust you – Sally persuaded me of that."

"Still, there are over four thousand private investigators in California," Baxter said. "Many of whom have far more sway and more staff and resources than I do."

"I already told you. Sarah Wilton recommended you. My husband taught me to keep things as quiet as possible. You've already worked with our sort."

With our sort, Baxter thought with interest. He was sceptical that the positive outcome Mrs Sullivan had just hoped might happen was possible, and instantly considered the possibility that the contractor might get nasty and blackmail Kent Sullivan. As it was, he decided to keep his mouth shut. They could cross that bridge if they came to it, but in the meantime, if Mrs Sullivan thought there was a chance to find and save her husband, he had no right to take away that hope. Plus, he'd be talking himself out of a job.

"All right. I'll take the case. I'll start looking for your husband right away."

This increased Charlotte Sullivan's tears and she snatched another fistful of tissues from the box to stem their flow down her cheeks. "Thank you, Mr Baxter. Sally said you would be able to help me."

"Then I'll get to work right away. First, I want you to tell me everything you can about the last time you saw your husband. You said he went out and never came back. Start there."

As Charlotte Sullivan began talking, Baxter brought out his notepad and got to work.

Chapter 3

Leonardo Snow did not have any friends, but if he did, they would have called him Leo, because that was how he always thought of himself. Leonardo was too formal. Too bookish. Not at all like him. His father, Montague Snow, was a failed abstract artist from north London who had named his three boys after the Greats – Michelangelo, Raphael and Leonardo. On reflection, Snow often thought he got off lightly. He was thinking that right now, as he poured himself a large Courvoisier brandy and strolled out to the balcony of his exorbitant luxury ski lodge in Aspen. He swirled the brandy in his glass and smiled wistfully at his late father's memory. The names weren't the only thing the old man had got wrong, but his mind soon turned to more pressing matters.

Like where did it all begin – with the building of the Temple or the building of the Tower?

He sipped the drink and turned to face a knock at his door.

"Enter."

A tall man came in. "Your guest is here, Mr Snow."

Snow stepped inside the room. "Bring him in."

They said the Temple, but he knew it was the Tower.

The man exited and returned a moment later with another tall man with a thick shock of brown hair, silver at the temples. He wore a smart grey suit and looked angry and confused.

"Senator Sullivan," Leonardo Snow said. "Good evening and welcome to White Fir Lodge."

The senator's eyes narrowed further with anger. He was a man with a fierce reputation in Congress and some had talked about him as a potential nominee for the party's presidential candidate. "Who are you and why have you done this to me?"

Snow poured another glass of brandy and offered it to the senator. Sullivan waved it away angrily. Snow shrugged, set the tumbler down in front of Sullivan and then strolled casually over to his window, taking in the breathtaking panorama of the snowcapped Rockies and beneath them, beautiful, pristine alpine slopes stretching gracefully down to the valley below.

"This is one of the best views in the entire region, Senator," Snow said. "I suppose you had an opportunity to enjoy it when your flight came to land here a few moments ago."

"To whom am I talking?" Sullivan demanded.

"My name is Leonardo Snow. You do not know who I am, yet."

"No, sir. But may I remind you that I am a senator of the United States Congress, Mr Snow. Under section 351 of Title 18, United States Code, it is a federal offence to kill or kidnap a member of Congress carrying a substantial sentence if found guilty, and — "

Snow talked over the top of him. "Senator Sullivan, none of this is of any concern to me, and you will understand why when I tell you who I am. If you'd like a clue, then let me tell you I will never let anyone inside the Tower."

Snow noted an instant change in Sullivan's countenance. His eyes widened, his face flushed. He swallowed hard and began fiddling with his hands.

"My God..."

"Not quite, but halfway there," Snow said. "I am the Grand Guardian of the Conclave of Darkness. You understand what this means."

Sullivan gave a single nod and now dipped his head, staring down at the floorboards between his John Lobb loafers. "It means I am a dead man."

"Indeed it does, Senator."

Snow turned and raised the glass to his lips, taking a good, rounded sip of the expensive brandy while looking out across the stunning mountainous view beyond his study window. "I'm reminded of Lucia Sergius Catalina – you're aware of this historical figure, I take it?"

"I am," Sullivan said. "He was a soldier and politician in ancient Rome."

"And a *traitor*," Snow said icily. "He was one of the main powers behind the Catilinarian conspiracy, a brutal coup d'état which attempted to remove Marcus Tullius

Cicero and Gaius Antonius Hybrida from power in 63 BC. Of course, it failed when Cicero exposed Catalina's treachery. The traitor fled Rome. He was eventually killed in battle in modern-day Tuscany, regaining a shred of honour. You will not be so lucky."

"I am no traitor!" Sullivan said. "All I want to do is give the world the gift that we have been hiding from it for so long!"

"That's what Beausire said," Snow said. "At least, something similar, right before Nocturnus killed him."

Sullivan's face scrunched up in confused anguish. "Wait, you're telling me that Marcus Beausire is dead?"

Snow nodded casually as if confirming nothing more important than the day's weather forecast. "I sent Sanguis, Nocturnus and Cerberus, three of my most loyal guardians to deal with the matter. He was executed a few short hours ago and Philippe Laroche is also dead, stabbed with a silver dagger, as Conclave Law dictates, in Paris less than twenty-four hours earlier. You are the last of the three. With you, the last dim, glimmer of the Fellowship of Light dies forever."

Sullivan was now staring back down at the floor, seemingly unable to comprehend what had happened and how fast it had happened. "How could you murder those men? They were good men and they wanted only the best for the world."

"They were traitors and thieves," Snow said. "In that regard, they were no different from you, Senator. And you will, in turn, suffer a similar fate as theirs. My second in command Necro is extremely keen to send you into the next world, but before he does, we have some business to attend to, do we not, Senator?"

"I don't know what you're talking about," Sullivan said.

"I think you do."

Sullivan went quiet. "Please, let me phone my wife before you kill me."

"I'm afraid I can't do that. You see, we know all about the Fellowship of Light – your little league of three traitors. Not only would I not be surprised if you had arranged a secret code to communicate what is happening here tonight with your wife, or whoever else you choose to telephone, I would be disappointed if you had *not* created such a thing. You have proved you cannot be trusted under any circumstances and in doing so you have forfeited your right to say goodbye to your loved ones. Now, to the other business. You will hand over anything else connected to your treachery."

"You're a bastard, Snow!"

"It has been said before, but it is no more than a matter of opinion and in your case the opinion of a man who will be dead within the hour. What I *can* offer you is the usual ritual murder of traitors in our organisation, which as you know means being stabbed to death with a silver dagger. You should be grateful for this because I could make your death last many hours of agonising pain and suffering before you're finally dispatched. Our Law allows such a thing and no one is a finer craftsman when it comes to this sort of thing than Necro here. Here are photographs of your fellow traitors."

Snow clicked his fingers and Necro showed the senator a series of images on his phone.

Sullivan nodded his head; he understood there was nothing he could do but accept his fate. He had known Marcus Beausire and Philippe Laroche extremely well, and he knew Marcus would probably have begged for his life. When he saw the photographs of Marcus and Phillipe's corpses, having died brutal stabbing murders just hours before, every last ounce of life drained out of his soul.

"I have nothing on me," Sullivan said. "Nothing relating to the Conclave."

"You're lying! Necro, please search our guest! Then take him outside and kill him. I don't want any of his blood on my floors – I just had them varnished and polished at extreme expense."

Snow now turned and addressed the senator for the last time. "Senator Sullivan, you have been found guilty by the Conclave of Darkness of the most egregious sin it is possible to commit against us – treachery. You betrayed us by unlawfully forming a breakaway group under the leadership of Philippe Laroche called the Fellowship of Light, whose only purpose was to steal our most closely guarded secret – the secret history of our world – and bring it into the light, allowing the people of this planet to understand the ultimate truth. For this, you have been duly found guilty and will be executed immediately, according to our Law. Your death will bring to a close the Fellowship of Light."

"Please! Is there anything I can do to change your mind?" Sullivan could hardly believe his own ears when he heard himself begging for his life. He had always promised himself this would never happen if he was ever in this position, but now faced with the certainty of his own brutal and bloody demise, he found the words tumbled from his lips, spilling over like so much water, almost uncontrollably, as if his soul was crying out of its own accord.

"Please Senator," Snow said. "Don't embarrass yourself like this. You were given a great honour by being elevated so highly inside the Conclave. You were brought inside the inner sanctum and showed the Secret of the Tower, and then you decided you wanted to take that secret and give it to the world. It was the most appalling betrayal of our trust to form the Fellowship of Light with those other two traitors and try and give the world our most profound secret. You must have understood it would always end like this if you betrayed us?"

Sullivan had no chance to respond.

Snow now watched as Necro, a large assassin of disconcertingly unknown provenance, grabbed hold of the senator by his shoulders, wheeled him around in a circle and walked him to the balcony doors. As he approached the door, another man in a black suit opened the door and stepped aside, allowing Necro to guide the senator outside onto the balcony.

Snow picked up his brandy glass and was enjoying another spicy, warm mouthful of the expensive spirit when something happened that profoundly shocked him. The senator, whom he had presumed had been terrified into total submission, had been fooling them all. He broke free from Necro's grip, sprinted to the balcony doors and landed a hefty left hook on the other man's face, knocking him over onto the floor. Then he ran out onto the balcony and vaulted powerfully over the rail, vanishing into the evening alpenglow.

Rather than anger, Snow felt a surge of excitement. The thrill of the hunt was on.

"Get up off the floor, Scorpio! You and Necro are to get after the senator. I don't want him to leave the property. Find him and kill him immediately!"

Chapter 4

Baxter caught his first break with the location of the wine merchant. They were based in Beverly Hills, the exact same part of Los Angeles where he now lived and worked. Their specific location was on the north side of Bedford Drive and now he pulled up in a parking space outside on the street, closed his door, fed the meter and took a long look at the place. Unsurprisingly, given its location and purpose, it was housed on the ground floor of a renovated historic building in Spanish revival architecture style. Baxter must have driven past this place a thousand times in all his years in the city but he'd never stopped to pay particular attention to upmarket wine merchants so this was the first time he had ever really seen it up close.

He locked his car and stepped into the shade of its cream-coloured door canopy. Written on it in gold were the words: DEVEREAUX WINE MERCHANTS. It looked like the kind of place that would be only too happy to relieve Baxter of most of his weekly pay for a couple of bottles of rare champagne.

He stepped inside and his presence was alerted to the owners by a subtle tinkling sound from the bell above the door. The shop exuded opulence exactly as he had expected it would. A place like this would count among its number some of the wealthiest people in the city, including many celebrities and even world-famous actors. There was parquet flooring polished so highly he could see himself in it like a mirror when he looked down at his shoes, which sadly were not polished. Endless collections of rare and expensive bottles of wine and champagne and sherry from around the United States and the rest of the world were neatly lined up on polished oak shelves. There was a tasteful and comfortable seating area in the corner – all leather studded chairs and fan palms – and the entire place was lit with a soft, low ambience from high-quality recessed downlighting.

As if by magic, a tall man with dyed blond hair in a style around twenty years too young for his face stepped out from behind a door and appeared behind the counter. Baxter saw the way he looked him up and down and watched his smile fade. It wasn't the first time Baxter had made that kind of impression on someone like Mr Devereux.

"May I be of assistance, sir?" the man asked.

Baxter noted a kind of unique mid-Atlantic accent that made him hard to place, that was so common in places like this. It was times like this when he wished he could flash his LAPD badge and finish the rest of this guy's smile off, but as it was, he had to take a more tactful approach.

"I'm hoping you can help me, Mr Devereux – I take it you *are* Mr Devereaux?"

"I am."

"Great," Baxter said with an affable smile. "I'm a private investigator working for a high-profile client who believes something happened to her husband and the last place he told her he was going was to your wine store to pick up some champagne for her sixtieth birthday. The problem is he never came home."

Baxter noticed the man's face grow more serious and his eyes were widening. "I see. I've never encountered anything like this before. We've had the police in here for various misdemeanours concerning certain customers, but never anything like this. High-profile, you say?"

Baxter wasn't surprised this was the detail that Mr Devereux was most interested in. "Yes. I presume a place like this is well covered with security cameras?"

"Well, yes it is, but it depends how far back you're talking about."

"Not far back at all – less than twenty-four hours."

"Then we would probably have that footage, but I'm not sure that I have any legal obligation to show it to you. No matter what's happened to your client, we have a duty of responsibility to our customers – quiet confidentiality and all that."

"I understand," Mr Devereux. "Before I was a private investigator I was a detective in the LAPD and I understand the law in this area very well. Accessing CCTV footage on private property, which is what your wine merchant is, at the end of the day, requires compliance with several important state and federal rules. I'm not demanding anything here. I can't show you a warrant. I'm making a polite request. To see the footage from last night when my client's husband disappeared."

Mr Devereux looked like he was suddenly suffering some sort of internal pain, at least he did by the look on his face. "I'm not sure I can give you what you want, Mr Baxter. It seems I might get into trouble if I start sharing CCTV footage with you."

Baxter gave an affable shrug. "Seems like you might get into trouble if you *don't* share the footage with me."

Devereux's eyes narrowed and he cocked his head slightly. "I'm sorry, I don't see what you're driving at."

"See, the thing is Mr Devereux, my client is a very important and high-profile man. His wife has specific, important and private reasons why she does not, at this stage, want to involve the police in a formal capacity, which is why she came to me. As you may know, the majority of missing people are found if action is taken quickly to locate them before too much time passes. The only lead we have right now is your wine merchants. If something were to happen to my client's husband, it would certainly make the news not just in California or even the United States but the entire world. And of course, your business would then be implicated in his disappearance and probably not for the better."

Mr Devereux started to look nervous. "I see. Yes, I can see how that might work out and certainly not in our favour. We pride ourselves on being not only the purveyors of the finest wines in Los Angeles but also with our very discreet approach to customers. Some of them buy rather more than you might think and in the cases of the more famous clients, this in itself would be a news story, if you see what I mean."

"Yeah," Baxter said. "I see what you mean. So are you going to let me look at the CCTV footage from last night or not? You don't want any of that trouble do you?"

Baxter phrased his last question carefully. He knew not only from research papers he had read over the years but also his extensive experience, that if he phrased the question in a certain way he could influence the answer. If he asked 'do you want a cup of coffee?' The answer could be yes or no, but if you said 'you don't want a cup of coffee, do you?', the answer was more likely to be no because he'd just told their subconscious that they don't want a cup of coffee. In this case, he played the same trick, telling Mr Devereux that he didn't want to end up in any of that trouble. And he got the answer he was looking for.

"No, I don't want any of that trouble in here. If you want to come round the back, I can take you to our small office where we keep the security system."

Baxter nodded, smiled and said thanks. He thought that was a great idea.

Chapter 5

The local town's gym was always dimly lit, just the way Mason liked it. Having been a British Army Boxing Champion more years ago than he cared to remember, and having spent the intervening years always keeping his hand in the sport, Mason felt most at home whenever he was in the boxing ring. Today was no exception. His hands were wrapped in fight tape, his calloused knuckles obscured by it. This world, the world of leather punchbags and sweat, the world of blood and tears, victory and loss, was his world and it had been his world since he had become a man decades ago.

Mason launched a series of sharp, accurate punches at the bag. It absorbed the ferocious blows without complaint, just as it always had done throughout his life. If only his opponents took their beatings as well as this, he thought. He continued piling his fists into the well-worn bag, the nice deep satisfying thudding sound as he fired hooks, jabs and crosses at it, each one flowing seamlessly from the last. This was the payoff of decades of training and experience, coming together to enable the perfect symphony of devastating power and swift and lethal accuracy. He wasn't as skilled as he had been back when he won the Army

Championship. He wasn't as dangerous either. But he cared about it just as much – it helped keep him fit and strong and it had come in handy on many occasions in his work at Titanfort, MI6 and most recently on the two missions he had done with Dr Holly Hope.

He danced around the bag, keenly aware of the importance of footwork in boxing, throwing more hooks, jabs and crosses as he went. Even though he was fighting nothing more than a punchbag, he now performed a feint and then moved in to clinch his opponent. The close-range grappling hold was something that had come in more than a little useful over the years, and now he was able to fire a series of devastating uppercuts into the bag. Had it been a real person this would have been their rib cage. He felt his heart pounding in his chest and now pulled back into a defensive position, before dipping his head, then executing a perfect bob and weave before simulating a parry and ending the punchbag's 'attack' on him with a powerful cross aimed at where his opponent's head would have been.

Knockout.

Mason pulled back and dropped his arms to his side as he stared at the punchbag, now swinging around wildly on a rope attached to the ceiling mount above him. His heart was still pounding hard and he was breathing fast. He wiped the sweat out of his eyes and walked over to his water bottle, taking a long deep swig before setting it back down on a bench and sitting beside it. He loosened the Velcro wrist straps on his training gloves and took them off, letting them fall onto the floor between his feet. He was slower and weaker, but he still had it. There had been many to challenge him, some even tried to copy his style, but they all failed in the end.

There was only one Mason.

But he was tormented and tired and sent his mind to the only place he found happiness – to the prosaic business of olive growing.

Mason had found a new calling in life. The old days – Army Boxing Champion, Rescue and Retrieval Specialist, Spy, Assassin, - were all behind him now. Life these days was a more serene affair, usually involving an early start with a simple breakfast of coffee before heading out and working on the farm. He loved nothing more than whiling away the hours out in his olive grove, tinkering with irrigation equipment or checking the fertility level of the soil. His latest interest was conducting negotiations with one of the local cooperatives to press his oil and export it back to the United Kingdom where it would be sold in pretty little glass bottles on the shelves of hundreds of supermarkets up and down the country. Life was good.

The opposite of life being good was a telephone call from Rosalind Parker. Rosalind had been his last boss in his final few months working for a covert section deep inside the British Secret Intelligence service known as the Department. She was a good woman and had been a fair and decent boss, but she was a ruthless manipulator of people and had extremely senior figures within the British

Government lean on her from time to time to get something unpleasant done. Mason had been at the business end of that arrangement and had learned to loathe her telephone calls. Luckily, she had not called him now for many weeks and he was beginning to think she had forgotten all about him. That was just fine with him. That was exactly the way he wanted it.

Mason picked up his gloves, and his water bottle, and then shouldered his bag before walking out to the reception area. He gave a nod to the woman on the desk who gave him a warm smile in return and then he pushed his way out into the car park around the front of the gym. It was time to go home to the farm and begin another quiet week minding his own business.

Chapter 6

The wild rhythmic beat of the music pulsed through the air, filling the enormous, packed stadium with an electric, frenzied atmosphere. Over 50,000 people had packed into Soldier Field to watch a woman dressed in a pink sequin jumpsuit prance around from one side of the stage to the other while crooning her latest hits.

Alicia Kane was not enjoying the experience. She had worked as a bodyguard in many different circumstances, ranging from the world's richest man to politicians, to rock stars and even talentless caterwauling like this, but this one was stretching her patience to the limit. As miming went, this one wasn't the worst she had ever seen but the noise produced certainly was. Luckily, she had an earpiece in her right ear so at least she'd still be able to hear on one side of her head tomorrow morning.

She was standing at the side of the stage waiting for the act to finish. At the front of the stage, on the ground standing between the stage-front and the security barriers were a dozen large security bouncers, roughly the same size as sumo wrestlers. They wore blue shirts with SECURITY written on the back in yellow and most of them had beards. They were all covered in tattoos. Alicia was not here as crowd control, but to ensure that the singer got from the stage to the dressing room and from the dressing room to her SUV convoy without harm. It was a good contract and promised to be some of the easiest money Alicia had ever made.

But there were risks. The singer in question was one of the most famous acts in the world at the moment and had received multiple death threats from a host of unstable characters on the internet. Alicia and her small team of close protection bodyguards were all armed with concealed handguns; hers was in a shoulder rig under her leather jacket. She had watched this act five times already in various cities across the United States and was keenly aware that the act was now on the last song of the encore. It was an afternoon performance, not uncommon for the singer due to the fairly young age of her average listener, although the singer did perform late-night gigs that were somewhat raunchier.

Alicia stayed back in the shadows at the side of the stage, the exact polar opposite of the bright pink exhibition now running forward to the edge of the stage and waving the microphone in the air, screaming at her fans to join in with the final chorus.

The crowd surged forward, their hands desperately outstretched into the air in a vain bid to touch their goddess. The screaming was wild, sometimes even drowning out the cacophonous racket being produced by the band on the stage.

Alicia silently mouthed the final words to the final chorus and then after an expansive and pretentious drum fill, the entire show came to an end with a thunderous boom and an explosion of tinsel bombs all over the crowd. The lights went off, the stage fell black. The crowd screamed even louder. The singer threw down her microphone and strutted off in the direction of Alicia.

Alicia turned to her number two, Scott. "OK – let's get the diva off to bed."

Siren, the singer's stage name, was a fitting epithet as far as Alicia was concerned. Alicia had often thought she would rather listen to a siren for an hour and a half than one of these gigs, but then she wouldn't get paid as well for that.

"Get me the hell out of here!" Siren said to Alicia.

"With pleasure," Alicia said to herself, turning and following the diva as she left the stage, turned right, pushed through a fire door and began walking down a breeze-block-lined corridor on her way to the dressing rooms.

Alicia, Scott and another man in the team followed Siren along the corridor until she turned right, then the star slammed the door on the four of them. The fourth and final member of Alicia's crew, Lee, had been standing guard outside the dressing room.

Alicia turned to Lee. "You check that room?"

"I did," Lee said. "Just a few seconds ago. I've been standing outside since."

"I wonder how long we're gonna have to stand here for?" Scott said.

"Until Her Holiness is ready to grace us with her presence again," Lee said. "As is her royal custom."

Jackson laughed. "Her Holiness. You really crack me up, Lee. She is kind of hot though."

Alicia gave Jackson a dirty look and was about to say something when the dressing room door swung open and Siren suddenly appeared.

"Right, we're leaving now. Take me to the cars."

Siren looked like she had been crying. Her mascara was running down her face and she was holding a mobile phone in her right hand. Mercifully, she had changed out of the pink sequin suit and was wearing jeans and a hoodie.

Alicia and her team of personal security officers escorted Siren through the labyrinthine backstage area until reaching one of the back doors, which they now opened and then stepped outside into the freezing night air. There was a decoy convoy around the main entrance which had successfully drawn the majority of fans, but there were a couple of dozen people here mostly, Alicia noted from experience, autograph hunters. These were not fans but professionals whose job was to acquire as many autographs as possible from celebrities, signing items like books or compact disc cases or posters and then selling them, usually on eBay for a profit.

Siren's management had a blanket policy of never signing anything outside venues so now Alicia and the team pushed the autograph hunters back as Scott moved forward and opened the back door of one of the Cadillac Escalades.

Alicia heard a gunshot. Everyone screamed. The autograph hunters scrambled in various directions and Alicia pulled her leather jacket lapel back and drew her Glock. She scanned in all directions looking for the shooter.

"Get her inside the car!" she yelled.

After that things moved fast. Alicia heard sustained automatic gunfire being fired in short professional bursts. Half a dozen of the autograph hunters fell to the floor, raked with rounds and left dying in the gutter. There were more screams and chaos erupted everywhere.

"In the car!" she screamed again.

She now counted four assailants, all wearing balaclavas and holding MP5s. She fired on one of the men, killing him instantly. Two of the others now turned on her and fired. She jumped for the ground in a forward roll, going under the lead Escalade and appearing on the other side, leaping to her feet. Using the Escalade's bonnet for cover, she fired at one of the two men and shot him in the head killing him.

Police sirens roared in the background. The autograph hunters who had survived the initial assault were now nowhere to be seen, Scott took three rounds and fell on the floor dead. Alicia never hesitated, never even looked at him. Jackson was trying to pull Siren into the car. Then one of the two surviving assailants fired into the driver's window and killed the driver of the Escalade. This was a professional hit. A black panel van pulled up beside the Escalade and the side door swung open. Alicia fired at the man who had killed the driver, killing him instantly, but the surviving assailant fired three more rounds, hitting Lee in the shoulder and knocking him to the floor. Alicia fired on the final assailant, killing him where he stood, allowing Jackson, who was now inside the Escalade to roll down the window and fire on the panel van. Lee now clambered to his feet and jumped into the front of the Escalade, pushing the driver through the door, turning the key in the ignition and revving the engine.

Alicia ran around the back of the Escalade and fired on the van, taking out its two rear tyres and one of the men inside. He screamed in pain and fell forward onto the tarmac, hitting it with a wet crunch. Alicia now jumped into the Escalade. Scott was dead on the pavement, but Lee, Jackson, Alicia and Siren were still alive. Jackson was still holding Siren's head down in the back of the car. Lee stamped on the throttle and sent the Escalade surging forward with a tremendous ear-bending wheel spin. As the smoke from the burned rubber cleared, Alicia leaned out through the back window and fired on the driver of the GMC panel van, killing him in his seat.

"Sit rep?" Alicia called out.

"Fine," Lee said. "I'm OK – just a flesh wound, but they got Scott."

"I know," Alicia said. "What about you Jackson?"

"Completely unharmed," he said. "Luck of the Irish."

Alicia looked at the African American bodyguard. "Good to know, J."

"And nobody is gonna ask me how I am?" Siren asked, her voice muffled as Jackson was still pushing her head down into the seat.

Jackson looked at Alicia. "Do I have to let her go?"

Alicia reluctantly said yes. She wanted to smile, but Scott's death had made her burn with anger at the events of the night. She didn't know him well, and he had only just joined her team, but she was responsible for him and now he was dead.

"Where are we going?" Lee asked from up front.

"We're getting Siren to her apartment and calling the cops," Alicia said. "Then I'm drowning myself in hard liquor."

Chapter 7

The office around the back of Devereux's upmarket store was not quite as sumptuously decorated as the front of the shop, but still offered Baxter a relatively comfortable chair while Devereux fired up the computer and navigated to the correct section of CCTV footage that he wanted to see. Baxter was scrolling on his phone and caught a glimpse of a story about a fatal shooting in Chicago – some kind of terror attack against a singer called Siren. He wondered what the world was coming to and put the phone in his pocket.

"I'm just pulling it up now," Devereux said over his shoulder. "I can't believe something might have happened to Senator Sullivan."

"I never said it was him," Baxter said, sitting up.

Devereaux turned. "He was the only customer of importance we had in here yesterday, Mr Baxter. I'm no fool."

"Fine, it's Sullivan, but we don't know anything bad happened to him yet and I would very much appreciate your discretion in the matter of his possible disappearance. As you can imagine, Mrs Sullivan is distraught and specifically asked me to try to maintain as much confidentiality concerning this matter as possible. She has concerns not only for her family's safety and well-being but also wider concerns in terms of the nation itself. As you may know, Senator Sullivan is a very high-ranking member of Congress and sits on several important committees. His disappearance will certainly raise some serious concern if not outright panic. I should report his disappearance in the next few hours if I can't locate him and I made that clear to Mrs Sullivan. His disappearance may be connected to his government work, in which case this matter has to be passed up way above my pay grade."

"You mean like some kind of espionage or blackmail thing?"

"Let's not get carried away, Mr Devereux," Baxter said. "The only reason I'm discussing this matter with you is because I know from a matter of great experience that the vast majority of disappearances are solved within a few hours and turn out to be perfectly innocent. Senator Sullivan has got some ongoing private issues and he may have just needed a little bit of space and time to think them through. Let's not get into the James Bond stuff straight away."

Devereux smiled for the first time since Baxter had walked into his store and now returned to his business at the computer, using his mouse buttons and scroll wheel to deftly locate the section of tape that Baxter was looking for.

Baxter sat up now, leaning even further forward in his chair to get a closer look at the CCTV footage on the screen. Back when he had first joined the LAPD, if there was any CCTV footage at all was a blessing and then it usually turned out to be like trying to see something through a black-and-white blizzard. Today's brand new digital technology made life a hell of a lot easier for men like Baxter and now he was staring at a crystal-clear, full-colour image of Senator Kent Sullivan pulling up in his Tesla outside the wine merchants. He watched the senator, a tall, lean man with perfectly styled silver hair, climb out of the Tesla, and lock the car with his remote, which he then slipped into his pocket. He then walked slowly to the entrance canopy Baxter had used just a few moments earlier. The senator looked calm and relaxed and not at all anguished in any way.

"Well, there he is," Devereux said. "We'll just follow him into the store. Look over here on this screen now."

Baxter watched as Devereux stepped into the store, now being monitored by a second camera. He walked over to the European wine section where he lingered for a while at Portugal – this made Baxter's mind turn to Mason and his olive grove for a few moments – but then they were on the move again, stepping across to Spain and Italy before finally winding up at France. He spent longer here, before turning and walking over to the desk and speaking to Devereux.

Devereux looked at his haircut and shook his head. "I need to fire my hairdresser."

Baxter's eyes glanced quickly at the back of Devereux's head and quietly agreed with him. Then, he returned to the CCTV screen and watched the two men engaging in a short conversation.

"What's he asking you?" Baxter asked.

"He's asking me if we have any chilled champagne. I remember it clearly. He'd found some of the bottles he was looking for over in the regular French section, but they were not chilled. I told him that we did have many bottles of champagne and other wines in the chiller cabinet over on the other side of the store. Watch and you'll see him go over there."

Baxter watched the two men end their conversation and then Senator Sullivan turned to his right and walked to the far side of the store. About halfway on his voyage, he disappeared out of sight of the CCTV camera.

"That part of the store's not covered?"

"Yeah, it's covered," Devereux said, clicking a few more buttons on his mouse. "Look here on this screen and you'll see that part of the store is covered."

Baxter now watched Devereux appearing from another angle as he moved to the chiller cabinet section of the merchants. Again, he lingered and Baxter watched the senator's head moving up and down and from left to right as he took in the contents of the expansive chiller cabinet. It took up the entire east wall of the store. Slowly, the senator crab walked from left to right as he made his way down the cabinet until finally finding what he was looking for. He swung open one of the large chiller doors, reached inside and pulled out two bottles of champagne. He closed the door and returned to the desk.

Baxter now watched him reverse course through the various CCTV cameras until he returned to Devereux at the counter.

"What exactly did he buy?"

"Two bottles of Dom Pérignon," Devereaux said. "I was hoping he was going to ask for a bottle of the Oenothèque, but at five grand I knew it was a long shot."

Baxter sympathised, especially as he hadn't earned that much money all month.

"Did he say anything to you while he was paying? I mean anything at all."

"Nothing," Devereux said. "Many of our clients are people with famous faces, including Senator Sullivan. We're in Beverly Hills, so a lot of our clients are world-famous stars of the big screen and they do not appreciate, I have learned from experience, having that mentioned to them while they're here paying. The strict policy at Devereux's is to treat every customer as if they were an entirely anonymous and private citizen. I recognised Senator Sullivan when he came in because he has been in the store many times, and we have spoken in the past about some of his political work – I hasten to add, that he brought the subject up. On this occasion, he simply asked how much the wine cost, paid for it and left, as you'll see now."

Baxter watched Senator Sullivan act out what Devereux had just described. The senator placed the wine bottles inside a cloth bag and then returned to the front door. He opened the shop door, stepped outside and was now out of sight. Devereux now selected the outside camera once again and Baxter immediately noticed something had changed outside.

"There's some kind of van behind Senator Sullivan's Tesla," Devereux said.

"Yeah," Baxter said, his heart quickening. "That's what I just saw."

Chapter 8

"And now that van has got my attention," Baxter said. "Keep the tape playing please."

Senator Sullivan now appeared from underneath the creamy entrance canopy and walked back over to his Tesla. Baxter watched him put his hand in his pocket, take out his remote and unlock his car. Then, Sullivan walked to the back of the Tesla where he opened the boot and put the two bottles of wine inside. At this moment, Baxter watched as the two front doors of the van parked up behind the Tesla, opened and two men climbed out. Sullivan reached up and grabbed the Tesla boot, swinging it down until it was shut. Then, the two men struck.

One of them pulled a pistol from a concealed rig under his suit jacket and approached Sullivan as he made to walk back to the driver's seat. The man grabbed Sullivan by the left shoulder and put the muzzle of his pistol into the small of Sullivan's back. Words were exchanged. To his credit, Senator Sullivan did not look panicked or phased at all. He remained calm, reflecting on his years as a fully-trained US Air Force officer. Now that man wheeled Sullivan around and walked him to the back of the van. They were out of sight in this position for a few seconds. Baxter could see one of the rear doors of the van open and then close, then the man with the gun walked to the driver's door, put the gun back in his rig and climbed in and closed the door. The other man walked forward to the Tesla, then he climbed into it and closed the door. Both vehicles then pulled away and were gone. The entire kidnapping had taken less than twenty seconds.

"My God!" Devereux said. "He was kidnapped?"

"Seems that way," Baxter said, his voice growing cold. "Run that tape back a second and let me get that licence plate."

Devereux ran the footage back a few seconds until the GMC van reversed back into view.

"I can't see it – it's not clear enough," Baxter said. "Can you zoom in?"

"No problem at all," Devereux said.

Baxter waited patiently for a few seconds as Devereux clicked more buttons and then scrolled the mouse wheel, zooming in on the GMC's licence plate. Baxter wrote down the sequence of six letters and numbers on his phone and then slipped it back into his pocket. He turned to Devereux.

"Mr Devereux, I need to thank you for what you've done here today. This is an important development and I'm going to report it to Mrs Sullivan immediately. I must ask you to keep this recording safe because I have no doubt the police are going to be involved in this matter at some point in the near future. Until then I ask you to keep this to yourself. I will contact the police at the correct time."

"Yes, I think I can agree to that," Devereux said hesitatingly. "I'll keep the footage safe. I'll put it on a flash drive."

"Thanks, Mr Devereux. Now it's time for me to get going. I have an important call to make."

Baxter walked through the shop, out of the front door and emerged from the entrance canopy into the bright Californian sunshine. After the cool of the security room, it felt good to have the warm sun on his face as he pulled his phone back out of his pocket and made a call.

"Teddy, it's me, Baxter. How's it going?"

"It's going alright," Teddy said. "But it'll be going better when I can retire out of the force and lead a life of luxury like you."

Baxter and his old Sergeant Edward Spartan laughed for a few moments and then Baxter got down to business. "I'm sorry to say, Teddy, this isn't a social call."

"Shoot."

"I need you to run a check on a licence plate and I need it fast. This is probably gonna be the biggest case I've worked on since I set up the agency, Teddy. It could turn out to be something really serious."

"Yeah?" Teddy said, a hint of salacious interest in his voice. "What are we talking about here?"

"I can't say, Teddy. Not yet."

"Got it. Maybe we'll talk about it over a poker game one day. Give me the number."

Baxter read out the number to Teddy, who was still working in the force as a uniformed sergeant. Moments later he heard his old friend's voice come back on the phone.

"You got anything for me?" Baxter asked.

"Yeah, and I think you're gonna be very interested when I tell you."

Chapter 9

Kent Sullivan tumbled in the snow, nearly crackling his head open on the trunk of a lodgepole pine. Staggering back up to his feet, he brushed the snow off himself and turned in the darkness to look back up at the enormous luxury ski chalet at the top of the slope above him. Never in his life had he been so grateful for his training in the USAF all those decades ago. That training had taught him not to panic when someone pulled a gun on him and it had also taught him when and how to evade what was about to happen to him up there on the balcony of that chalet.

He calmed himself, thought of his wife sitting at home terrified about what must be happening to him and resolved to get away and get back to her at all costs. He also now knew that the Conclave was run by a man named Snow, and he knew about the Fellowship of Light's plans to reveal the truth to the world. Those plans now had to be expedited massively. The Conclave of Darkness had clearly rumbled their plans and had already executed the other two members of the Fellowship. Sullivan knew he had no time to waste.

He heard shouting inside the ski lodge and looked up to see Snow and his men on the balcony pointing down at the forest he had managed to reach. He heard other men shouting inside the lodge, and more streaming out of doors on the ground floor. He was fifty yards away, but he could see they were armed with MP5 compact machine pistols – the kind special forces used in dangerous hostage situations or other close-quarter combat. They were relatively light and easy to carry and the perfect weapon for hunting someone like him.

He had to think carefully. He considered hiding and waiting until morning when he could use daylight to facilitate a safer escape, but when he heard the snapping, snarling and growling of dogs, he knew hiding was no longer an option. He had to run. With Laroche and Beausire both dead, he was the only one left who could bring the truth to the world. He spun around leaving the ski lodge behind him and headed deeper into the woods. He did not know this part of the country but he knew he was in Aspen. He understood the way the ski villages worked. Off to his left, in a break in the canopies of the conifer forests surrounding him, he saw the unmistakable sight of chairs hanging from a ski lift. He knew civilization would be at the bottom of that ski lift. Staying inside the forest and keeping his head low, he moved quickly but as quietly as possible through the snow tracking exactly parallel to the ski lift as he made his way down the slope.

Remember your training Kent, he thought to himself. *Remember your wife. Remember Charlotte. Remember your kids.*

The Babylon Agenda

He heard the men shouting, ordering him to stay where he was. It was a bluff; they didn't know where he was but he could tell from the volume of their voices they were closer than he thought. He was suddenly terrified by the sound of gunfire roaring in the forest. He threw himself to the ground and rolled behind the cover of a Douglas fir. The rounds continued. His head was cradled in his arms – it had been instinct – but now he pulled his head back until he was able to sneak a look up the slope and try to gauge where the men were. It was impossible to see, but he did notice a bright muzzle flash somewhere off to his far left. They seem to be going in the direction of the ski lift. That made sense. He had looked through the window when Snow had been talking to him earlier, and seen they were in an extremely isolated position. He doubted there was more than one way up and down to a place like this, so they would naturally presume that was where he would head.

Maybe he had to think again, but he had to keep his wits about him. There was a lot of rugged terrain around this area and the risk of slipping and falling from a great height was not minimal. For now, he could see the slope was descending at a steady gradient because of the trees, but once he broke free from them and found himself out in a snow field, not only would he be exposed, but his risk of stumbling over a steep ledge would be higher.

He pressed on through the woods, slowly cutting across at a forty-five-degree angle towards the ski lift. He saw one of the ski lift towers now, anchored into the snowy mountain slope and attached to it the heavy high-tensile steel cables slowly fading from sight in the mist as they ran their way down to the next tower. He heard dogs barking behind him, they were closer than ever. Perhaps no more than one hundred feet and closing in every second. He heard another peal of gunfire echoing eerily out across the valley to his right. His heart pounded in his chest. He had no choice but to make a break for it. He left the cover of the trees and sprinted out across the exposed snow field towards the ski lift tower. He planned to run beneath the high tensile cables from tower to tower until eventually working his way slowly down the mountain, understanding there may be some climbing involved. He had no equipment, but behind him was certain death so he would take the chance. It wouldn't have been his first time climbing up a mountain or down one.

Then he heard the sounds of a snowmobile roaring behind him. His world was illuminated by bright LED arc lights in front of the snowmobile as it turned the corner of the forest he had been running through up at the ski lodge and turned to face him. It bore down on him menacingly, lighting him up like a Christmas tree. Seconds later, he was surrounded by men in white snow camouflage combat fatigues, all of them holding MP5s. He stood perfectly still and slowly raised his hands into the air. He knew what was about to happen and he knew he only had seconds left to act. His most sacred duty to the Fellowship had to be fulfilled before these men killed him and took his life. The

The Babylon Agenda

door of the snowmobile opened and then he saw Snow pull himself up out of the vehicle and, standing up inside it, lean over the door and casually call out to him.

"What a foolish thing to do Mr Sullivan! Putting me to all this effort and yet I still get exactly what I want."

"I don't think you're gonna get what you want, Snow!" Sullivan called back through the swirling snow.

Sullivan darted to his left, knowing he could easily be hit by bullets but deciding to take the risk. The men opened fire and the bullets raked into his upper legs. Sullivan knew he only had seconds inside the tree line to do what had to be done before the men finished him off. Staggering forward he felt to his knees and crawled to the trunk of a pine, then he ripped through his suit jacket, ripped the buttons off his shirt and tore the amulet from his neck before pushing it down into the roots and covering it once again with snow. The snow looked untouched and now he rolled over onto his back, finding just enough energy to do up his buttons and pull his tie up as the men marched over to him and formed a semicircle.

The next thing he saw was Snow appear, standing over him grinning. He pulled a silver dagger from his pocket.

"You know why my men did not shoot to kill you, I presume?"

Sullivan nodded. "They choose not to kill me because Conclave Law says I must be stabbed to death with a silver dagger."

"Yes, because you are a traitor."

"I am not a traitor – you are the traitor, Snow! The entire Conclave of Darkness is a hideous and depraved mockery of what the Masons were originally set up to do."

"It is the Conclave that discovered and guards to this very day that which you wish to expose to the light, that which you wish to tell the world. Our society began at the Tower, Senator Sullivan, not the Temple. It is the Tower that guards the truth about our world. Why do you want to give that away?"

"Because it's the right thing to do for us!" Sullivan said, grimacing with pain as his blood seeped out of his body into the snow.

"I think not, Senator," Snow said. "Doing what you intend to do will bring chaos, misery, destruction and terror to everyone in the world. What we know we must keep to ourselves. It is a sacred responsibility, so sacred that this is why the Conclave never even told the Masons what we had discovered."

Snow cleared the men out of his way and knelt beside Sullivan. With no further words, he thrust the silver blade into his torso over and over again in the most violent way. He wiped the dagger clean on Sullivan's suit, put it back in his holster and stood up to his full height. After he had straightened his tie and suit jacket he looked down at the dying senator and smiled.

"That is the end of the Fellowship of Light and your search for the Tower."

Sullivan said nothing. He was too weak to speak as the blood pumped from his body and turned the snow red all around him.

As a matter of elevated security due to his status as a US Senator, Sullivan had a full GPS set on his telephone at all times. He knew any investigator, police or private, would be able to locate the location he was currently in. This would therefore be his last GPS location. Any investigator would be able to find this place. He could only pray that they would also find the amulet.

He watched Snow now make the sign of the cross over his chest before ordering his men back up the slope to his luxury home in the White Fir Lodge. He told Necro to leave the snowmobile and that he would drive it back up later.

Sullivan's blood pressure was so low he was losing sound and vision. The last thing he thought was how grateful he was that Snow and the rest of the Conclave clearly had no idea that the Fellowship had located the Tower, although the three of them had not had the time to excavate it and see if it really did contain the whole truth Snow was so keen to learn and hide from the world. Snow believed the Fellowship was still searching for the Tower.

The last thing he saw was Snow leaning over him, this time not smiling but deadly serious.

"Ave Maria, gratia plena, Dominus tecum. Benedicta tu in mulieribus, et benedictus fructus ventris tui, Iesus.

Sancta Maria, Mater Dei, ora pro nobis peccatoribus, nunc, et in hora mortis nostrae. Amen… Proditor!"

Chapter 10

"So what have you got for me, Teddy?"

Baxter was in his car and driving back to his office. It was a warm sunny day in Beverly Hills and he had his window rolled down and was enjoying the breeze blowing into the car. He was also enjoying the first disc in the Complete Village Vanguard Recordings, Bill Evans's 1961 live classic. He was listening to 'Alice in Wonderland'. Music as it was supposed to be, at least that's what he thought. Better than any of that, he was playing it on a compact disc and not one of these stupid little plastic sticks that everyone seemed to use to listen to music these days. Vinyl was best, then discs for the car. Not the stupid little plastic sticks, please. No sleeve notes, no class, nothing to touch.

You're getting old, Baxter.

"I think I got something that maybe can help you," Teddy said. "You're still listening to Bill?"

"Yeah, I'm still listening to Bill."

Baxter smiled and turned the volume down slightly so he could hear Teddy better. His one concession to modernity was a hands-free kit for his mobile phone, and he was having a little trouble hearing his old friend. Teddy was a Bill Evans fan too, but neither of them needed the distraction right now, even though LaFaro was well into one of his famous double bass solos.

"OK, well go ahead, Teddy. Let me have it."

"The license plate was easy to trace," Teddy began. "It was hired from a rental company the day before but never returned. It's already been reported as stolen."

"You get any names of who hired it?"

"As you probably already guessed, they were all fake. At least we can't find anybody with those details on our system and they're not at the DMV either. But what we did get was the number plate picked up on some cameras."

Baxter pulled up at the lights on Santa Monica Boulevard and signalled right. He was first in the queue and desperate to get back to his office and report his findings to Mrs Sullivan. He was drumming his fingers on the steering wheel along to the perfectly timed beat of Paul Motian and eager to hear more, from both Bill and Teddy.

"What kind of cameras?"

"The kind of cameras that followed that GMC from Beverly Hills to LAX."

"I like it, Teddy," Baxter said with a smile. "I like it very much. Keep talking."

"They went directly to the airport after kidnapping Sullivan and when they got there they drove immediately to one of the private aprons. The whole thing's on airport security cameras. I got a buddy there. Enrico."

"Go on." As Baxter asked this question, the lights changed from green to red and he put the car into Drive and pulled in a smooth right-hand arc onto Santa Monica Boulevard. The traffic was light and the flow was good but now the sun was pitching in through his window and he manipulated the visor to block its hot rays. It wasn't hot enough for the window to be rolled up and the air conditioner to be put on, so he carried on with his current setup, only now moving his elbow up onto the door seal and pushing back in his seat as if he was a Beach Boy in 1966, which reminded him to find his Pet Sounds CD when he had time and bring it out to the car.

"Well, they took the senator out of the GMC van and walked him over to a Learjet. The party boarded, the aircraft taxied, and then they were out of there. Bang."

Baxter was suddenly curious. "How come these guys can drag a kidnapped senator in the back of a GMC and bundle him into the back of a private jet without causing any suspicions? Surely, somebody at airport security must have realised something was wrong and acted?"

"There wasn't any bundling," Teddy said. "The party stepped out of the van and moved in a perfectly normal fashion. Cool as cucumbers."

"They must have threatened the wife," Baxter said.

"That's what I was thinking," Teddy said. "They had plenty of time on the drive between Beverly Hills and the airport to make it clear to Sullivan that if he played up when they got to their destination, he'd regret it. That's the obvious choice."

"OK, so they're on a private jet – a Learjet – and they've just taken off out of LAX. Did you get the registration number of that aeroplane? Do we know where it went?"

"I did get the registration data and the flight plan out of air traffic control and that plane flew to Aspen, Colorado. I'm sorry, but that's where the trail ends, at least as far as I'm concerned. I don't have any jurisdiction in Colorado."

Baxter understood. Teddy was a sergeant approaching retirement in the Los Angeles Police Department and he was a former LAPD Lieutenant now retired and set up in private practise as an investigator. Now, Teddy's journey was done and Baxter would have to make the next stage of the investigation himself. He was crossing the junction of Beverly Drive now, with Beverly Garden Park on his left. Some children were playing out on the newly-cut grass. They were laughing and throwing balls at one another and playing with a dog and above their heads, was an enormous canopy of bright blue sky. It was a perfect day in Beverly Hills, but not perfect for Senator and Mrs Sullivan.

Baxter prepared to turn right and pull into the street where his office was located. He had decided to speak to Mrs Sullivan by telephone rather than drive across town and visit her in person. He wanted to think about what Teddy had told him before he made contact with her. Go through all the possible ramifications of what he had heard. Sometimes, the tiniest detail could push an investigation off on an entirely different angle and lead to a different conclusion. He wanted to be confident that he knew everything that could be known about the facts before calling her. This was, after all, the biggest case he had worked on as a private investigator. Something also told him it could be the most dangerous.

*

Baxter was taking a sip of the hot, freshly ground coffee he just made in the little setup he had in his office when Mrs Sullivan answered her phone. He had decided to call her. Her voice was the same as when he had spoken to her before – nervous, uncertain and yet with a hint of anger or defiance that reflected how she felt about whoever had reached into their lives and snatched her husband away from her.

"Mr Baxter?" she said. "I take it you have some news for me about my husband?"

Baxter was looking down at the little pad of notes he had written after arriving back at his office. It had been an effective and constructive few hours of work and he was pleased so far with how the investigation was going. But he had learned not to sound too happy when speaking to clients. If the investigation was going well for him, they were still usually going through hell, at least in the earliest phases of a case. Sometimes he was able to bring joy to people – most of the time, but not all of the time. Then everyone was happy, but right now he might be content with the way things were shaking out, but he knew Mrs Sullivan was still missing her husband and had no idea where he was. For now at least, neither did Baxter.

"There's good news and there's bad news, Mrs Sullivan."

"I'm not sure how to respond to that."

"I'll say it straight, Mrs Sullivan, because that's how I am. I know that your husband made it as far as the wine merchants and did buy two bottles of champagne. I also know that he was kidnapped by two armed men driving a black GMC panel van when he left the wine merchants. They also stole his car. The car has not been found yet and the panel van was a rental. They took your husband in the panel van to LAX airport."

"The airport?" Mrs Sullivan sounded surprised.

"They boarded a private jet at the airport and flew to Aspen, Colorado."

"Aspen?" She sounded even more incredulous. "Why would anybody kidnap my husband and take him to Aspen?"

"There are many questions I don't know the answers to yet," Baxter continued. "I don't know who these men are. They used fake details to hire the van and their faces, which we have from security cameras at the airport, have been run through police computers and none of them have been identified. That just means none of them has criminal records. It also means we can't ID any of them. As to why they took him or flew him to Aspen, that's something I still have to find out."

"Is my husband still alive, Mr Baxter?"

"I can't tell you that."

There was a long pregnant pause.

"I see. And you're telephoning me now so I can sanction your flight to Aspen?"

"That is correct, Mrs Sullivan. I'm going to need to get over there as soon as possible if I'm to stay on your husband's trail while it's still hot. I take it it's OK for me to go ahead and book a flight?"

"Of course, Mr Baxter. Please do whatever you can to bring my husband home. You have carte blanche."

Mrs Sullivan hung up the phone with no niceties and left Baxter thinking to the tune of the disconnection tone. He set his phone down into the cradle and leant back in his chair thinking about the conversation he had had both with Teddy earlier on today and now with Mrs Sullivan.

He ate some cold, chilli-crunch shrimp pasta out of the carton and drank some warm strawberry lemonade. Then he picked the phone back up and dialled the number for LAX Airport.

Chapter 11

Baxter was standing in line at the Delta Business check-in desk at Los Angeles International Airport wishing he'd remembered to bring his old, worn Sony Walkman with him. Not only would that give him something to listen to on the flight up to Aspen, but it would enable him to turn up the volume right now and enjoy one of his favourite Bill Evans songs instead of listening to the sound of the idiot behind him, whining into his cell phone about his job, wife, boss, brother and dog.

Maybe, Baxter mused, *you* might be the problem, man, and not all the others.

But he had left the Walkman on his nightstand because he had left in such a rush, so now he had to make do by mentally reconstructing Waltzing for Debby, and now and again quietly humming along to enhance the experience. He liked the song, even though his ex-wife was called Debs, so he was unable to listen to it or think about it without being reminded of the failure of his marriage. He was gradually getting over it, but there was no point lying to himself. Things were still raw and painful even after all this time, and worse than that, he'd had a telephone call from her a few days ago saying she was seeing someone else.

The Babylon Agenda

Baxter shuffled forward without complain until he was standing at the desk. He disconnected the jazz classic that was currently playing in his head and went through the same process with the woman behind the desk that he had gone through so many times he couldn't even remember. Everything was in order, and he was only taking carry-on luggage so the procedure went past in a few short minutes and he was on his way to security screening. He passed through the metal detector and after his carry-on luggage had been scanned, he made his way to the departure lounge where his flight was already boarding.

He stepped aboard the Delta Bombardier CRJ-900 and the flight attendant directed hm to his business seat. He stowed his small bag in the cabin above his seat and was grateful to collapse down into the comfortable chair and take the weight off his feet. Most of Baxter's private investigation work was within the confines of the City of Los Angeles, although he did from time to time have occasion to go out to places like San Diego, San Bernardino, or even San Francisco. Flying out to the Rockies and visiting Aspen on a case was a first for him, although he always maintained a strictly professional mindset so there would not be any time to enjoy the scenery. His mind was already thinking about the case, but when he drifted from the subject he usually found himself thinking about his memories of the times he spent with Dr Holly Hope, Jed Mason, Alicia Kane and Guy Wilde. He still couldn't believe that he had worked with them to locate not only the Ark of the Covenant but also the Holy Grail.

He was aware of someone bumbling around next to him and turned to see a woman in her forties, wearing a smart charcoal-coloured business suit, swinging her bag in the bin above their seats. When she had completed the task and closed the lid, she looked down at him and gave him a warm smile.

"I hate flying in smaller planes like this. How about you?" she said.

"I kinda like it," Baxter said, shifting in his seat a little so he was able to look at her.

She now sat down beside him and filled the air between them with a very expensive and pleasant scent of perfume. She turned to him and held out her right hand, somewhat awkwardly because of the angle she was sitting in the chair.

"I'm Martha Crockett. Pleased to meet you."

"I'm Wesley Baxter."

"Well, good to know you, Wesley."

"People just call me Baxter."

She looked at him slightly strangely, smiled and nodded her head, then reached for the magazine in the mesh pocket in the seat in front. She pulled it out and set it on her lap without opening it. Then she leaned her head back on the headrest and closed her eyes before blowing out a long deep exhalation.

"Boy, what a day that was," she said.

Baxter smiled politely. "You can say that again. Why are you going to Aspen? Business?"

"Oh no, I live in Aspen," she said. "I was in Los Angeles on business. Can't say I'll be sorry to see the back of it though."

Baxter loved LA, but he didn't take it personally. The city had changed beyond all recognition in his lifetime and he understood when people who weren't used to such a sprawling gargantuan metropolis found it difficult, noisy, dangerous or uncomfortable.

"What about you?" she asked. "You're from LA?"

"Born and raised. I'm on my way to Aspen for business."

"What's your business? If you don't mind my asking."

"Not at all. I'm a private investigator."

Her eyes widened and she pulled her head back a little in surprise.

"Oh, wow! I've always wanted to meet a private investigator and now I finally have. I must have had a pretty sheltered life, I guess."

"If you've never met a private investigator then you've led a privileged life, take my word for it."

"That bad, huh?"

"It's not all bad," Baxter said, almost wistfully. "But people only usually contact private investigators when there's big trouble in their lives. That might just be a cheating spouse, or maybe something much worse. We deal with the dark side of life. Theft, gambling, infidelity, fraud, and sometimes even kidnappings, or murders. And before I was a PI, I was in the LAPD for a long time."

She looked at him smiling. "No kidding?"

"No kidding," he said. "I was a plainclothes lieutenant by the time I retired."

"So I guess you have seen it all. You work alone?""

"Yes and no. My PI business is just me, but I have a small team I work with on international cases."

He was overegging the pudding, but what was the harm? She was a good-looking woman.

"Impressive."

Baxter turned away from her and realised his smile was fading. She was right of course; he had seen everything. A lot of what he'd seen across his years in the LAPD in particular had been unsettling, some of it even to the point of scarring him for life. There were some things you just could never unsee. He considered that was why he had enjoyed his two missions with Mason and the team so much – because those days were so wild and crazy and unexpected, they filled his mind up with brand new memories and helped push back some of the darker psychological material he had collected in his decades working homicide in the City of Angels.

He came back from his thoughts to see that Martha was buckling herself into her seat, the flight attendants had closed the doors and the plane was gently trundling out along the taxiway. He looked out of the window at the city lights beyond.

The Babylon Agenda

He thought now of Alicia. The truth was, he was never sure what it was she did or where she did it. She had spoken to him about Seattle but also Chicago. She worked as a bodyguard, but was there some sort of a history with the CIA? He knew that wherever she was right now, she wouldn't be taking any crapola. Of that he was sure. He was more confident in imagining Dr Holly Hope working away in some library or academic department or other at Harvard University. He had never met anyone like her before – she was like someone from a Hollywood movie – the way she solved puzzles and codes. Her mind was brilliant. As for Guy Wilde – to call him a unique individual was somewhat of an understatement. The old British hippy looked a bit rough around the edges, with his scraggly grey mop of hair and his old dusty boots, holes in his heavy metal T-shirt, and his old, scuffed WWII leather bomber jacket. But he was the warmest, wisest company Baxter had ever enjoyed. That just left Jed Mason. Mason had talked to him about some of his past, and Baxter was aware of the Englishman's time in the British Army as well as a mysterious organisation based in New York City called Titanfort. This had something to do with the American intelligence community, or at least that's how Baxter had interpreted it. After this, Mason joined the British Secret Intelligence Service. But Mason rarely spoke about himself or his background. And Baxter could understand that. He felt the same way.

He turned to his right just as the Bombardier was lining up on the runway. He was now able to look through the small jet's porthole at the famous parabolic arches at the heart of LAX Airport. Then after a brief pause, he heard the aircraft's ailerons and flaps set for take-off and then the engines came on full throttle. He was pushed back into his seat as the small jet roared along the runway and then moments later – much faster than in a regular passenger jet – they were lifting off and racing out across the coast. The aircraft banked hard to starboard and he was able to look through his window and see the early evening lights of western Los Angeles glittering like thousands of jewels below. He saw Santa Monica Pier and then his neck of the woods – Beverly Hills – before the jet straightened up and punched through the clouds. The moon was bright and lit the top of the clouds an almost liquid silver colour. The sky above was black – the stars blotted out by the brightness of the moon.

Baxter checked his watch and calculated he had just enough time for a good nap before landing in Aspen and checking into his hotel. Then he had a day to find Senator Sullivan.

Chapter 12

Baxter didn't materially have much in life but he had a sharp mind and great intuition. He knew the leads he had on Sullivan all ran out after that plane took off to Aspen. He also knew Aspen was a very small place and that anyone who could afford to fly a private Learjet from LA to the Colorado Rockies, would not be staying in anything but one of the most expensive residences in the area – owned or rented. He also knew that some of the best security footage in the world was recorded by the human eye.

After getting nowhere at the arrival desk in the small airport, he made his way out to the area where the car rentals were parked. He noticed a young man in a big puffy coat and wearing a beanie on his head who was standing outside an office of one of the car rental companies. Baxter strolled over to him with his hands in his pockets and his carry-on luggage over his shoulder. Baxter was Baxter. Casual, relaxed, slightly down at heel and worn around the edges but he had one of those faces people just seemed to take to. Now he deployed it.

"Hey there," he said.

"You looking for your car, sir?"

"As a matter of fact, I'm not," Baxter said. "Although I might be looking to hire one today."

"Sure. We can hire one out here – you don't have to do it over the phone or online."

"That'll be great."

"Looking for anything in particular?"

"Just a little run around. Nothing too special. I have some business here in Aspen for a couple of days."

"What about this Cadillac sedan over here?"

Baxter followed the man across the parking lot where he saw a cherry red sedan – maybe three or four years old. Just perfect for what he wanted. He turned and looked at the young man.

"This looks just great, thanks very much. How can I pay you?"

"We take all the major credit cards."

"I probably should have called you and made a booking in advance on the phone," Baxter said. "But I was just in a real rush and didn't have the time."

It was a lie but one essential for his work. Baxter wanted to sniff around the car hire companies after arriving in Aspen until he found somebody who looked like he might have seen something. Now he put the final part of his plan into action.

"I was wondering if I could ask you a question?"

"Anything to do with the rental agreement is handled inside the office."

"Actually, I was wondering if you'd seen someone I was looking for come through this way in the last few hours."

The man looked at him and narrowed his eyes with confusion. "I don't understand."

Baxter produced a passport photo of Senator Sullivan that Mrs Sullivan had given him in his office earlier that day and held it up so the young man could see him. "I think this guy came through here within the last twenty-four hours. He would have landed on a private jet – an expensive Learjet. He probably would have been surrounded by other serious-looking men in black suits. I'm trying to find this man for his own safety. Have you seen him?"

"Are you some kind of investigator or something?"

Baxter nodded. "That's right. I am a private investigator from Los Angeles."

"So those couple of days business – just running around town in the sedan – are about finding this man?"

"You got it. Can you help me?"

The man shifted uncomfortably from foot to foot. He glanced over his shoulder at the office and then back to Baxter. "I don't know, this seems a little weird."

Baxter reached into his suit pocket and pulled out his wallet. He opened the wallet and pulled out his old police badge. "If it makes you feel any better, I was in the LAPD for forty years. I'm retired now. I run a small private investigations agency out of Beverly Hills. This man is an important politician and I must find him. I believe the men he was with may be trying to harm him."

Baxter now put the badge back in the wallet and the wallet back in his pocket. He pulled out a crisp $50 bill. "Can you help me?"

"I saw him," the young man said. "And you're right – he was surrounded by several other serious-looking dudes in black suits. I saw the Lear come in as well – that's not uncommon around here by the way – so that's not what stood out. There's a lot of little jets like that flying in and out of here all the time. What stood out to me was the men surrounding this guy. I thought he was some kind of actor and maybe they were his security or something."

"He's no actor," Baxter said. "He's a US Senator and he might be in trouble. Can you help me?"

Baxter held the $50 up and handed it to the young man who took it immediately and put it in his pocket, glancing again over his shoulder at the office.

"They took off in a white Rolls-Royce Cullinan," the young man said, visibly impressed. "I've seen it round here once or twice in the last few weeks."

"Thanks very much," Baxter said. "You've been a lot of help to me. Considering who this man is you may have been more help than you could possibly imagine."

*

It did not take Baxter very long to find the white Rolls Royce Cullinan. It took him less than sixty minutes with his drone. He drove the Cadillac sedan out to a public park, then activated his drone, took it off and flew it systematically around the most expensive properties in the town. In less than one hour, images of the white Rolls Royce parked out the front of a luxury ski lodge to the southwest of the town were beamed back in real time to his iPhone. He made sure to keep the drone several hundred feet above the property so as not to alert anyone inside of his presence, and he used the zoom facility to check the rest of the place out. He noticed the property was close to a ski lift bringing people up to a luxury resort a few hundred metres behind it. It was then he saw something strange in the snow. It looked like fresh snowmobile tracks, he zoomed in some more and saw footsteps. All of this piqued Baxter's interest. He took note of the address, brought the drone back to base and packed it away in his bag.

You got to love modern technology, he thought. *But I'm not giving up my compact discs and vinyl.*

Baxter picked up a grab-and-go lunch from the Heavenly Bakery Company near where he was parked and took it back to his sedan. He messily ate the turkey and Swiss cheese croissant as he drove out to the address, enjoying a mocha latte to wash it down. He couldn't listen to any of his favourite music, even though he'd brought one of his CDs – *Explorations* by Bill Evans, because the damn stupid car only had a port for a flash drive and no CD player.

Baxter finished his lunch and wrapped the cardboard coffee cup up in the croissant bag, squished it up and put it on the passenger seat. The property where he'd seen the white Rolls Royce parked was to the southwest of the city on an estate full of luxury chalets on a south-facing slope, but he decided to drive to the luxury resort above it and park up there. It was a beautiful drive on a recently ploughed road and snow still hung heavily on the fir trees flanking either side of the road. A few minutes later, Baxter was pulling up to the resort and climbing out of the sedan.

He was in an area signposted as Southern Gulch and could already see the property below where he'd seen the white Rolls Royce. The air was cold and crisp, and his breath smoked in a huge cloud in front of him as he began the walk with his bag over his shoulder towards the property. Before he got too close to the property, he decided to step into some woodland so he would stay out of sight as he drew closer. He wanted to get a closer look at those footsteps he had seen with the drone. He cursed himself for not having thought ahead and brought some proper footwear – his socks were now soaking wet with melted snow and his shoes squelched as he walked through the forest to his destination.

When he reached the centre of the forest, he saw something that horrified him. Here amid dozens of pine trees, the footprints led to an area of heavily churned-up snow. It was filthy, it was muddy and, Baxter was certain, bloody. Had they killed the senator here? Baxter wasted no time in his search for the truth. He placed his bag down on the snow, unzipped it and pulled out a small handheld

The Babylon Agenda

metal detector. It was an essential piece of his kit and he'd used it many times on previous cases.

Keeping one eye on the chalet through the trees, he swept the metal detector quickly around the area. It bleeped frantically at the base of one of the pine trees. Baxter returned the detector to his bag, zipped it back up and began clearing the snow away with his hands. He could see it had already been disturbed and patted down but he broke through the surface of it and made his way to the tree roots. After a careful search, he found a small gold amulet that had been pushed inside, beneath one of the roots. It was not particularly well hidden and his experience told him that this may well be deliberate. Pocketing the amulet in his suit pocket jacket, he picked up his bag and made his way back through the woods to his sedan. Inside, he closed the door, switched the engine on and got the heaters going. The amulet was a small fiddly affair and took some manipulation before he could open it. When he opened it, he found a small tiny piece of canvas rolled up into a tight scroll less than half an inch high. When he unfurled it, he knew he had to make a telephone call to someone. Pulling out his phone, he hit the number which he had stored on speed dial and prayed she was in.

Moments later she picked the phone up.
"Hello?"
"Holly, this is Baxter. I need your help."

Chapter 13

The second Baxter had described what he'd found inside the amulet, Holly knew she would be flying to Aspen. Within minutes of the call ending, she had already booked a one-way flight to the famous Colorado ski town, packed a small bag of personal belongings and called a cab to take her to Boston Airport. She flew with American Airlines with an hour's stopover at Dallas Fort Worth and landed in Aspen well after dark. By the time she got through the small airport and stepped outside into the beautifully crisp high-altitude air, she looked up to see a dazzling wild grove of stars and was even able to make out the Milky Way. This was slightly harder to achieve back in her hometown of Boston so she gazed up for a few moments but was disturbed by the sound of a car horn honking. Looking back down to Earth, she saw the somewhat more prosaic sight of Baxter waving a hand at her through the window of a cherry-red Cadillac sedan. She waved back and walked over, climbing in beside him.

"Great to see you, Holly!" Baxter said, pulling away from the airport.

"And it's great to see you too, Baxter. I wasn't sure I'd see any of you guys again."

"Me neither. I was just getting settled into life back in LA and then this happens." Baxter was cruising the nice smooth ride out of the airport south into Aspen. "I've gotta say, I couldn't believe it when I saw what was inside the amulet."

"I couldn't believe it when you told me," Holly said. "But I'm glad you did."

Baxter glanced over at her. She was staring through the windscreen, her face lit by the gentle glow of the oncoming traffic. "Life been treating you good, kid?"

"I can't complain," Holly said. "Life in Boston is good. Harvard is good. I enjoy my research."

"You sound bored."

She sighed and crossed her hands on her lap. "It's just that after what we went through together I…"

"I feel the same way Holly," Baxter said. "None of us are superheroes but what we went through was extraordinary."

"Well, I don't know… Mason and Alicia are kind of out there a bit."

"Not as out there as Guy Wilde," Baxter said and they both laughed. "But you know what I mean."

Holly nodded. "I've never sought adventure, Baxter. I'm the bookish kid. I was always comfortable there. I felt safe there. Whenever we went anywhere as a kid I always looked for the nearest library. There was just something about exploring those places, the smell of the old books, that quality of silence you get in those places. That is my world. But all of a sudden..."

"All of a sudden you found yourself racing through the streets of Rome, being shot at by a secret society. Hey," he said with an affable shrug, "it happens to us all."

Holly laughed again.

Baxter was indicating right. "Did you have a chance to book accommodation?"

"No, I just came out here. That was stupid."

"Forget about it. I booked two rooms at this little hotel up here. It's nothing special but it's a warm bed and a good breakfast."

"Sounds great to me."

There was a long silence as Baxter finished the drive, and pulled into the hotel car park. He switched off the ignition and the dashboard lights flicked off. Then the two of them climbed out of the car, closed their doors and walked into the hotel reception area. Baxter did the business, and moments later the woman behind the desk was sliding two keys towards them.

Then he checked his watch. "Listen, it's not even ten pm. I'd rather discuss this tonight if possible. What I told you about the amulet was only half the story."

"What do you mean?" Holly asked.

"Let me buy you a drink first."

*

"So you think they murdered this Senator Sullivan?" Holly asked.

Baxter gave a sad nod of his head and took a long slug of his bourbon. "I think he probably is dead, yes. You see, Mrs Sullivan was worried he'd been snatched – possibly because somebody wanted a ransom or wanted to blackmail him over some defence contracts, that sort of thing. When she told me, it all sounded very plausible and I had no reason to change my mind until I got here to Aspen and saw the bloody snow in the forest below the luxury ski chalet I told you about. When I found the amulet with these weird markings, I thought… he's dead, right? This is more secret society crap."

"I wouldn't like to say," Holly said. "But given the nature of those markings…"

"On the phone, you said they had something to do with the Freemasons?" Baxter asked.

"More or less," Holly said, "but not exactly. Sorry if I sound confusing but that's because I am confused. The images you described to me, are not precisely Freemasonic in style, but similar."

"Well, why not see them for yourself?" Baxter said, reaching into his pocket. He handed Holly the amulet.

Holly opened it up, a little more nimbly than Baxter had described his attempt, and unfolded the little tiny strip of canvas that was inside. She looked at the symbols on it and saw Baxter had described them extremely accurately. There were no real surprises except for how intricately they were drawn and with such care.

"These symbols," she said. "As I say, they're almost Masonic in their design but not exactly. You can see where some of them have their provenance as Masonic symbols, but they've been changed, they've been altered. I don't know why. If I saw them on the internet or anywhere else I would probably just ignore them as so much nonsense. The fact they were in an amulet around the neck of a senator who you think has been murdered, I think raises some questions. The fact he had hidden it before being killed, if that's what you think happened, tells me I need to pay attention to these symbols."

"And what are you getting?"

"It's not hard – if it's supposed to be cryptic it's not very well concealed. It's a message written in something similar to the Masonic cypher, but as I say, with some differences. It says: JM Witherington, 1733/16NW, 33:33↓Ineptias.

"And that means?"

"I think your Senator Sullivan wants us to read a book written by this Witherington person."

Baxter leaned forward. "And where would we find that?"

"1733/16NW. It's an address – No. 1733, 16th Street Northwest."

"Which is where?"

"He means the House of the Temple Library in Washington DC. That's at that address – I've been there before more than once. I'll call ahead and see if someone can meet us there."

"What about the bit at the end?" Baxter asked.

"I think I know what it means. If I'm right, Sullivan wants us to find a book in the library, then we go to Page 33, down to Line 33 and look for some nonsense words."

"I have a bad feeling about this, Holly."

"Me too, and I'll tell you why. A few days ago, I read online about the tragic street-stabbing of a French historian named Philippe Laroche in Paris, who also happened to be the Master of the Grand Lodge of Paris. And then yesterday I read in the news about another man – a Professor of Theology from the University College of London who also happened to be a Grand Master Mason named Marcus Beausire – was found dead, also stabbed, in a historic Portuguese mansion."

"And you think they're connected with Sullivan?"

"Two professors and a US senator, all three of whom were Masons, all stabbed to death in mysterious circumstances within a few days? You know what I think?"

"That we should call Mason?"

She nodded and smiled. "I'll call him when we're done here and tell him about everything we know so far. If he's in Portugal he might be able to investigate the murder that happened there."

Baxter scratched his chin. "I wonder why Sullivan wants us to go to the library?"

Holly sipped her drink. "I guess we'll find that out when we fly to DC in the morning!"

Baxter raised his glass and they toasted. "Looks like we're on the hunt again!"

Chapter 14

These days all of life was an open road to Guy Huxley-Wilde. That was just the way he liked it, especially if that open road was a long desert highway somewhere in a very sparsely populated Middle Eastern country. Right now, Wilde was opening the throttle on his beloved Harley-Davidson and tearing down Iran's Route 22 on his way to Tehran in the darkest hour before dawn. It was a good time to travel if you wanted to avoid unnecessary attention.

Since leaving Ashgabat in Turkmenistan a few days ago, he'd been driving the backroads on his bike to avoid any unwanted attention. This would represent a major drag due to the Bronze Age necklaces he was smuggling out of the country. They were beautiful blue things, made from lapis lazuli pearls, but they were also 4000 years old and belonged to the Turkmenistan Government. Happily for Wilde, he had a buyer of black market relics waiting for him in Tehran who would pay handsomely to get his hands on the necklaces, the only problem being the substantial prison sentence he would serve if he was caught with them on his way out of Turkmenistan and into Iran. Wilde was a pretty mellow and open-minded sort of guy, but he'd draw the line of spending ten years in an Iranian prison.

But Wilde had no fear of that. He'd been doing this for so many years now it had become entirely second nature to him. No one seemed to give him much bother these days, with his wild mop of hair and his scuffed boots and ragged bomber jacket. He had half a dozen old paperback copies of Rough Guide books stuffed in his bag and always managed to convince any interested parties that he was bombing his way around the world after retiring from the British Civil Service. It was all lies of course. Wilde was the heir to a large country estate back in England but the quiet, pastoral life was never something that appealed to him and from a very young age all he had ever wanted to do was travel the world, like a 21st Century nomad on his beloved steed of steel and chrome. That was why he was good at what he did. He never really turned any heads and when he did he was able to talk his way out of any difficulties in just a few minutes. As a consequence, he had made a lot of money over the years but most of it he had given away. He was a man of few needs and even fewer wants, and he had more money than he could ever possibly use sitting in his country estate back in England.

He saw the sign for the campsite he had been looking for inside the Golastan National Park and after checking his mirrors he indicated right and decelerated before finally pulling off the road and driving uphill through a densely wooded area on his way to the park. He'd been here before because this was one of his regular relic-running routes. It was a calm, relaxing sort of place with a beautiful lake surrounded by trees. He followed the smaller road for another mile or so before it became a track, then he turned left and went off the track, driving his Harley over some rough ground for a few minutes, his headlamp lighting the forest. Then he pulled up in his favourite spot. It was a little hidey-hole he always used while he was driving on this road and it was beginning to feel a little bit like a home away from home. He pulled to a stop, kicked his stand out and switched the engine off. Then he climbed off the bike, took his helmet off, put it on the seat and walked around in circles for a few moments, stretching his arms and yawning.

Once he began to come back into reality after his long ride, he realised how much he loved this place. It didn't look much like home though. There were finches and blackbirds and starlings, and he saw those often enough back in England, but this was also a land of white-tailed eagles and griffon vultures. There were oaks and spruce trees, hawthorns, blackberries and walnuts, which were also common enough in England, but then there were also wild tomato plants and pomegranate trees.

Wilde was pleased to be here; he took a deep breath and then wandered over to the shore of the lake where he sat down and began to mellow out, staring out across the water. To make the moment even more perfect, he reached into his leather jacket and pulled out one single Cohiba Siglo IV. It had been given to him as a thank you by the man who had fenced him the Bronze Age necklaces a day or two ago in Turkmenistan. It was a medium-strength

Cuban cigar, costing around one hundred and fifty American dollars with a burn-time of just under an hour. It had an earthy, woody taste with a hint of chocolate and coffee, and Wilde always fancied he could detect a tang of black pepper and leather on the retro-hale, but perhaps that was controversial.

He fired it up and got it going in no time at all, then leaned back against the tree trunk, stretched his long legs out and began to relax properly. He enjoyed puffing on a cigar, especially after he'd been on the road for a long time and was staring out across the placid lake, lit by moonlight, an extremely serene experience. If life was about anything, Wilde strongly believed, it was about the serious pursuit of serene experiences. With that in mind, his mind immediately turned back to the sight of Jed Mason unloading a magazine on a bunch of unpleasant mercenaries, although exactly where that was he couldn't remember. It wasn't that Wilde was a busy man and had too many experiences to properly organise them in his memory, it was more that he was one to let things go, let things hang out. He had been fortunate enough to visit many locations in the few days he had spent with Mason, Holly, Alicia and Baxter, but so many of them had begun to blur into one in his mind especially those that involve the heavy use of automatic weapons. As far as he was concerned, the only business he ever truly wanted with a gun was smuggling a vintage one on the black market somewhere.

Wilde puffed on the cigar again and looked up to see the first stars of the early dawn fading away in the sky right before his eyes. He'd be making a campfire soon enough, and then pitching his tent for a day's sleep. It was one of those little one-man bivouac affairs that he picked up for next to nothing at a flea market in Isfahan not long ago. It did the job – it was waterproof and kept him warm enough, at least it did in conjunction with the sleeping bag he carried with him. It was important for a man in his business to be able to pull off the road and sleep somewhere independently, without the eyes of a curious hotelier crawling all over him. One never knew when the authorities would come calling for a man like Guy Wilde. When he thought that, a big smile crossed his face; he enjoyed his life a hell of a lot more than he probably should.

Jedediah Mason. He wondered what the old sod was doing right now. Probably getting ready for dinner on his olive farm – where was that now Spain? No, it wasn't Spain, it was Portugal. He remembered it was Portugal, and there was a woman involved too – he thought her name was Bernadette but that didn't seem right. It seemed too French for Portugal but then again maybe she was French. Wilde was not the world's best at paying attention to details. He puffed the cigar again and rolled the smoke around in his mouth before blowing it out across the lake. It was lighter now, there was a short twilight in Iran, and reluctantly he got up with a groan and brushed himself down before clamping the cigar in his mouth and unpacking his camping equipment from the bike.

It took a seasoned pro like Wilde less than ten minutes to have the entire thing set up, and then he was igniting his little campfire and opening up a can of beans. He cracked open a warm can of Iranian lager, not exactly life at the Ritz but he was happy enough, and then sat back down again in the entrance to the bivouac and stared into the fire as he ate his beans and drank his beer. After breakfast, he would sleep through the day and then make tracks again just around dusk. It was a life that appealed to only a special few. A secret part of him wished Holly Hope would call him again, but then again did he give her his number? He couldn't remember that either. Either way, it was a moot point. He was certain – as sure as there was a sky above his head – that he would never hear from Holly or any of the rest of them ever again.

Chapter 15

Holly Hope loved a visit to the capital, and this was even more exciting thanks to her new *raison d'être* – tracking down whatever Kent Sullivan had hidden inside the library in the House of the Temple. She had no idea how they were going to find what they were looking for in the library, but a cursory search of the internet told her the House of the Temple had been open to the public since 1915 for guided tours. A further check showed it was open Monday to Thursday between ten in the morning and half-three in the afternoon. She wasn't sure when she had made her previous visits, but their flight was minutes away from landing in Dulles a little after midday, so they had plenty of time to take a cab and get there before it closed. How they found time to do what they needed to do in the library when they were inside was another matter.

"It's after we get into the place that the problems begin," Baxter said, drumming his fingers on the arms of his seat as the plane began to descend through the clouds.

Holly nodded. "That's what I was just thinking. Any ideas?"

"Some."

The plane rumbled and shook as it flew down through a massive bank of rainclouds. "And?"

"Still working on them. Get right back to you."

Holly smiled. She was already happier than she had been for months. Work at Harvard was good and it was satisfying, but sometimes she felt isolated and cut off from the world – a world she had tasted for the first time on her mission to discover the Ark of the Covenant with her new friends, Jedediah Mason, Alicia Kane, Guy Wilde and Wesley Baxter, the last of whom was right here beside her on the flight. But were they her friends? Maybe work colleagues was a better way of putting it, but then again was even that correct? After all, she had only spent a few days in their company, when everything was all added up together. She didn't care.

She thought about Jed Mason a lot – perhaps a little too much, if the truth was known. The truth was that she found him attractive, and why was that so wrong? He was tall and lean and fit, he was kind, generous and brave. On the other hand, he could be cold and distant and often got lost in dark memories. He also found it hard to laugh at jokes. He wasn't perfect. And yet he crossed her mind more often than she would have thought likely, especially given the large distance between the two of them. She was still in Boston as she had spent almost her entire life, and he was living in Portugal. He was far across the other side of the North Atlantic and worse than that he seemed to be in some sort of a relationship with a Portuguese woman called

Benedita. Mason didn't talk about her much but just enough for Holly to know there was something there. Such is life, she thought and abandoned the subject.

As to the others, she thought about them all considerably less. She knew next to nothing about Alicia Kane other than she was the hardest, toughest woman she had ever met. If she was to be believed, then she was probably working as a bodyguard right now, probably in her hometown of Chicago. Holly didn't think anyone on the team knew much about Guy Wilde. He was some kind of strange English aristocrat who for whatever reason had dedicated the most recent part of his life to smuggling small weapons and relics across borders, mostly in the Middle East. But he was a great guy with a fantastic sense of humour and also considerably wiser than most other people she had met. He had once told her that he made it a point to study the language, culture and philosophy of whatever country he was in and tried to soak up as much of that wisdom as possible. It showed when you talked to him.

Then of course there was old Baxter, the sixty-something private investigator who was squashed down in his seat to the right of her. A little overweight, always looking like he was ready for bed, he had thinning hair and bags under his eyes, and his clothes were always slightly crumpled and his shoes scuffed. He looked like he slept in his office, the truth be told, but he was also slightly nervous on missions, she had noticed. Maybe he felt out of his depth –she knew she certainly did. Baxter was warm and probably the most loving person on the team at least from her point of view. But she was glad to know all of them and secretly hoped that the little adventure she and Baxter were sharing would turn into something bigger and that she would be given cause to call Mason and Alicia and ask for their help. At least some of her hopes had come true when she phoned Mason the previous evening after her conversation with Baxter and explained everything she knew. When she asked him if he could go along and investigate the Portuguese murder scene where Beausire was killed, he had been reluctant, as usual, but eventually agreed. He said he'd call her when or if he found anything of use. That was enough for her, but she now hoped they would get a chance to meet in person.

The journey from the airport to the Dupont Circle was a little under thirty miles and the cab driver promised he could do it in around three-quarters of an hour. She relaxed in the back seat of the taxi while Baxter sat up front and chatted to the driver. The journey from the airport into Washington took them east on Route 66 and just north of Arlington before crossing the Potomac and driving into the city at Foggy Bottom. Mason had cracked a rare joke about the name of this place once; she hadn't found it funny, but maybe it was British humour. They now turned left and drove past the White House before taking another right and then eventually driving north on 16th St NW. They pulled up. Baxter paid the driver in cash – Holly noticed he always used cash when he was out on the streets – and

The Babylon Agenda

then after the two of them watched the driver pull off into the traffic, they turned and made their way up the steps to the entrance.

Holly had done her homework on the flight just as she always did. The House of the Temple was modelled after the Mausoleum at Halicarnassus, and building work began in 1911. It was finished four years later in the autumn of 1915. Situated exactly one mile due north of the White House, which was just one of those details that the Masons seemed to love so much. Now she stared up at its beautiful white marble, Doric columns and was reminded of some of the beautiful architecture she had enjoyed in Rome.

"This place looks like a building in ancient Greece," Baxter said.

"It's supposed to," Holly said. "It was modelled on the Tomb of Mausolus, which was one of the Seven Ancient Wonders of the World."

"You know, it sure was great the way they used to make buildings look so pretty in the old days. Why does everything today have to look like a Borg Cube?"

She faced him. "You're a fan of Star Trek?"

Baxter reddened a little and shrugged. "I've watched an episode from time to time. Of course, I'm more of your classic first series kind of guy than the actual Borg episodes."

Holly smiled. "Sounds like you know all about the Borg."

"Like I said… you know since Debs left and everything… it's just me in the evening and maybe I get around to watching some of this stuff on TV. You have to realise, it's not planned or anything. It's just whatever's on."

"Set your lasers to stun!" Holly said with a smirk.

"If you must know, I listen to music most nights when I'm thinking about my cases. It helps me think. I usually just put on a little bit of classic jazz, that kind of thing."

"Beam me up, Baxter."

He looked at her now with a big smile on his face. "This amuses you?"

"A little," Holly said. She was enjoying herself more than she had done in weeks.

They continued their way up the steps. Baxter said, "You don't watch Star Trek?"

She shook her head. "No, not really. I don't watch television at all."

"I thought nerds like you loved Star Trek."

"Who says I'm a nerd?"

Baxter suddenly looked mortified. "Hey, I'm sorry I didn't mean anything but I kinda thought…"

Holly stopped at the top of the steps just outside the entrance to the House of the temple. "Baxter, just relax. I'm kidding. Everyone knows I'm a total nerd. I'm the Queen of the Nerds. Now there's a name for one of your Star Trek episodes."

Baxter pushed the door open and gestured for Holly to walk through into the lobby. "The Queen of the Nerds? I'd watch that."

Chapter 16

Holly's call had woken Mason before dawn and after some coffee, he had climbed in his beaten-up pickup truck, and driven out of his farm at first light. It was early and clear, and the roads were almost empty. That was one of the reasons he loved living in rural Portugal so much, especially after his experience of trying to drive in the south of England. That was an entirely different kettle of fish. He sat back in his seat, turned on the radio in a vain attempt to improve his Portuguese, and followed his GPS, which he had programmed to take him to the Quinta de Regalia. Before Holly's phone call, he had never heard of this place and he had no idea where it was, but she sounded pretty serious and she seemed to know all about this Beausire character, so when she told him that she thought his murder had much wider implications and may involve a secret society he knew he had no choice but to go and check out what she had asked as soon as possible.

Mason was on the highway for a long time before turning off and joining an A road. His main goal at this point was avoiding the city of Lisbon, and thankfully he was approaching from the city's north. After a small amount of traffic on the A16 skirting around Mem

Martins, he turned right and found himself approaching the town of Sintra from the east. Every time Mason drove through Sintra he was a little bit more depressed than the last. The first time he had seen the town, it was an idyllic picture-postcard image of a Mediterranean town, tucked away in the dry sun-brushed hills with older people lazily strolling through the shade of weeping figs or oleanders, but today he noticed with dismay graffiti sprayed all over the walls and gangs of hooded youths hanging around on the street corners. What they found to pass their time in a place like this baffled him.

He drove through the town and exited at the western end, driving up the hill towards the Quinta da Regaleira. The property was an enormously elaborate romantic palace with an adjoining chapel, surrounded by sumptuous parkland. Secret grottoes, wells, lakes and fountains were situated in various places around the estate, all of them working together to create an enormous tourist magnet. He'd even read about an elaborate tunnel system stretching from the chapel to the main house and prayed he would be spared having to go down there as part of his investigation. His life had already turned into enough of a Robert Langdon novel as he could bear. But the place was still very beautiful, or so were the pictures he had seen of it online after researching it. It was more than a money-making machine; the entire property was listed as a World Heritage Site by UNESCO.

He pulled into the car park, locked his car and walked around to the main entrance of the luxurious property, pausing to take in the main façade, and its impressive display of gargoyles and Gothic pinnacles stretching up into the bright blue Portuguese sky. Its main feature was a beautiful octagonal tower, but if Mason had understood Holly correctly, he wouldn't be spending a lot of time inside the palace, because he was looking for something entirely different somewhere else on the estate.

He asked the woman at the reception where he could find the famous Masonic Initiation Well. The beautiful smile on the woman's face now faded as she patiently explained that the area had been cordoned off by police. She said there had been an unfortunate event at the bottom of the well very recently and as a consequence it was not open to the public. When Mason asked what the event was, even though he already knew, he was told that it was confidential police business, but she thought a man had been killed there. Mason explained that he would like to know where it was all the same although he had no intention of going there today. The woman's smile returned and she handed him a paper leaflet, turned it over to its reverse and pointed at a map. In perfect, but beautifully accented English, the woman then traced his route from where they were standing down to the Initiation Well. Mason thanked her in Portuguese, took the map and then went back out the way he had come from, pausing for a moment on the top of the steps to get his bearings.

Mason made his way across the fairytale estate, not pausing once to take in any of the beautiful sights. He had an aesthetic sense and was able to appreciate beauty when he saw it, but today he had a mission to complete, although he hoped it was a very short one. Checking his battered Mondaine wristwatch, he was pretty sure he could be back on his olive farm before it was too late this afternoon and hopefully able to do some more work, before settling down to some food and a glass of wine. Anyone other than Holly Hope he would have told to get lost, but he found he could never say no to the beautiful nerd from Boston.

The Initiation Well was built into a slope so it was accessible from both the top and the bottom. Mason approached it from the top end and saw the police barrier tape stretched all over the entranceway. He noticed with interest that there were no security guards or police present, but people visiting the estate were nowhere to be seen, behaving as good citizens and avoiding the area cordoned off by the authorities.

Mason was not a good citizen and instead pulled the barrier tape up, slipped beneath it and went inside the top of the Initiation Well. It was exactly as Holly had explained, stretching down 27 metres to the bottom where there was a beautiful mosaic floor with a five-star motif laid in it. If Holly was correct, that was where Marcus Beausire gasped his last few breaths. He began walking down the spiral staircase, gradually counting off the 23 niches built into the stone on the side of the wall. Holly had explained to him that the nine flights of stairs stretching down to the bottom were often rumoured to be connected to the Knights Templar due to their having nine founding members. However, she had told him that she favoured the explanation that the nine flights of stairs symbolised the nine churches of Hell from Dante's Inferno. She told him that the place was heavily connected not only with the Templars, but had also hosted Rosicrucian and Freemasonic rituals over the centuries. It was this last one that Holly was convinced was responsible for Beausire's murder and that of two other men she mentioned when she spoke to him on the phone.

Mason continued down the steps, trying to imagine as he went the horror that must have been passing through Beausire's mind as he made his way down the very same staircase just over a day and a half ago. But, this time it was day and not night. This time, Mason was walking casually in the warmth and not being hunted by a team of murderous pursuers. He reached the bottom of the well and looked down at the inlaid stone compass which was adorned with a Templar Cross and tried to imagine Beausire's last few moments here. Then he got to work.

Holly had told him how Baxter had found a small golden amulet hidden in the root system of a fir tree very close to where the private investigator believed an American senator – Sullivan – had been murdered. According to Baxter, and Holly's theory, Sullivan and Beausire were one of three members of something called the Fellowship of

Light. There was another one called Laroche, also stabbed to death in Paris.

Mason began with a visual inspection of the area where Beausire was killed. Holly was speculating from something she had seen in Sullivan's amulet that the three men – this Fellowship – constituted some kind of breakaway group from a sinister organisation she believed was called the Conclave of Darkness. This information Sullivan had cryptically left behind inside his amulet, as planned should the worst happen. She believed they had some kind of agreement that if they knew their deaths were imminent, they would remove the amulets from around their necks and hide them near their bodies. This was so their murderers would not find the amulets and steal them. How this had anything to do with Masons, Holly was not sure. Mason thought all this was pretty far-fetched, but gave Holly the benefit of the doubt.

Mason watched a small party of Korean tourists wander up to the base of the well, take note of the bright yellow police barrier tape and then wander away muttering to themselves. Mason was pleased that the well was still sealed off from the general public as it gave him some peace to conduct his search. He began with a cursory visual inspection but seeing nothing out of the ordinary, or anywhere Beausire could have hidden his amulet, he went to the only place where it would be possible to hide something – the wall.

Working his way slowly around the circular stone wall, Mason painstakingly checked every single nook and cranny until he found a small loose stone a few inches from the floor. It was impossible to remove with his fingers, so Mason pulled out his pocket knife and used one of the blades to work it free. When it was cleanly out of the way, he was able to look inside and saw a small gold amulet. He reached inside and took the amulet and then pushed the stone back into the gap. Then he brushed away a small amount of rubble and rock chips that he had created so as not to draw attention to the hole, pocketed the amulet, walked over to the police barrier tape, ducked underneath it and then stepped out across the sun-dappled lawns into the estate.

He had no interest in what was inside the amulet; all he wanted to do was report that he had successfully found it to Holly and tell her what was inside. He would take a photo of the interior contents, if indeed it had any, and send it to her and then he could get back to his olive grove. Then he felt a thunderous strike in the small of his back that blasted him forward off his balance and sent him flying into a verge full of plants.

Chapter 17

The woman in the dark suit with her hair up and her hands held behind her back was standing patiently in front of a closed wooden door. It was the door to Leonardo Snow's private study on the top floor of the White Fir Lodge and standing outside it was usually an unsettling experience.

So why did she do it? Why did any of them work for a man like Snow, the Great Guardian of the Conclave of Darkness? The answer was simple enough and twofold. First, it offered her the chance to kill people with impunity – so long as sanctioned by the Conclave, and second, post-service retirement was exceptionally well-funded. She supposed there was a third reason, too – who else would hire someone with a track record like hers? Larceny and wrongful appropriation, grand theft auto, fraud and false statements, financial advantage done by deception, aggravated assault. She forgot the rest, but that was why she worked for Snow.

She was also a proud member of the Conclave of Darkness. She liked the feeling of advantage and superiority it gave her when walking through a crowd of 'normies', as she liked to call them. She knew so much more about the world than any of those fools would ever know. But there were downsides – serious failure in the Conclave meant termination, and that meant much more than a simple ending of a contract. It meant the ending of her life. Happily for her, she had never failed. Inside the Conclave, her nickname was the Chameleon, because her skills were centred around blending into any environment. She could play the part of anyone with total authenticity. No one ever questioned her. She was the consummate actress and always got the results the Conclave was looking for. Like right now.

"You may enter."

The man, whose official Conclave 'Nomenclature' was Necro, had told her this after having received the order to do so from Snow himself, via an earpiece. He was a big tall man, built like a French-door fridge, with scarred, tanned skin and a platinum tooth to match a silver earring. No one inside the Conclave knew where he came from, and no one recognised his accent. Maybe Snow knew, but no one else would dare to ask. Necro's position in the organisation as Snow's main bodyguard meant he was untouchable.

"Thank you, Necro," she said.

She stepped inside the large wooden study and closed the heavy door behind her. At first, Snow was nowhere to be seen. Then she was aware of a rustling sound up on the mezzanine level and looked up to see him pushing a book back into a shelf. When he saw her, he turned and made his way down the sweeping spiral staircase until they were face to face.

"Ah, Locusta! You have something to report to me about our little rabbit."

"Yes, sir," she said. "His full name is Wesley John Baxter. He is a private investigator working out of Beverly Hills in Los Angeles. He has a small office which he has optimistically named Baxter & Associates, even though he is the only one working there. He was a cop in the LAPD for many years eventually rising to the rank of lieutenant, a plainclothes detective working in homicide mostly in Santa Monica. He quit the force and became a gumshoe."

"Why are we talking about him?"

"He was contacted by Charlotte Sullivan with regards to her husband's death."

"Why him? You have described him as a nobody."

"Mrs Sullivan was referred to Wesley Baxter by Sally Wilton who had used his services in connection with her husband's affair."

His eyes widened. "You're talking about the wife of Edmund Wilton?"

Locusta knew why Snow had suddenly taken interest in what she was talking about, pretty much for the first time since she had stepped into his office. Edmund Wilton was one of the wealthiest men in the world who had on occasion made the much-coveted Number 1 ranking, at least in the United States of America, and had been killed a few months ago in a terrorist attack in the Vatican. But that was not what interested Snow about him. The Great Guardian of the Conclave of Darkness had taken a sudden interest because what the world did not know about Edmund Wilton was that he had been a very high-ranking freemason for many years, and had also held informal talks with Snow about joining the Conclave of Darkness.

Wilton had been almost completely persuaded by Snow that what they called the Grand Secret, would have to be kept from the rest of the world and neither of them was convinced that the wider Freemasons organisation would be prepared to do such a thing once knowledge of the secret moved across their ranks. In the end, Wilton had been killed before making a final decision on the matter, but she knew Snow was all but convinced that he would have 'crossed the house' as Conclave members said, and stepped into the Conclave as a very high-ranking member. More than any of this, she knew now Snow would take a much more intense interest in the activities of Mr Baxter than he might otherwise have done because he had been wrapped up in an investigation centred on Wilton and now he was sniffing around Sullivan's death and that was a trail which led back to Snow.

"That's right. Edmund Wilton," she said. "Sally Wilton was suspicious that her husband was conducting an affair behind her back in Beverly Hills, so she hired Baxter to look into it. She and Mrs Sullivan are friends so when Mrs Sullivan became concerned about her husband's disappearance, she called Sally and asked her for the name of the man she had hired to track down and expose her husband's affair. That is how Baxter is involved in this and that is why we are talking about him."

"Continue."

"After Mrs Sullivan discussed the matter with Baxter he immediately prioritised the search for her husband and made it his number one case. I don't think he has too much else going on. He made contact with the wine merchants where Mortis and Lupus snatched Sullivan after you ordered them to do so. He then tracked them to the airport via a contact in the police force in the LAPD, which took him to Aspen."

"And when he got to Aspen?"

"He spoke to a junior worker at one of the car hire companies who gave him your car's details."

"I see. How did he get from the wine merchants to the airport? I mean specifically."

"He looked on the security footage at the wine merchants who gave him the van Mortis and Lupus rented."

"I see. Those two men have both failed the Conclave. I take it you've cleaned up all of these loose ends?"

"Yes," Locusta said. "The wine merchant, Sergeant Edward Spartan and the young man at the car hire company have all been terminated. Their deaths were all made to look like accidents."

"Good work. Then you are to terminate Baxter and that will be an end to the matter."

"I'm not sure that will be the case. When I was talking to him, he told me he works with a small team when he is working on international cases. There's a good chance he has already been in contact with these people with regards to Senator Sullivan's demise."

She watched as Snow took the information in, silent and solemn as usual. He was hard to read – not quite inscrutable, but almost – and now he turned and walked over to his large picture window. With his arms folded behind his back, clearly contemplating the information she had just supplied him with, he gave out a long sigh. She knew better than to interrupt him when he was deep in thought. He was a profound and complex thinker but he also had a short temper. Disrupting him was not advised. It was better to let him think in peace for as long as he wanted, today that turned out to be not very long at all.

"Where is Baxter now?"

"He boarded a flight to Washington DC with an academic from Harvard called Dr Holly Hope."

"I see. There are several locations where Sullivan could have hidden information in Washington DC. You are to go to the city with Scorpio and his team and track them down."

"Should we execute them?"

"Not until you are certain you have the entire team. There is little point in terminating Baxter and Hope if they have passed the information about Sullivan's murder, or more pertinently perhaps why he was murdered, on to any other parties."

"But when we're certain we have everyone," she asked hopefully, with hope rising in her heart, "we can execute them all then?"

"When you are certain you have the entire team, the Conclave will approve their executions. In the meantime, brief Scorpio about your journey to Washington DC and then get after Baxter. Oh and before you go – Mortis and Lupis are downstairs awaiting further orders. Terminate both of them for their failure at the wine merchants."

"Yes sir," Locusta said. "With the greatest of pleasure."

"Good work, Locusta."

She liked her Conclave Nomenclature 'Locusta'. It had a nice ring to it. Much nicer than being Martha Crockett, her latest character. But Martha had been right for a harried businesswoman on her way back from Los Angeles to Aspen, the kind of woman a tired PI might want to shoot the breeze with for a few hours. She smiled at the memory of her conversation with Baxter, but now she was Locusta again.

Baxter might have warmed to Martha, but he wasn't going to like Locusta at all.

Chapter 18

Holly's previous visits meant she knew that admission into the House of the Temple was free, but as she made her way up the impressive stone steps at the front, and looked at the mysterious carved sphinxes on either side of the grand entrance, she knew she would have been happy to pay almost anything to be here.

"Those things are pretty impressive," Baxter said.

"Each one of them weighs 17 tons," Holly said. "They were so heavy that they were carved exactly where they are today. The one with its eyes open is a symbol of power and the one over there with its eyes closed is a symbol of wisdom. Also notice that as you walk up these steps, they're numbered in groups of three then five then seven and finally nine. That's deeply significant in freemasonry."

Baxter shook his head and laughed. "Those guys think of everything."

He stepped ahead of her and pushed open one of the large grilled bronze doors and the two of them went inside an enormous, breathtaking atrium. Holly counted eight colossal granite columns which stretched from the polished black and white marble floor up to an ornate ceiling crisscrossed with oak beams. She was struck by the beautiful juxtaposition of the neoclassical architecture outside the building, the Art Deco design inside the building, and the strange Egyptian figures which adorned the atrium walls.

She and Baxter came to a stop in front of an impressive white marble table that reminded her more of an altar, constructed of two large two-headed eagles which reminded her more than a little of the Ark of the Covenant she had found in France some months before. Written on the front in beautiful gold lettering were the words: SALVE FRATER.

"What does that mean?" Baxter asked her.

"It means 'Welcome Brother' in Latin," Holly said.

"Don't take it personally," Baxter said with a smile. "You being a woman and all."

They walked across the beautiful grand black and white marble and Holly felt like she was inside an ancient Egyptian palace.

Jonathan Richards, whom Holly had spoken to earlier on the telephone, now walked over to them and shook their hands.

"Hello and welcome to the House of the Temple," he said. "As you know, we are open to the public and free to visit but if you'd still like me to show you around I'm perfectly happy to do so and have some free time. I was very impressed by your credentials, Dr Hope."

"Thank you, and your offer to show us around would be wonderful," Holly said.

"Of course. What are you researching again?"

"I'm currently working on the relationship between Christian theology and the Masons, so I'm extremely grateful that you found the time to meet me today and let us in to show us around."

As Jonathan smiled, clearly impressed by her credentials, Holly felt a tinge of guilt that everything she had just told him was a total lie, but she knew from her experiences on the previous two missions with Jed Mason that it was the only way to get results – at least quickly.

"If you follow me through here we'll go to the temple room," Jonathan said.

Holly and Baxter followed Jonathan into the temple room through a set of enormous giant leather padded doors, passing a massive marble chair that Jonathan called the Tyler's Seat. Carved into its back were the cautionary words this time in English: KNOW THYSELF.

The temple room was an inspiring vault with a startlingly high ceiling rising above a beautiful, intricately designed space fit for a king. Holly was impressed and stared in amazement at wooden benches carefully covered with gold inlaid pigskin, the velvet imperial purple curtains framing a beautiful stained-glass window of brilliant ambers and oranges. In the centre of it all, an imposing green marble altar flecked with gold, in front of which was a golden purple prayer cushion. On the far wall was a huge wooden throne inside a canopy draped with purple and gold curtains, behind which an elaborate stained-glass window depicted the rising sun. Beside it was the third written message the House of the Temple had given her in as many minutes: TIS THE MYSTIC TIE THAT MAKETH ALL MEN BRETHREN.

Baxter leaned in close to her and lowered his voice. "You can call me crazy if you like, but this place looks like something from Ghostbusters."

Jonathan now took them through to the library, and Holly was extremely relieved to see that they were the only two people in there, although as they'd made their way across to it she had noticed a party of visitors assembling in the foyer by the white marble table.

The library was as grand as any she had seen, with circular walkways of parquet flooring, lined on either side by floor-to-ceiling bookshelves. Wooden seats with red velvet cushions were dotted here and there for readers as well as specialist booths for more serious researchers.

To say she was at home here was a gross understatement. Jonathan strolled ahead of them, dropping details about this book or that view through this window, when Holly turned to Baxter and quietly spoke in his ear.

"Exactly how are we going to get him out of here?"

"Leave it to me," Baxter said.

With no further explanation, Holly watched Baxter turn around and walk out of the library in the direction they had come. She walked over to Jonathan who was now leafing through an enormous book on top of a reading table, situated in front of a beautiful vase of fresh flowers. The sun was slanting at an angle through the stained glass window and lighting everything in a kaleidoscopic array of colours. Although she was already on a mission, Holly wanted just to spend the rest of the day or preferably the week in here. She was about to make her excuses and go to find the section that she was looking for to find Senator Sullivan's book when all of a sudden a shrill fire alarm filled the library.

Jonathan looked at her, calm but slightly surprised. "I'm afraid I'm going to have to ask you to leave. Everyone has to evacuate the entire building when the alarm sounds."

"Of course," Holly said with a smile. She already had the advantage of Jonathan, because while he was visualising a fire raging somewhere inside the building, Holly already had a damn good idea what had happened. When she stepped out into the lobby and saw Baxter with a smile on his face everything came together.

"Don't tell me, cigarette lighter under the smoke alarm in the restroom?" she whispered.

"No," he said, shaking his head. He half-pulled out a box of matches from his right pocket and smiled at her. "But you're in the ballpark. Quick follow me!"

With no further warning, Baxter took hold of Holly's elbow and pulled her behind a large marble column, one of the eight inside the atrium, as they watched Jonathan and two or three other members of staff shepherding out the large tour group through the bronze grilled doors at the front.

The Babylon Agenda

Baxter looked at Holly, his face suddenly all business.

"Holly, I don't wanna put any pressure on you, but you've got about five minutes before they see we're not out there and someone comes in looking for us."

It was time for Holly to shine.

Chapter 19

Mason was eating a mouthful of dirt in a rose bed that someone had just kicked him into and realising that his day was not going to be as easy as initially thought. Scrambling out of the beautiful bed of flowers, and scratching himself badly on the rose thorns as he extricated himself, he spun around to see a man in a plain grey suit, with a white shirt and no tie. He was well built, muscular and very agile, but he also had a face on him like thunder. He instantly lunged again towards Mason, absolutely fearlessly.

He fired a rapid series of punches into Mason's face, forcing Mason to bend his head back and take two or three steps back into the rose bushes to avoid being pummelled. Mason now tripped on the dirt in the bed and catching his jeans on the base of the roses fell backwards into them once again, crashing down on his back and feeling dozens of thorns stabbing into him. He cried out in pain, knowing the only way out was to roll through more of the roses and come up on the other side of the bed. He gritted his teeth and conducted the manoeuvre, leaping to his feet on the other side of the bed, and now the two men were divided by the rose bed.

Mason took the first chance he had since the assault to stuff the amulet in his pocket and now trampled back through the roses to give the other guy as good as he'd already been given. He lunged towards him, easily sideswiping a defensive hand out of the way and punching him in the side of the head, forcing the man to stagger backwards until he crashed up against the enormous movable rock at the base of the Masonic Initiation Well. The rock was there so that the entrance could be completely hidden, but today it had provided a nice surface for Mason to jam this man up against as he fired a rapid series of punches into his stomach before firing a wild backhand slap across his right temple and knocking him over beside the rock.

The rocks that had once been used to conceal the entrance were covered in green moss and ferns and other plant life, and now Mason clambered up on top of a lower rock in front of them and launched himself at the man, fully intending to land on him and finish the fight. Instead, the man saw what he was attempting, and rolled out of the way, forcing Mason to land with a hard smack on the muddy gravel in front of the entrance.

Mason leapt up to launch another attack on the man, who now pulled a knife from his belt and slashed it in the air in front of Mason's face.

"Give me the amulet!"

"What makes you think I have an amulet?"

"I saw you stuff something in your pocket. I saw you looking around inside the entrance at the bottom of the well! I know what you've done. You've come here to take the amulet and I want it back."

"If you think I've got an amulet then you better come and take it."

"This isn't a game, whoever you are! You have no idea what you're meddling with. Give me the amulet now and we can both walk away from here with no further harm. If you refuse to give it to me, then I shall have to beat it out of you."

"You sound optimistic."

"I am well trained by the Conclave and I'm prepared to give my life in defence of our secrets. You have no idea what I will do to take that amulet from you or if you get away from me today, to track you down and kill you before you can do any harm with it!"

"What's so special about the amulet?"

"You can't be a member of the Fellowship if you're asking that question."

"What's the Fellowship?"

The man was shifting his weight from foot to foot, gripping the knife in his hand with blood running down his lip from one of Mason's strikes.

"The Fellowship of Light is a group of traitors, one of whom left an amulet in the bottom of that well behind me. Hand it over and this can end now."

"I'm afraid I can't do that," Mason said. "I've been asked by a very good friend to retrieve it for her and I'm going to give it to her because I gave her my word."

"You would die for your word?"

Mason would not die for his word. Mason would do many things but that was not one of them; on the other hand, he was more than a little sure that this man did not have the hand-to-hand combat skills to kill him today. However well he considered himself trained by this mysterious Conclave, it wasn't up to the standards demanded of Mason during his specialist training across the years, especially with Titanfort.

Mason beckoned him forward. "If you want it, come and get it."

The man lunged again, this time attempting to drive the knife in his right hand up into Mason's rib cage, but Mason knew this was coming. He sidestepped him and brought his hand crashing down on the hand holding the knife. The blade clattered to the floor, Mason kicked it away into the gravel and then swung his right hand up into the man's nose hearing a satisfying crunch at the end of its journey. As the man reached up to his nose with his hands, as Mason knew he would instinctively, Mason brought his knee up into his groin and then grabbed him around the back of the neck and brought his head towards the ground. Then Mason raised his other knee and kneed him in the face.

Mason had thought this would be enough, but as the man fell backwards onto the floor, he could see he was still conscious, but heavily dazed. He crawled onto his hands and knees and then attempted to crawl across the gravel to pick up his knife. Mason saw his chance to end the fight. Mason stepped over to him kicked him hard in the ribs and then twice as hard in the face, cracking his head back and knocking him out instantly.

Mason looked around the sumptuous gardens of the Quinta da Regaleira to ensure that no one had seen the fight. He was satisfied that the entire business had played out in private such were the extensive gardens of the place. He pulled the amulet out of his pocket to ensure it was still safe, present and correct, and seeing that it was, he placed it back in his pocket and then strolled around the gardens the quiet way back to his car. He had a telephone call to make.

Chapter 20

Holly and Baxter stepped back into the library as quickly as they could, knowing that they would be under camera surveillance and they only had moments to act. Baxter decided to hang around at the entrance door and delay anyone should they come and disturb them, while Holly now ran around the library to the section she was looking for – Ancient Babylonian Mythology.

Faced with hundreds of priceless leatherbound books that had been created across various centuries and carefully and beautifully collected and curated by the House of the Temple, the nerd in her wanted just to start reading and damn the mission, but the teammate in her understood that she had to work fast. Taking Sullivan's message inside his amulet out and reading through it once again she found the name of the book that she was looking for. It was called *The Birth of Babylon* by JM Witherington. She had never heard of the author before and suspected that he may be a fictional character and that the entire book was a fake just to conceal Sullivan's message. If it was a real book, written by a real author it would at some point be in demand by a researcher whereas a fake would only be found by a casual browser who found it on this very shelf.

She found the book in less than sixty seconds. It was a beautiful red, leatherbound tome with gold inlay and gold embossed letters on the spine. She pulled it off the shelf and opened it to the page Sullivan had specified in his message – Page 33.

"You better hurry up!" Baxter shouted over the alarm. "Someone's walking over here. It's not Jonathan but some kind of security guard. He doesn't look very happy."

"Keep him talking Baxter! I need a few more seconds."

Holly scanned Page 33 using Sullivan's coordinates until she found line 33 and what she was looking for. Carefully hidden in the text in the thirty-third line down were nonsense words: 'Audre misdescribed seducement'. It meant nothing to the casual reader – perhaps a typesetter's error, but to her, it could mean everything. She took her phone from her pocket and took a photograph of the page, including the nonsense.

Then she slid the book back up onto the shelf and ran around to the entrance where Baxter was arguing with the security guard.

She waved her glasses case at the security guard. "Sorry, my fault! Full apologies, but I lost my glasses back in the library and when the alarm went off I realised I'd forgotten them, so I ran back in to find them. Stupid me."

"Well, that's very irresponsible, Ma'am," the security guard said. "When a fire alarm goes off you're supposed to evacuate the building permanently, not come back in if you've forgotten something. As it turns out, we think it's a false alarm but we're going to need you to leave the building anyway until that's verified."

"That's no problem with me," Holly said.

"And that's no problem with me either," Baxter said. "Come on, Darling. Let's go and find somewhere nice to eat lunch."

And with that Holly and Baxter walked out of the House of the Temple Library, across the marble lobby, down the Masonic steps and onto 16th Street.

"I think we really should go and get some lunch, don't you?" Holly asked. "That will give us a chance to get stuck into these crazy words!"

"Yeah, why not?" Baxter said. "I'm really hungry. You know what I'd love more than anything else? A great big chunky steak and a pile of fries. You think there's anywhere good around here to do that?"

"I'm sure we could find somewhere like that," Holly said. "But what I want to do is have a think about exactly what the nonsense words mean that I found inside Sullivan's book."

Baxter pointed up ahead. "If we go down here and turn right, we should be able to get a taxi into Georgetown. Maybe there's some good places to eat there."

Holly agreed and the two of them walked to the corner of the street and turned and then Baxter saw the cab and hailed it. The cab slowed and indicated, before pulling over and braking to a stop right beside them.

"Easier than getting a cab back home in LA," Baxter said.

He opened the rear door and Holly was climbing inside when a bullet punched a hole through the rear window. Baxter turned to see a man with a silenced gun standing on the pavement, wearing a long black leather trench coat and wearing dark glasses. There were screams and people ran for their lives, but the man was calm and measured and walked slowly forward, firing a second shot which was aimed this time at Baxter.

Baxter ducked down behind the door narrowly avoiding being shot, then screamed at Holly to get inside the cab. She jumped in behind him and screamed at the driver to get going. The driver didn't need to be told again, but then another round punched through the windscreen, killing the driver instantly. Baxter never hesitated. He clambered over the front seat, opened the driver's door, pushed the dead driver out onto the road and climbed down into the driver's seat. Then he slammed the door and stamped his foot on the throttle, surging the car forward towards the gunman.

Chapter 21

Mason returned to his pickup truck and climbed inside, slamming the door shut behind him. Now with a little time to spare, he took the amulet out of his pocket, opened it up and found a strange piece of tightly rolled-up canvas. He unfurled it and it revealed a strange line of what looked to him like Egyptian hieroglyphics. He didn't know what to make of them, but he knew a woman that did. He took out his phone and called Holly.

"Holly, hi! It's Jed. I got hold of that amulet that you were after. You were right by the way: it was hidden close to where they found Beausire's body, just inside a wall cavity hidden by a stone at the bottom of the Masonic Initiation Well."

"That's great, Jed! But I can't really talk right now!"

"Why? What's going on?"

"We got to the House of the Temple, the Masonic building in Washington DC I was telling you about. We got there and we found Sullivan's clue inside a book that he'd hidden on a shelf, but as we were coming out on our way to lunch some guy started shooting at us on 16th Street. He killed a cab driver and now Baxter's trying to get us away to safety somewhere."

Mason sat up in his car seat, horrified by what he was hearing. He was concerned by the fact that while Baxter had good experience with the LAPD, he'd been retired a good while and always seemed to be a little nervous on missions. As for Holly Hope, she stood no chance in a firefight whatsoever. Her other skills were considerable and expansive but in an entirely different field. Without him or Alicia there, he was extremely concerned for their welfare.

"What the hell's going on exactly?" he asked. "Are these guys tailing you in a car?"

"Yeah, they are," Holly said. "It's one guy. He was the one who was shooting at us – a great big tall man in a long black trench coat. He climbed into a black sedan after he took some shots at us while we were climbing into a taxi. He's giving chase now but he's on his own, I think!"

"That's something at least," Mason said. "If he's on his own, he's not going to be able to get a decent shot off with any accuracy and he's going to be firing with his left hand as well. When he shot at you back at the taxi cab was he firing with his right or left hand?"

"I can't remember," Holly said. "Wait! Baxter remembers! He said he was firing with his right hand."

"That's good news at least," Mason said. "Not only has he got to control the car he's driving but he's also firing with his weaker hand. Baxter should be able to evade him for long enough to get somewhere safe. Is there anywhere you can go?"

"Baxter wanted to go to the local police station, but I talked him out of it. I think we're dealing with some pretty heavy-duty secret society stuff here, Jed. I believe the men who murdered Laroche, Beausire and Sullivan are part of some breakaway group from the Freemasons. I mean these guys aren't doing regular Freemason stuff like raising money for charity and working for good causes, I think these guys are some sinister splinter group that have got a very sinister agenda."

"You told me they were called the Conclave of Darkness, is that right?"

"I think so. Sullivan referred to it in the canvas strip inside his amulet. But my point is, we don't know who they are or where they are. They could be anywhere. If I'm right and these nutcases are mostly Masons that broke away and formed this group, then they're all over the place, especially in law enforcement. If we go into a police station and seek sanctuary, we could be handing ourselves over to the Conclave!"

"While I was getting the amulet out of this Portuguese well, I was attacked by someone who said he'd been trained by the Conclave. So, they're global, for sure."

"You were attacked too?"

"Yeah, I was attacked, which makes me think you're right when you talk about how extensive their network is, as I say. I don't know if they're hacking into phone calls or what they're doing but they seem to be a step ahead of us."

"And they also seem to be extremely – " Holly screamed and stopped talking.

"Holly?" Mason asked. "Are you okay?"

"It's okay, Jed!" Holly said, and Mason felt free to breathe again.

"You're sure? Damn it, I wish I was there."

"It's okay, the guy got a shot off and it ricocheted off our roof. I thought we were a-gonna there for a second, but Baxter's keeping ahead of him. I was going to say this group is not only a step ahead of us all the time, but they also seem to be extremely desperate to get their hands on these amulets and the secret messages they contain. I've got to tell you this now, while I still can. As I said to you, the message inside Sullivan's amulet led us to a book he had hidden inside the House of the Temple Library, and in that book, there were some nonsense words. I believe these are some kind of anagram that will point us to some special site that he wants us to find. I believe that Marcus Beausire has done the same thing and that there will be a clue in his scroll, inside the amulet, that will lead us to a book somewhere probably in a Masonic building somewhere in England, because that was where he was from. I believe inside that book there will be more nonsense words that make a coherent anagram. I believe Philippe Laroche, who was killed earlier in Paris, will also have a message hidden in an amulet somewhere near where he was killed, and the same thing will go for him. I believe that when we have all three of those anagrams solved correctly, we will be able to find whatever it is that they are trying to tell us about."

"And whatever the Conclave are trying to stop us from finding?"

"Exactly," Holly said. "And I don't know about you, but I'm excited about it! It's just a shame about this total maniac behind us. They always have to ruin everything."

"Don't worry about getting excited about anything just yet," Mason cautioned. "We don't know what any of this is truly about yet."

Mason heard the sound of another gunshot exploding in the background and Holly screamed a second time, but she soon came back on the line.

"Listen, I think we're going to need to get the team back together. I don't know about you but we can't handle what's going on here in DC and I think things are only going to get worse."

Mason inwardly sighed but was so horrified by the sound of Holly and Baxter coming under fire and him being able to do nothing about it, they had no choice but to agree with her. If he didn't, they were going to get themselves killed.

"Okay, I agree. Let's get the team back together one more time. You call Alicia. I think she's in Chicago. Get her down to DC as fast as possible. I'll try and get hold of Wilde, although bugger knows where he is."

"Okay, Jed – that sounds like a great idea," Holly said. "It's great to hear your voice again after so long by the way. Really missed these adventures."

Mason wanted to ask if she was completely crazy. He was sitting in the beautiful sumptuous sunlit grounds of a Portuguese mansion, with nothing but the sounds of a gentle breeze whistling in the leaves and soft birdsong, and enjoying the prospect of a relaxing afternoon on his farm. Holly was being hunted through the streets of Washington DC by some kind of assassin who was currently shooting at her with a handgun. And here she was telling him that she was excited to hear his voice and wanted to be part of another mission with him.

It's true what they said about still waters running deep, he mulled.

"Okay, Holly. That's great, but I want you to concentrate on surviving for now. Just make sure you and Baxter get away from this guy and get somewhere safe. And I want you to call Alicia and get her down to DC – tell her anything you have to but get her there. You need her. I'll do the same with Wilde if I can. Then we'll try and arrange to get together somewhere at some point soon and discuss this whole nightmare from start to finish."

"Okay, Jed! Bye for now."

"I'll speak to you soon."

Mason turned his phone off and put it in his pocket, praying that he really would be able to talk to Holly soon.

Chapter 22

"Okay, Jed! Bye for now."

"I'll speak to you soon," Mason said.

Holly hung up.

"What did he say?" Baxter asked, glancing at Holly in the rearview mirror.

"He says he's happy for us to get the team back together again and we should call Alicia as soon as possible."

"That sounds like a good plan to me," Baxter said. He swung the wheel hard to the left and screeched onto the next road, still unfortunately pursued by the psychopathic gunman behind them.

"What did he say about us getting to a police station?"

Holly shook her head. "He agrees with me about that. If I'm right and these guys used to be Masons, then they would have recruited primarily from the Masons and that means they could be literally anywhere. If the Masons are heavily represented in any group, then it's law enforcement police officers, lawyers, judges."

"You know what? Now you say it, a lot of the guys back in LA were in the Masons," Baxter checked his mirror and swerved hard to the right, just missing a red light. "Damn this guy."

"Right," Holly said. "Masons are good guys, but what about if some of those working in these institutions and jobs joined the Conclave? We have no idea when we walk into a police station if we're talking to someone who has nothing to do with the Masons at all, or maybe they are a Mason, or worse than that they're a member of the Conclave. We need to find somewhere neutral to hide until Alicia can find us."

"Hey, listen. I'm not without my chops you know," Baxter said, though rather unconvincingly. "I was in the LAPD for a long time. I discharged a weapon many times."

"I know Baxter, but this is different. These guys are crazy and high-speed. We need Alicia, you know that."

Baxter paused a moment and then nodded sadly. "Yeah, I know that. I kind of like her company in a strange kind of way."

"Yeah, me too," Holly said, glancing behind her and seeing the black sedan was closing in. "Where the hell are we going to go?"

"I have no idea," Baxter said, "but I don't seem to be able to shake him off."

Baxter had been driving south from the House of the Temple and was now rapidly approaching the White House. He broke through some red lights and turned to the right, driving down between the White House and the Eisenhower Executive Office Building. Holly saw him check his mirror and craned her neck to look in the rearview mirror herself. They both saw their pursuer was still behind them.

"I've got an idea," Baxter said. "Take out your phone again."

"What do you want me to do?"

"Call the police and tell them you think there's been a kidnapping. Give them the licence plate of the car behind."

"Hey, that's a good idea. That might just work!"

"It'll work. They have to look into that kind of thing. They take it very seriously."

Holly made the 911 call and gave the operator the best story she could come up with. Her daughter had just been kidnapped by a man driving a black sedan, and she was able to get the licence plate. She gave the number of the licence plate and then she gave the road they were currently on. Then she hung her phone up.

"Okay, keep driving, Baxter. That's done. Now start praying."

"With a little bit of luck, a local unit in the vicinity will be on their tail in seconds," Baxter said.

As if on cue, they both heard police sirens and Holly turned to her left and saw a local Washington DC police cruiser that had been parked on the side of the road start up its flashing lights and pull out onto the road at speed, heading in the direction of the black sedan.

"There's one already!" Holly said.

"There's another one pulling in behind him as well," Baxter said. "I think we might have got him!"

Holly took out her phone and made the third phone call in as many minutes. "Hey Alicia, it's me, Holly."

"How are you doing, Holly?"

"Not good. I'm getting shot at by an assassin in Washington DC, and I've just been on the line to Mason who's working with us in Portugal. I think we need your help. I think we're going to get the team back together. How do you feel about that?"

"I feel pretty great about it," Alicia said. "I just spent the last two weeks babysitting the biggest brat on Earth. Now I find out I'm gonna go chasing another secret society. How do you think I feel about it?"

Holly smiled. "That's great. We're gonna need you down in DC as quickly as possible. How quickly can you get here?"

"I can be there within two or three hours at the most. I just need to go home, pack some things and then I'll organise a flight. Where are we meeting?"

Holly swivelled around in the back seat and looked through the rear window. The black sedan behind them was now being forced off the road by four separate police cruisers, lights blazing and sirens wailing. Within a few moments, the man driving the sedan had been pulled out of the car and was being forced onto the bonnet with his hands behind his back. Other officers searched the interior of the car and the boot. She looked up ahead and saw Baxter smiling at her in the rear view mirror. When he gave her a big thumbs-up, she sat back in her seat and relaxed.

"Let's say the Hilton in Kalorama. Is that good for you?"

"That sounds great, Holly. I can't wait to see you both again. By the way, what do you mean Mason's working with you over in Portugal?"

"It's a long story, Alicia," Holly said. "It's got something to do with a breakaway group from the Masons and they seem to be all over North America and Europe. We've already found a partial clue in the House of the Temple right here in DC and I think it might be some kind of Latin poem or something, that I guess could lead us somewhere. I'm not sure. We had cause to ask Mason to look into a similar event that had happened over in Portugal and he found something too. It's all coming together, Alicia! It's all coming together again. It's great we're getting the team back together."

"Anybody called Wilde yet?" Alicia said.

"Mason's gonna try and call him later, but I think we all know he's gonna be the hardest to get in touch with. I really hope we can track him down though, because he's so useful getting hold of things for us that we need and also he has so many contacts."

"Yeah, he's definitely a serious part of the team, when he's not high."

"Alicia…"

"Sorry. It'll be great if we can get all five of us back together. Listen, man, that guy still shooting at you?"

"No, he's long gone, thanks to a suggestion by Baxter. I'm gonna hang up now and we'll see you at the hotel in a few hours."

"Gotcha, Holly."

Holly hung up the phone and explained to Baxter what she had planned with Alicia. He slowly turned the car in the direction of Kalorama and they settled down for a gentle cruise. It was all kicking off again, and Holly was as excited as a child on Christmas Eve.

Chapter 23

Baxter was more than a little glad to find himself standing at the bar of the Hilton Hotel, waiting for his order to come. His last-minute idea of having Holly call the police and tell them she had witnessed a family kidnapping, giving them the licence plate of the car that had pursued them, had probably saved their lives. For most of the high-speed driving Baxter had done in the LAPD, he had usually been the one doing the chasing. Plus these days he was considerably older and his reaction times were much slower. Another thing that had occurred to him was how strange it was that the gunman had not tried to kill them, at least not in his opinion. He had a clean shot at Baxter, and yet he had missed. In his view, the gunman was trying to kill the taxi driver to stop them from getting away so he could get hold of them and do whatever it was he wanted with them.

He turned with the two cold bottles of lager the barman had just given him and strolled across the bar area to a table in the corner where Holly was sitting. As usual, she was hunched over the table, with her head in her hands and her elbows resting on its surface, staring down into her phone and muttering to herself. If he didn't know who she was and what she was doing, he could be forgiven for thinking she was on the edge of madness. That was exactly what Baxter loved about Dr Holly Hope.

He placed a beer in front of her and then shuffled down in the seat beside her. After taking a long and much-deserved sip of the ice-cold beverage, he felt his body winding down and destressing by the second. As he let himself slide down into the comfortable seat, he turned to his friend and asked her if she had made any progress with the information she had managed to obtain from the book Sullivan had hidden in the Library of the House of the Temple.

"Not really," Holly said with a sigh. "And I really hate it when that happens, you know what I mean? I hate not being able to make sense of things. That's one of the reasons I love research; it allows me to work my way through, starting from a large amount of disparate information and gradually discarding what's unnecessary, and collecting and collating what is necessary, and then eventually I'm able to fine-tune my way to get what I want. It's a very satisfying process for a girl like me."

"It sounds a bit like detective work," Baxter said.

She smiled and thought about that for a moment. Then she took a sip of her beer and pushed her phone away, sitting back in her seat and relaxing.

"I guess it is very similar to detective work," she said. "The only difference is, I'm usually trying to track down ancient scriptures, and you're trying to track down murderers."

"Yeah," Baxter said with a sad shrug. "I tracked down a lot of murderers in my time, and cheaters, frauds, philanderers, even a few everyday burglars and bank robbers. These days are a bit more mellow unless you count getting hired by a senator's wife to look into his disappearance and murder."

"Have you told her yet?"

"No, not yet."

Baxter felt terrible just thinking about how Senator Sullivan was almost certainly dead. But he was not one-hundred per cent certain and that was why he had said nothing to Charlotte Sullivan.

"Between you and me, Holly, I think the guy is gone. Just seeing that place down in the woods, and the blood. The amulet. Also, we know from the newspaper reports you told me about Marcus Beausire that he was murdered and left an amulet near the death scene. It's just too much of a coincidence for me to draw any other conclusion, other than the sad fact that Kent Sullivan was murdered by the Conclave. But the truth is, I have no direct evidence and it would be wrong of me to report that to Mrs Sullivan at this time."

"And what about the police?" she asked innocently. "Are you going to tell *them* you think he's been murdered? I mean you must know somebody in the LAPD you can trust."

Baxter was in two minds about this. He was fairly certain – as sure as a man with his experience could be – that Kent Sullivan had been murdered in that snowy forest, but with even the tiniest fraction of doubt in his mind, he was unhappy about telling Mrs Sullivan. He was equally unhappy about telling anyone in the LAPD. For one thing, while there were definitely good friends in the force he knew he could trust with his life, he knew those men would have to report the murder up the chain of command and that was where things could get tricky.

After what Holly had said about the Conclave being constructed of breakaway Masons, and what she had said about so many policemen being Masons, Baxter was certain at some point up the food chain there was a good possibility that his investigation and discovery of Kent Sullivan's murder would eventually land on the desk of somebody involved with the Freemasons. There was no harm in that – he knew many men who were Masons and had even been asked to join a lodge himself. They were good people who did good work. The problem was, what if the one whose desk the report landed on happened to be someone who had broken away and joined the Conclave of Darkness? That was when things could get much more serious and in his opinion, unnecessarily so.

"I think we both know why that's not a good idea, Holly," Baxter said.

"Yeah I guess so, it just feels weird to know somebody's been murdered but not reported to the authorities. It just feels unethical. It doesn't sit well with me at all."

"It doesn't sit well with me either," Baxter said, taking another sip of his beer and relaxing even further. "But the fact is, if your theory about this so-called Conclave is correct, we're just painting a giant neon arrow pointing in our direction if I send this report to the LAPD. I think for now, the wisest choice of action is to keep things as quiet as possible.

"I can go along with that."

"Good. Now tell me, what do you think Kent Sullivan was hiding with the scrambled words you found in the book back at the House of the Temple?"

"As I've already said, they seem to be part of some kind of poem or something but beyond that, I'm afraid I don't know. I mean they literally could be anything – the part of the solution to a safe code, geographical coordinates, some kind of other word system that refers to something in another library. At the moment it's scant information and we need more."

"I guess that's what Mason's got inside his Portuguese amulet," Baxter said. "Or at least I hope it is. By the way, shouldn't Alicia be here yet?"

Holly nodded and took some more beer. "Yeah, somewhere around now, anyway."

"You think something's happened to her?"

"Absolutely not."

"How can you be so sure?"

"Because she just walked into the hotel," Holly said with a smile widening on her face. "Take a look over there in the lobby."

Baxter smiled too when he looked up and saw the tall muscular woman who had saved his life on many occasions stride into the lobby of the hotel as if she owned the place and stand there for a second, scanning for any sign of her friends. She was wearing dark blue jeans and a three-quarter-length black leather jacket, and her hair was down. She had the air of someone who was always in control and took no nonsense from anyone. She turned on the heels of her black polished boots and began to walk towards the bar, presumably figuring this was the most obvious place to find her friends. When she saw them and realised she was right, she gave only the ghost of a smile – Baxter would expect nothing less and then walked over not to them but to the bar. She loitered there for a few moments and then when she turned around, Baxter saw she was holding a bottle of lager of the same brand he had ordered. She walked over to them, sat down chinked their two bottles, and sipped a third of the bottle down in one go before setting it down on the table and blowing out a long sigh of relief.

"How you doing guys?" she said.

"I'm good," Baxter said.

"Yeah, all good here too," Holly said. "Thanks so much for coming, Alicia. I thought maybe we could handle this one by ourselves but when that dude started shooting at us,

I was on the phone to Jed, and he thought it was a good idea if we pulled you into the mission."

"That's no problem at all," Alicia said. "I'm glad to be here. If you knew what I've been doing for the last two weeks you'd understand."

"What have you been doing for the last two weeks?" Baxter asked, genuinely interested.

"Babysitting an asshole," was all Alicia said before drinking more beer. "So, is Mason coming here or what?"

Baxter would have been interested to learn more about her job babysitting the asshole, but it seemed like Alicia was keen to change the subject, which is why she had brought up the subject of Mason so smoothly. He decided to take the hint she had dropped.

"Mason's working over in Portugal," he said. "When Kent Sullivan was murdered, I found an amulet near his body. He must have been wearing it around his neck and managed to hide it before he was killed. Holly did her thing and managed to connect him to other men who were murdered over in Europe, one in Portugal recently – a man named Marcus Beausire. Holly gave Mason the location of Beausire's murder and he drove over there because it is very close to his farm."

"Isn't life full of happy coincidences," Alicia said.

"Well, I think it was an hour or two drive away," Baxter said. "When he got there, he went to the location of this man's murder – it was some kind of Masonic Initiation Well they've got going on over there. You know the kind of thing, used by these secret societies for hundreds and hundreds of years?"

Alicia was working her way through the last third of her lager. "Yeah," she said at last. "After hanging around with you guys, I *do* know what you mean."

"Anyway," Baxter said, finishing his little story. "When he got there, he managed to find an identical amulet to the one that had belonged to Kent Sullivan. But the problem is Holly here thinks that there should be three. And the third one belongs to this other man who was murdered in Paris recently, by the name of Philippe Laroche. We think these three men created a kind of breakaway group from the Conclave of Darkness, called the Fellowship of Light."

"Is this mission gonna involve rings or Wizards?" Alicia asked.

Baxter didn't get the reference, but Holly laughed.

Holly said, "No, it's not going to involve Wizards, but you never know – maybe there's gonna be some rings involved, or jewellery."

Still confused, Baxter ploughed on. "So, that's why Mason's still over in Portugal. We plan to meet together in London."

"Why London and not Paris?" Alicia asked. "I thought you said this Laroche dude's missing amulet was in Paris?"

"It is, or should be," Holly said. "But inside Beausire's amulet, the one Mason found in Portugal, was a clue telling us to go to the Museum of Freemasons in London. That is where Beausire hid his part of the anagram. We need to go there first, and then we can go to Paris and look for Laroche's amulet.

After we find that, if we can, then hopefully inside will be a clue leading us to *his* part of the anagram and then we'll have all three sets of their clue, leading us to… who knows?"

Alicia didn't bother to hide her scepticism. "You know where to look for this amulet when we get to Paris?"

"Not yet, but we'll cross that bridge when we come to it. I'm determined to find out just exactly what the Conclave of Darkness is trying to stop the Fellowship from telling the world."

"Okay, well that all sounds great to me," Alicia said. "Have you guys booked the flights to London yet?"

"Not yet, no," Holly said. "We wanted to make sure you were cool with everything before we did. I'll go ahead and book them now. It's such late notice, I think we're looking at three regular seats on a normal commercial carrier."

Alicia shrugged and finished her beer, smacking the bottle down on the table and causing several other drinkers to turn and frown at her. "I couldn't give a damn how we get there, just so long as we get there. I'm keen to get on with this thing and find out what's going on."

Baxter couldn't have agreed with her more.

Chapter 24

Locusta was not happy. She was sitting in the bar of the same Hilton Hotel that had previously hosted Wesley Baxter, Holly Hope and Alicia Kane, having traced them there just moments too late. She was drinking a hot black coffee, and the man opposite her was drinking neat bourbon.

"You're lucky to be alive, Scorpio," she said.

"Me? Why am I lucky to be alive?" the man said with a snarl.

"Because I told you that we're trying to follow them, not kill them."

"I wasn't trying to kill them, I was trying to kill the driver. I wanted to slow them down because of how long you were taking back in the library."

"I'll take as long as I need in the library or anywhere else," Locusta said. "I was executing orders given to me directly by the Great Guardian, namely to kill junior conclavist Jonathan Richards for his grave error in allowing Holly Hope to find whatever Kent Sullivan hid in that library. Snow is absolutely livid. It took him a lot of time and effort to get a member of the Conclave inside the House of the Temple, to have eyes on the ground, so to speak. He finally gets Richards in there and then Richards finally gets his chance to shine and he blows it."

"You shoot him?"

She nodded her head. "With a silencer at the back of the library. I took out the security guard for good measure as well. Senior Concave members in the Washington DC Police Department are already working on a cover story. I think I heard something about Jonathan Richards having a heart attack, and the security card getting shot in a robbery somewhere."

"I'll give us this much," Scorpio said. "We're certainly very inventive."

"Necessity is the mother of invention, Scorpio. You do realise I had to talk Snow out of having you killed, as well?"

She saw Scorpio's face grow white. His usual cocky smirk faded away and he decided to take a few moments out by drinking some of his bourbon. When he finally resurfaced he seemed to have found his voice again.

"Who was he going to order to do it?"

"Who do you think he was gonna ask to do it?" Locusta said. "I'm right here in the field with you. Not only that, I'm also his most efficient and prized operative. If you make another screw-up like that Scorpio, I promise you I will put a bullet between your eyes."

"And I love you too, darling," Scorpio said.

"This isn't a joke, Scorpio," Locusta said, sitting back in her chair and blowing on her coffee to cool it a little. "This is very serious business."

"How do you know it's serious business? Don't tell me the old man has let you in on what the hell's going on?"

"The old man, as you call him, or Mr Snow as he likes to be called, has confided in me more than most, but I have not been brought entirely into his confidence. Perhaps after we bring this mission to a successful close he might tell me more. In the meantime, I have no choice but to ensure I continue obeying him without question and ensure I can deliver the exact results he wants during this mission."

"And what might those exact results be?"

"The Fellowship of Light are already extinguished," she said. "That apparently is not enough. Now we have another group – some rogue collection of nobodies who have come from nowhere, who have somehow got wind of what's going on. They've taken vital pieces of information from the amulets of Kent Sullivan and Marcus Beausire and – "

"How do you know they got the amulet from Marcus Beausire?"

"A report from Leo this morning. Apparently he got his ass kicked at the Masonic Initiation Well in the Quinta da Regaleira. At least he had the nerve to report it to headquarters. Not sure if Snow is going to terminate him or not. Anyway as I was saying, this group of nobodies seemed to have found these vital pieces of information from Sullivan and Beausire and so we know what they're going to do next."

"They're going to try and find Philippe Laroche's amulet!" Scorpio said.

"Not yet," Locusta said. "I believe they'll start searching for that but not until they've found whatever clue trail Beausire hid in his amulet. Remember, Sullivan's amulet led them to the House of the Temple Library here in DC, but Beausire was a Brit. If he hid anything in a library, that library is going to be in London, where he lived and worked."

Scorpio sighed. "If we'd known the Fellowship of Light had created these amulets with their little clues in them and had this little plan of theirs to leave a trail behind if they were murdered, we could have looked for that amulet ourselves."

"But we didn't know, did we?" Locusta said, sipping her coffee. "As far as we were concerned, we'd tied up all loose ends and brushed up all the last odd jobs. When we murdered them we thought that was the end of it, but little did we know they had created this little plan that will allow them to talk from the grave."

"But only if we let them."

"Exactly," she said. "Only if we let them. Those are our new orders – we are no longer waiting to see how many people are in this little group, clearly being run by this Boston nerd, Dr Holly Hope. Our new orders are to get to London and find the clue left behind by Marcus Beausire before they do. Then we are to ambush them and execute all of them."

"But there's another one, isn't there?" Scorpio asked. "I think someone in Europe intercepted Mason's phone call to a man called Wilde. He was somewhere in the Middle East, no one's sure."

"He's not directly involved, whoever he is," Locusta said. "For now he can remain free-range, but when we've killed the four of them who *are* directly involved, we will of course have to snuff him out too. That is Conclave Law – anyone who has been in contact with the Fellowship of Light, even by extension, must be extinguished."

"Sounds fair to me," Scorpio said. "Have we got flights to London?"

"Yes, we have. And I'm already in touch with some of our people there, to find out where Beausire might have hidden his clue. I'll bet it's in a Masonic library, just as Sullivan's was. When this is wrapped up, we go to Paris and find Laroche's amulet. That will be the end of it."

"Surely Laroche's amulet will be somewhere near where he was murdered, just as with Sullivan and Beausire?"

Locusta almost laughed. "You can be so naïve sometimes, Scorpio. Remember how the three men were murdered before you speak. Beausire had been drawn to the Initiation Well to see if he could be negotiated with, when he refused to do so and tried to evade us, he was murdered. In other words, he had no way of knowing he was going to die, so he acted on the spot and thinking on his feet, he hid the amulet near where he was murdered. The same goes with Kent Sullivan. He was snatched to be brought to Snow and interrogated before being killed. He managed to escape, vault over the balcony in Snow's study, and sprint into the forest. He had a few seconds to hide the amulet before he knew he would be cut down and killed."

"And what's your point?" Scorpio said, finishing the rest of his bourbon and checking his watch.

"My point, Scorpio, is that that is not how Philippe Laroche was murdered. Laroche was the ringleader of the Fellowship and was told several days in advance that if he did not desist with his plans to expose the Conclave's secret history to the world, he would be murdered. As a consequence of this, my dear slow, hard-of-learning little friend, Laroche could have hidden the amulet anywhere."

"Right," Scorpio said, getting it at last. "I understand. You say we have people on the ground in London who are already looking into the Beausire library business?"

"That is exactly what I just said," Locusta said. She checked her watch and finished the remaining coffee in her cup. "And we're going to be joining with them in just a few hours. Get ready to fly to London, and get ready to kill Holly Hope and her friends."

Chapter 25

Guy Wilde had pulled into his next resting place on the long dangerous drive down to Tehran and was repeating the same procedure from the day before, making a small fire and preparing his bivouac so he could sleep through the day before another night ride when his phone rang. He looked at it, confused and a little annoyed and then scratched his head when he saw there was no caller ID. That was not particularly unusual for him, or presumably for anyone else involved in the illicit trade of relic smuggling, but he did like to keep his contacts list neat and up to date so he generally knew who was giving him a call. He considered leaving the phone call in case it was some kind of trap. He shrugged his shoulders, knowing he could get out on the road fast enough on his faithful old Harley, and answered the phone.

"Good morning, this is the Ritz Carlton. How may I help?"

"I'd like to book a room for one please," Mason said. "And make sure the minibar is full to the brim."

"Jed!" Wilde said with a wide smile breaking out on his face. "Is that really you?"

"You got it in one old friend. How's life treating you?"

The Babylon Agenda

"You know how it is, ups and downs, rough and smooth, that sort of thing. How about you? How's the farm? Is it a farm? I mean, if you're growing olives then isn't that more of a grove than a farm? I've never been entirely clear on that."

"No, me neither," Mason said. "But we can call it a farm for now, if it makes it easier. Thing is, I've been dragged away from my farm by a certain academic over in Boston."

Wilde felt his heart speed up as he built his fire. "Holly is onto something?"

"Yeah, you could say that. Baxter called her up. He was hired to find a missing person – get this, an American Senator! This guy disappeared while going out buying wine and never came home. This was totally out of character for him, plus his wife knew he wasn't in a particularly good place at the moment – debts and so on and she got very worried for him. So, she is certain something bad happened to him. She calls her best friend Sally Wilton – as in Edmund Wilton's wife – and she puts her onto Baxter, who's in his office one day when he gets a call from Mrs Sullivan. Next thing you know, he thinks this guy's been murdered in the Rockies, and Holly's now got involved because he's got something to do with some weird breakaway group from the Masons, they're calling the Conclave of Darkness. Alicia joined up with them when they started to get shot at."

"I thought my life was busy smuggling some Bronze Age necklaces from Ashgabat to Tehran."

Mason chuckled. "That's not what you're doing, is it?"

Wilde now lit the fire and watched the flames grow. "A man's got to bring home the bacon somehow."

"Hey, it's not my business," Mason said with another laugh.

"But what you're talking about is *my* business?" Wilde asked, growing a little more serious. He poked at the fire in front of him with a twig and started to make tea. "I mean, I'm not being funny or anything, but if Baxter and Holly and Alicia are in Washington getting shot at, and you're in Portugal, what has that got to do with me exactly?"

"Because Holly said that she thinks this has got something to do with Babylon."

Wilde raised an eyebrow, suddenly a little more interested. If anything was going to get him on board with one of Holly's crazy missions, it was something to do with the world of antiquity, something to do with a place like Babylon, something to do with relics.

"Okay, you've got my interest, Jed. Please go on."

"So, she found out this group called the Conclave of Darkness is up to something dodgy, and she's not sure what. She translated some symbols inside amulets these guys had hidden – these guys who call themselves the Fellowship of Light. This Fellowship talked about something called the Babylon Agenda, it was written in one of the amulets. None of us know what that means yet, but we all know Babylon means Iraq, and Iraq means Middle East."

"And Middle East means me," Wilde said. "Is that about it?"

"Yeah, that's about the size of it, mate," Mason said. "Baxter is a private investigator based in Los Angeles, Holly's a Harvard academic with a mostly Christian theological background, Alicia is an ex-CIA spook and bodyguard, and I'm just an old boxing champ from the British Army who's a bit tasty with his fists. Truth is, if this has got anything to do with Iraq, we're going to need your expertise."

"I see… *expertise*," Wilde repeated with emphasis, still poking at his fire. "Yeah, well, I suppose I could be interested, especially if there's going to be a visit to Babylon."

"I can't promise that we're going to end up going to Babylon, but there's a reasonable expectation that that could happen. You know what these missions are like – if there's a splinter group of Masonic breakaways called the Conclave of Darkness, who are up to this so-called Babylon Agenda, then I'm quite happy to bet my lunch on us ending up somewhere in the Middle East. At the moment, we have no way of knowing, but if it happens we'll all be really grateful if you'd give us a hand. How about it old mate?"

Wilde had already made up his mind. "Yeah, I can get involved, but what exactly is it that you're gonna want from me?"

"That's impossible to say at the moment," Mason said.

Wilde thought he sounded genuinely regretful. "I see."

"I'm going to meet Baxter, Holly and Alicia up in London and we've got to find another series of nonsense words, or so Holly says. She says if we get hold of that, it's probably going to lead us to another location where we might find whatever it is this Conclave of Darkness is so keen to hide. I can't say where that will be, so for now we might need you just as a kind of telephone consultant. How does that grab you?"

"It grabs me just fine, Jed," Wilde said, happy to be involved in something a little bigger than his usual relic smuggling. "I'm in Iran at the moment and on my way to Tehran. If this does lead you out to Iraq, then I'll be able to get down on my bike in no time at all. It'll be fun to get together and do what we used to do in the old days."

"In the old days? It was only a few months ago!"

"Yeah, but you know what I mean," Wilde said jovially.

"I'll leave it there then, mate," Mason said. "Now you're fully briefed so just be ready for a phone call if we need one. If we don't need your expertise, but we find ourselves getting down to Iraq, I'll give you as much notice as I can so you can get down there and meet us."

"Sounds good to me, Jed. See you later."

"Till then, buddy"

Wilde heard Mason hang up the phone and then he switched his phone off and threw it in his bag, which was on the ground beside him, not far from the fire. He was already interested and had been as soon as Mason had mentioned Holly Hope and Babylon. He checked his watch and started making some calculations about how quickly he could get to Tehran and deliver the necklaces, just in case Mason gave him a call and asked him to get down to Babylon. The ancient city's ruins were only an hour or so drive south of Baghdad, a city which Wilde knew like the back of his hand. He could see why Mason and the others were keen to get him on board again.

Tipping his tea on the fire to put it out, and preparing to pack up his bivouac and get back on his bike, Wilde took a deep breath and mused how good it felt to be loved.

Chapter 26

How could an entire world have a secret history? This was a question Snow had asked himself many times, but in his case, it was a question to which he knew the answer. An entire world could have a secret history if it had a secret society guarding it and keeping it from the rest of the world. That was how an entire world could have a secret history. Of course, there would be troublemakers who wanted to spoil things and bring that secret history to the rest of the world. Dragging it into the light, exposing it to the scrutiny of the everyday man or woman. Leonardo Snow, as leader of the Conclave of Darkness, would simply never allow such a thing to happen. That was why he was expending so much effort not only in ensuring the Fellowship of Light and every trail they had ever made in their lives was fully extinguished but also that Dr Holly Hope, Wesley Baxter, Alicia Kane and now this Mason character joined them as quickly as possible.

Snow was still in his luxury ski chalet in Aspen – White Fir Lodge – and enjoying another large brandy as he stood out on his balcony. Far below, somewhere in the trees where Necro and his team dispatched Kent Sullivan, a group of his workers were cleaning away the last remnants of the murder. The three men he had left behind at the scene to clean it up had been executed for their sloppiness. Everyone in the Conclave knew Snow brooked no failure. Not ever. Those men deserved to die and it was their failure to do their job properly that had led this idiot gumshoe from Los Angeles to get hold of something Sullivan had hidden there and then hook up with some academic from Boston. It was all getting rather out of hand.

He sipped his brandy and looked out across the small town. He surveyed it like a general scanning a battlefield. It was peaceful enough, with those everyday men and women he had thought about earlier going about their everyday business. They were none the wiser about the reality of the world and believed the garbage they were taught in their history lessons. Above that little town, some of the world's most majestic mountains stretched up to the sky, their snowcapped peaks clawing at the bright azure of this glorious Colorado day. None of it meant very much to Snow, because as Grand Guardian of the Conclave of Darkness, he was fully aware of the secret history of the world. It was a knowledge which once one had learnt, one could not unlearn. It changed the way you viewed everything. It challenged your beliefs, perhaps it made you scared. Perhaps it made him scared, he was not entirely sure of that.

Behind him, his phone rang. He turned on the balcony, stepped inside the large dark wood panel study and lifted the Bakelite receiver to his ear. His other hand gently swirled the brandy in his glass as he answered the call. "Locusta. Report."

"We're getting on board a flight to London. Scorpio and I. We're in touch with two of our agents in London. They're already working on where Beausire might have hidden his clue."

"I take it Jonathan Richards was dispatched as I had ordered?"

"Jonathan Richards and the security guard who was in the building monitoring the cameras at the time are both dead. I've already been in touch with some senior members of the DC Conclave. There will be no trail and nothing will be made available to the public."

"Good work, Locusta. This is why you are my number one. I cannot stress how important it is that when you get to London, you find wherever Beausire hid his clue. Whatever those three bastards in the Fellowship of Light put inside those things, they seem to be giving Baxter, Hope and their friends some kind of clue trail to follow. Needless to say, I am rather interested and more than a little nervous as to exactly where that clue trail will lead them. I have a very grave responsibility. I am the guardian of the greatest secret in the history of mankind. I cannot let down all those hundreds of people who have come before me and kept this secret from the world. I must ensure that it stays safe for ever."

"Yes, Grand Guardian," Locusta said. "But when will you tell me this secret?"

"Certainly not whenever you ask me to tell you," Snow said. "The secret is not just restricted to the Guardian of the Conclave, for reasons of power or vanity. The secret is restricted to the Guardian because of its weight. It is a terrible burden to bear. I fear telling you will bring you more pain than happiness and joy."

He sipped his brandy and waited for the long pause that Locusta left after he had finished speaking. He supposed she was considering whether to ask him again or not, but decided against it, which pleased him. It showed good judgement.

"Do you think the Fellowship found the Tower, Grand Guardian?"

Snow bristled. "Let us pray not, but I doubt it. I have spent years looking for it and it has never revealed itself to me. When it does, the great secret will be confirmed, I know it in my heart."

"If the Fellowship were onto its location," Locusta said, "and left that information in the amulets in some coded form, this Baxter and his associates might stumble onto it."

"That is why you are going to track them and make sure we are always a step ahead of them. If the Fellowship traitors really did find the Tower, then I want that knowledge and I want it before these bungling fools get it."

"We'll be in London in just a few short hours," she said. "As soon as we get anywhere in the search for Beausire's clue, I will report again."

"Make sure that you do," Snow said. "This is the most important thing that you will ever do in your life, Locusta. Please understand that and make no mistakes."

Chapter 27

Mason's flight to London Heathrow Airport was one he had made on countless occasions and passed by quickly and without event. He was through customs control quicker than usual and rapidly found himself in a cab driving east into London. The drive was easy enough, with traffic increasing as usual in Hammersmith and Kensington, slowing especially at the southeast corner of Hyde Park Corner before the cab driver turned into Mayfair, cruised past the Ritz then skirted around the southern end of Trafalgar Square before turning north and driving through Covent Garden until reaching his final destination – the Museum of Freemasonry.

The drive had been a trip down memory lane for Mason, but at no point elicited in him any desire to return to the Motherland. The opposite was the case. Every inch driving through the grey, rainy London traffic had only increased his love of his new life in Portugal and he had already started counting down the minutes to when he could return to his new home. He paid the cab driver and stepped out onto Drury Lane, where he had arranged to meet Holly, Baxter and Alicia in a small pub called The Crown. He pulled out his phone and navigated to a page he had bookmarked which allowed him to check the arrival times of aircraft coming into Heathrow. As he had expected, their plane had landed a good hour before his, so now he expected to find them inside the pub. When he stepped inside the old London tavern, he was not disappointed to see three familiar faces staring up at him from a cosy little nook in the corner.

He walked over to them, scanning the pub for anything out of the usual on his way.

"Fancy meeting you here!" he said.

Holly got up from her seat and gave him a long, lingering hug. Alicia managed her hellos by way of a simple wave and a downbeat 'hey'. Baxter stood up and shook Mason's hand, and then Mason asked them if any of them wanted a top-up. No one did, so Mason walked to the bar and ordered himself a pint of bitter. Then he returned to the table and sat down beside his old friends, realising that he had missed their company a little more than he might have told himself.

Without saying another word, Mason sipped his beer then set the glass down on the table and handed Holly the amulet, complete with the original canvas scroll still inside it.

"I think this is what you're looking for. I know I already sent the photograph over, but it can't hurt for you to have a look at the real thing. I didn't understand it at all. It was all just squiggles and shapes to me."

Holly was sipping a gin and tonic, so she set her glass down and took the amulet from Mason's hand. She opened it and unrolled the scroll of canvas inside, her eyes suddenly dancing all over it as if it were a fireworks display.

"I don't think there's anything here that I couldn't pick up on the photo," she said, "and we already know what we're looking for now. Somewhere in the Museum of Freemasonry, which is just around the corner, we should find a book called The Rise of Babylon, by JM Witherington. Inside that book should be some nonsensical words, so long as Beausire used the same system as Sullivan."

"Although at this time we don't know what those crazy words refer to," Mason said. "Right?"

"That's right," Holly said. "Fortunately at the moment we're just collecting the words and we have no idea what any of them allude to. They're obviously anagrams, but without all three I'm not sure we can get them right. The first line of nonsense from the book Sullivan led us to was 'Audre misdescribed seducement'."

"That really is nonsense," Mason said.

"But you can create an anagram in Latin that makes sense," Holly said. 'And that is *'ad secretum discendum ire debes'*, which means 'you must go to learn the secret'. This is not, in my opinion, a complete sentence and we need the other clues left in the books by Beausire and Laroche to complete the full clue. Until then, we just can't know what these mean."

"It's not the first time we've been chasing dragons and fighting shadows," Alicia said, sipping her beer.

Mason also took another sip of his bitter. This was one thing that London did better than Portugal. No matter how hard he tried, he just could not lay his hands on his favourite beers down there. There seemed to be a range of lagers from all over Europe, and some of the more mainstream high street beer brands from Britain, but some of these slightly more bespoke bitters were completely and totally impossible to get, as were all proper English ales as well. This was the only serious downside, as far as he could work out, to living in his new Portuguese home.

"Chasing dragons and fighting shadows," Mason said after he'd finished sipping his beer. "I like that. That kind of describes my entire life."

"Well, it's mine so you can't take it," Alicia said with a wink.

"Tell me more about these people that were chasing you in Washington," Mason said.

Baxter replied. "I don't think they were trying to kill us, I think they were just trying to stop us from getting away. They seem to be the standard issue mercenary, much like most of the men and women we've gone up against in the past. Just dressed in black, totally professional. Would blend in just about anywhere really."

"Where do you think they get their clothes?" Alicia asked. "Goons R Us?"

Mason smiled. "How many of them were there again?"

"There was just one shooting at us as we tried to get in the taxi," Baxter said. "And he was the same one that chased us around DC for a few minutes before we got the local police to pick him up. I don't suppose he was in custody for very long if this Conclave of Darkness is as well connected as we think it is."

"And we don't know anything more about them than that?" Mason asked.

"We do," Alicia said. "But don't get too excited. After Holly gave me a call asking me to join the mission, I spoke to some old friends of mine in the CIA and asked them if they could look into who was the owner of the luxury ski chalet in Aspen. The place is called White Fir Lodge and according to him, it's owned by a shell company based in the British Channel Islands – Jersey, to be precise. The only other information they could give me is that the company controlling that little enterprise is called Snow Industries."

"Which could mean basically anything," Mason said.

"No, I don't think so," Alicia said. "The owner of Snow Industries is a man called Leonardo Snow. Not much is known about him, but I do have some details. First of all, he is British, but we're not gonna hold that against him."

"Hey, take it easy," Mason said with a smile. "I'm outnumbered by Americans three to one at this table."

Alicia's smirk deepened and then she continued. "Snow was born in London back in the 1960s and became a stockbroker in the London Stock Exchange in his early Twenties. He became wildly successful, probably the most successful of his generation, before working on Wall Street as a corporate raider. He made a phenomenal sum of money, but then just sort of dropped off the map. He was never a public figure, so his presence or absence was never noted by anybody and that's all I know about him."

"But we can assume he was a high-ranking Freemason, and that he quit them to form his own group, this Conclave of Darkness," Holly said.

"That's just speculation," Baxter said. "I mean it's good quality speculation, but it remains speculation. If there's one thing I learned as a detective, it's that it's all good and well following an instinct and listening to your intuition and following up leads like that, but you can never be sure until you get to the end of the trail."

"I disagree, Baxter," Mason said. "I'm with Alicia and Holly on this one. The house is owned by Snow Industries, and Leonardo Snow used to be one of the world's most successful stockbrokers. He's very rich. Until I get a better target, this guy is number one in my sights as the head honcho of this so-called Conclave of Darkness."

"And with that said," Holly said, checking her watch, "I think we need to get round to the Museum of Freemasonry. Now we're all together, we can go see if we can get hold of this book by Mr Witherington. Let's hope it goes a little smoother than last time."

"Yes," Baxter said. "Let's hope it goes a little easier than last time."

Chapter 28

Mason led the way up the steps of the Museum of Freemasonry, an imposing building on the corner of Drury Street and Great Queen Street. As with so many of the buildings of this era, the building was constructed in the Art Deco style and was officially completed in 1933. Originally known as the Masonic Peace Memorial Building, today the actual museum is located on the first floor. Visiting hours were Monday to Saturday, ten in the morning until five in the evening, and ten in the morning to eight at night on the first Thursday of every month. Entry was free, and, Mason noted with relief, that they were right in the middle of visiting hours. Mason pushed the door open and held it open for the rest of the team to step inside the lobby and then they all moved inside.

They were met by a man at a grand reception desk, who called himself Michael Smith. Michael asked them if they needed any help and Holly immediately stepped up to the plate. She gave him her academic credentials, and seeing he was immediately impressed, she decided to replay exactly the same hand she had played in Washington DC at the House of the Temple's Library.

"I'll take you through to the library now," Michael said.

As they walked he chatted and told them about the place, something Mason could have done without, but he noticed Holly seemed to be enjoying it immeasurably.

"This is an officially registered museum," Michael began. "Here we look after many books and archives relating to almost everything you can imagine about Freemasonry, and we are closely connected with the United Grand Lodge of England. We have a very impressive collection of very special manuscripts and an enormous quantity of printed books here that all relate to Freemasonry in one way or another. I am absolutely sure you'll find whatever you need for your search right here, Dr Hope."

Michael led them through an enormous hallway, around the top of which ran a first-floor mezzanine behind an elaborate balcony of black balustrades. Situated around the space, on brightly polished parquet flooring, were at least two dozen glass cabinets filled with beautiful silver and crockery relating to the Freemasons in various ways. They continued through to the next room, which Michael introduced as the library.

"Here we are," he said. "You should be able to find everything you need! Perhaps if you tell me the name of the book, I will be able to lead you to it more directly."

"No, that's okay," Holly said.

Mason was relieved to hear it. They had held a brief discussion on this very subject on their way across the road from the pub on Drury Lane and decided that the least information given to anyone inside the building would be the best possible option. Although they had no idea of how extensive the reach of the Conclave of Darkness really was, none of them wanted to push their luck.

"That's fine then," Michael said, rubbing his hands together and bowing his head slightly. "If you *do* need anything at all then you know where to find me. Right there through the cabinet room in the reception area."

Mason watched the smartly dressed man turn and walk away at a brisk clip, before disappearing through the doors into the cabinet room.

He turned to Holly. "I take it you do know where to find this book."

"Yes, I think so," Holly said. "They seem to have stuck to the same plan for at least these two, maybe all three of them. The note inside Beausire's amulet tells us to go to the ancient Babylon section and find this book by JM Witherington. That's the same as Kent Sullivan's amulet. It makes sense when you think about it. They want these things to be hard to find, but not impossible to find."

"That's so good of them," Alicia said, looking around the old silent musty library. "You know, I wish I'd stayed in the pub for another beer. Are you sure you guys need me in here?"

"That guy came absolutely out of nowhere in DC," Baxter said. "And I'll tell you what Alicia, we really could have done with you back there."

She shrugged. "If you say so."

Mason happened to agree with Baxter. There was something about Michael Smith he did not like the look of, and decided to go back and keep an eye on him while Holly looked for the book.

"Listen, guys," Mason said. "I'm going to go and check out old Michael back there, while you guys look for the book. Baxter, you can keep a close eye on Holly and Alicia can keep watch here by the entrance."

Everyone seemed to think that was a good idea, so after Mason watched Holly and Baxter disappear off deep inside the library, he told Alicia he'd see her in a moment and then wandered off towards the Cabinet room. He pushed open the doors and made his way across the parquet floor back to reception. Only he never got to reception, because halfway across the floor he heard a scream and turned to his right and saw Michael lunging at him with a full-length ceremonial Masonic sword.

Mason nearly got run through, it was that close. He only just managed to dart out of the way and sidestep Michael before spinning around and turning to face his attacker, who by now had also turned around and was slashing the sword in his face.

"What happened to the jovial chap at the front desk?" Mason asked.

"You made a mistake coming here, Mason. All four of you have made a big mistake! The Conclave is your worst nightmare made manifest." He slashed the sword two more times and took a step closer. "We're not some idiotic religious cult from Sumer or a bunch of insane Luciferians. This is real business now. The Conclave of Darkness will finish all four of you. We'll finish all five of you – Wilde will get it in the neck as well. No one can escape the Conclave. We'll track you down wherever you hide and destroy you!"

"You sound like the inland revenue," Mason said.

Michael screamed with rage and lunged once again, wildly thrusting the sword at Mason's stomach, hoping to cut him open and spill his intestines all over the floor. Instead, Mason managed to sidestep him once again and bring his right hand crashing down on Michael's sword-bearing hand. He thought that would be the end of it and the sword would fall to the floor with a clatter, but Michael had a very firm grip on the sword's handle and instead brought his other hand up into Mason's face and took a good grip of the entire left side of his head, forcing him away with the force of a wrestler.

Mason struggled against the force of the hand pushing his head to the right, and only just found the solution by reaching his left hand down and grabbing Michael's groin. In shock, Michael instantly retreated, releasing Mason's head and spinning around with a flourish, slashing the sword wildly at Mason's neck. Mason bent his head back and took a step to the left just missing yet another blow from Michael's sword. Mason looked around for a weapon and saw another ceremonial sword in one of the glass cabinet cases, so now he tipped the entire case over causing a tremendous smash and only just had time to scrabble around in the broken glass and pottery and reach the handle of a blade before Michael brought his sword thundering down towards his neck yet again. Mason finally reached the handle, grabbed it, rolled forward across the smash detritus and leapt to his feet on the other side of the broken cabinet.

"That seems a little fairer, don't you think Michael?"

Michael grinned. "The Conclave don't play fair, Mason."

He ran forward through the broken glass and wood and crockery, slashing the blade wildly like some kind of pirate. Mason was a boxer by training and not a swordsman. But he had fenced before with friends in the past and he understood the basics. That he had found himself in a sword fight in the middle of the Museum of Freemasonry in central London, was however not on his bingo card for 2024.

Mason fought back, blocking Michael's attacks and swiping his blade out of the way before lunging forward at his stomach. The crashing cabinet had brought Alicia to the door of the cabinet room which she now pushed open and Mason turned to see her staring at him in disbelief. She was armed with her Glock, having been able to bring it into the country thanks to a friend at the CIA calling forward to British Customs and clearing the way, essentially concocting a fake story about her working on an undercover CIA mission. She now raised the weapon and pointed it at Michael, but Mason unintentionally swivelled around to slash his blade at Michael and got in between her and his opponent.

"Hey!" he heard Alicia say. "If you get out the damn way, Captain Hook, I might be able to take a shot!"

At that point, there was a tremendous roar of gunfire, and Mason wondered for a moment if Alicia had fired a bullet through his back. Michael turned for a moment to look over his shoulder. Mason looked in the same direction and saw a man and a woman dressed in black bursting through into the cabinet room from the reception area, both holding handguns. Michael now turned to face Mason with a grin.

"I told you the Conclave doesn't play fair!"

Chapter 29

Locusta and Scorpio screamed at Michael to hit the deck so they could get a clean shot at Mason and Alicia standing directly behind him. Michael obeyed, as Locusta knew he would do, and instantly rolled to the floor and out of sight, still gripping his sword. Exactly why this fool had chosen to attack Mason with a three-hundred-year-old ceremonial sword, she had no idea. She had a much clearer picture of what would happen to him if she reported his failure to stop Mason to Snow.

With Michael out of the way, she and Scorpio unloaded their magazines at Mason in the middle of the cabinet room, and Alicia stood behind him, but both of them were experienced in armed combat and didn't hang around to take the bullets. Mason had already dived out of the way behind one of the pillars holding up the mezzanine around the cabinet room, and Alicia had darted back inside the door into the library.

"Split up!" Locusta told Scorpio. "Get down there in the library, and kill Kane. Baxter and Hope will be in there too. I want all of them executed immediately."

"At once," Scorpio said, with a respectful nod of his head.

Locusta watched him take off across the centre of the cabinet room pausing for a moment, halfway along, to turn left where he unloaded three more rounds at the pillar which Mason was using to hide from them. She heard Mason grovelling around on the floor behind the pillar, trying to protect himself from the bullets with nothing more than a big ego and a sword.

"Now you're mine, Mason!"

She raised her gun into the aim in a two-handed grip and tracked slowly around to the left to get a clean shot underneath the mezzanine, but by the time she reached it, Mason had already darted around on the library side of the pillar.

"You can't escape from us, Mason," she said. "We're everywhere. If we don't kill you in here, then someone else will kill you out there."

"I'll take my chances, thanks!" Mason yelled back.

Locusta made her way, treading carefully, from pillar to pillar, towards Mason. Thanks to a briefing she'd had on the private jet on the way over the Atlantic, she was aware the Englishman was extremely adept at fighting with his hands, but she also knew he had no firearm at the moment and was armed only with a sword. She made her calculus of attack based on this knowledge, deciding to always try and maintain a good distance between the two of them. She could not let him jump out and attack her and engage in close-quarter combat. She was excellent at what she did, but no match for Mason in this department. She knew he would disarm her in seconds and then she would be finished.

"Why not just come out with your hands up?" she said. "That way I can make it quick with a bullet between the eyes."

In the background, she heard rapid gunfire from inside the library. Definitely two guns. The first fired three times, and then the second one returned fire with five rounds. She didn't know who was who. Maybe Scorpio was attacking Alicia, or maybe Alicia was attacking her colleague. Either way, she couldn't trust Scorpio to get the job done as well as she could. She had to presume for now he was failing in there.

"That's a very tempting offer," Mason said, "Call me old-fashioned, but I think I'd rather stay alive for a little longer."

"And go down to that little olive grove of yours?" Locusta said. She was trying to get to him. "Oh yes, that's right. We know about your little olive farm. I told you the Conclave is everywhere. I've been reading all about your little enterprise down there, your olive grove, your business arrangements with the local cooperative. But all of it is very boring compared to your budding relationship with that Portuguese woman – what was her name again? Benedita?"

"Don't go anywhere near her, or I'll kill every last one of you!" Mason said, his tone cold and deadly serious. "Don't test me on this. If anyone touches her, they'll be signing their own death warrant. I promise you."

"You'll kill every last one of us?" she now laughed heartily. "You have absolutely no idea what you're talking about. The Conclave numbers in its thousands. If an order is put out to kill Benedita, then she will be killed. If an order is put out to burn your farm to the ground, then it will be burned to the ground. There is nothing you can do about it and there is no revenge you can take. You may kill half a dozen of us, but then ten times that many will be set the task of finding you and killing you and all your loved ones. All you can do is pray for a quick death. No one survives contact with the Conclave."

She was closer now; she had already searched the first two pillars and spun around quickly to search the third. But he was not there either. She knew he was good and what he was doing was keeping a careful eye on her location and ensuring that he was moving from pillar to pillar back to the library without ever producing a clean line of sight between him and her weapon. She wanted to kill him before he could get into the library. Inside there now she heard several more shots.

"Praying for a quick death isn't much of an incentive to give myself up," Mason said.

"Exactly what will the alternative be? As I say, no one survives contact with the Conclave. Right now we're offering you a good deal. We will kill you and your three friends in there and Wilde over in the Middle East, but that is where the killing will end. If this goes on much further, my superiors will put the order out to kill everyone you've ever known. Is that what you want? You want everybody you've ever come into contact with throughout your life to have a fatal accident? Because that is what will happen. Stand up now and let me kill you and put an end to all of this!"

"What exactly is so important that you can make threats like this?" Mason called out.

She was aware that he had already made his way back to the final pillar, now no more than two metres from the library door. She decided on a new tactic, considering that he wasn't armed with a handgun. She stepped out into the centre of the cabinet room with a direct line of sight to the library door.

"We do not want anything," she said. "Want is for nobodies. We have everything we need and everything we want. The Conclave seeks to keep what we have, specifically to guard the secrets we hold. There is no way on Earth that the Great Guardian of the Conclave will allow a man like you or any of your friends to expose these secrets. The Fellowship has already been extinguished, and you are next. Yield to your fate. Let me extinguish your life."

She was surprised when Mason darted out from behind the pillar and threw himself at the library door. She opened fire, three rounds, and felt the gun recoiling in her right hand. She watched the bullets ricochet off the door, always a fraction of a second behind Mason and then he was gone. And she was left standing on her own in the cabinet room with nothing more than the library door swinging backwards and forwards for company. She cursed herself and sprinted inside the library, her gun raised into the aim and with thoughts of murder on her mind. She would kill Jed Mason if it was the last thing she did.

Chapter 30

When Mason crashed into the library, it was in the middle of a scene of chaos. The tidy, calm and order he had seen when first walking inside the room with his friends moments earlier was now completely gone. Several of the shelves had been pushed over and books were littered all over the floor. At least half a dozen of the windows had been shot out with bullets, and there was a strong smell of gun smoke in the air. There was no sign of his friends, but Scorpio showed himself naturally enough when he shot up from behind an upturned desk and opened fire on him.

Mason once again found himself in a forward roll, which was harder to execute than he had considered while still holding a cutlass. He heard gunshots, but this time not from Scorpio. He looked at the Conclave man and saw him quickly duck for cover under a hail of bullets, and realised Alicia was pinning him down so he could get closer to him. Between the two of them, they could execute some kind of pincer movement, but he knew he had only seconds to do it because Locusta was right behind him. While Alicia continued to fire heavily on Scorpio, Mason broke cover and sprinted along the aisle between the bookshelves and the blown-out windows until he was able to see Scorpio cowering behind the desk.

Mason drew his sword back and was preparing to bring it down in a slicing motion across Scorpio's back when he saw him out of the corner of his eye turned and fired. Mason only narrowly avoided being shot in the stomach and found himself smashing down onto the floor in between two bookshelves. He scrambled up and sprinted across the library towards Alicia just as Locusta burst through the doors and fired on him. Scorpio also fired on him. He threw himself to the floor behind one of the research booths and landed a few inches away from Alicia's boots.

"How's it going down there?" Alicia said. "You need any help because you seem to be doing just fine so far."

Mason was reminded of when she had saved his life in the Vatican, a memory he did not like to revisit very often. "Yeah, I'm just fine thanks. You try taking on two guns with a cutlass!"

"We're not swapping if that's what you're getting at," Alicia said. "Down!"

"I already am down!" Mason said.

Alicia fired on Locusta who had just skidded around the corner of the library shelves, hitting her in the arm and sending her into a wild spin down to the floor.

"Looks like I got the bitch!"

Alicia fired again, this time past Locusta and thought she had killed Scorpio. When he got up from behind the desk and skidded over to Locusta, she saw it was a flesh wound and she had torn a deep gouge in the left-hand side of his skull. She and Mason had taken cover behind the ends of two of the bookshelves when Holly called out from behind.

"We've got it!"

"What do you mean you've got it?" Mason called out.

"You'll see," and Holly said. "Let's get the hell out of here!"

"How?" Alicia cried.

"There's a fire escape over here."

Stepping back in a retreating action, with her hands still raised into the aim in a double-handed grip on her Glock, Alicia called out for Mason to get the hell behind her.

Mason thought that was a good idea and now springing over to Holly who was standing holding a fire door open at the back of the library.

"Where's Baxter?" Mason asked.

"Tell you later," Holly said, running through the door and now Mason held it for Alicia, who walked backwards out of the library emptying her magazine on Locusta and Scorpio, both wounded and angry. When she reached the end of her magazine, Alicia ran out through the door, slammed it shut and Mason turned to see Holly piling into the back of a London black cab. Baxter was already in the back seat and now Mason jumped in with them. When Alicia was in, she slammed the door and the driver, operating under orders Baxter had already given him, stamped his foot on the throttle and raced down Wild Street away from the Museum of Freemasonry.

Mason turned in his seat and looked through the back window just in time to see the fire door open and Locusta stagger out into the street. She had blood all over her left hand from the wound Alicia had inflicted on her shoulder, and now she raised her gun, single-handedly losing several shots at the back of the cab, but the driver had already turned a natural bend in the street and was zooming past the Covent Garden Electrical Testing Tower. He turned a hard left on Campbell Street and they were gone.

Baxter had been looking out the rear window too and was now ashen. "I don't believe it!"

"What's the matter?" Holly asked.

"That woman! The woman shooting at us back there – she sat next to me on the plane I took from LA to Aspen!"

Mason turned. "Are you sure?"

Baxter looked offended. "I've been a detective all my life, Jed. Sure, I'm sure! She called herself Martha Crockatt. She said she lived in Aspen but was in LA for business!"

"That means these nutcases have been onto us from the very beginning," Alicia said. "Tracing calls, tracking us with God knows what. That makes me feel a lot better."

"There's nothing we can do about it now," Mason said. "Everyone just try and calm down." He pushed his head back in the seat and closed his eyes, barely able to believe how narrowly they had just escaped with their lives.

"The Conclave of Darkness really are incredibly savage," Alicia said. "You know, I thought those other guys we went up against were bad, but did you see the way they were firing on us?"

"I saw," Mason said. "Is everybody okay?"

Holly nodded. "Yes, I'm fine thanks. I seem to have got away without any real trouble but I did find JM Wetherington's book and I also got the words Beausire wanted us to find."

"That's excellent news, Holly," Mason said. "If we'd gone through all of that for nothing, I don't think I'd be a very happy bunny. What about you, Baxter? Are you okay?"

"I'm okay," Baxter said. "As soon as Holly went up to find the book, I saw the fire door and decided that we might need an escape route. I went outside, trotted back along to Drury Street and got the cab. Reginald here was very good and obliging especially when I told him that there might be a little bit of trouble. He said it couldn't possibly be worse than Soho on a Saturday night, and he bet me £10 that he'd stick around."

Baxter put his hand in his pocket, pulled out his wallet and now passed Reginald the ten-pound note. "Thanks, Reg!"

"No trouble at all, Baxter," Reg said. "Where exactly do you guys need to go? To the docks?"

Mason saw everyone looking at him and then back to Reginald in total confusion.

"I don't understand," Mason said. "Why do we need to go to the docks?"

Reg looked in the mirror at what Mason was holding in his hands. "It's just that we don't get many pirates in here with cutlasses."

Mason realised he'd left the building with the sword and now smiled. "Just a quiet café will do, thank you, Reginald."

Chapter 31

Snow was on his private jet when Locusta called to report the failure of the London section of the mission. Outside his window, he was looking at an enormous storm slowly gathering strength and couldn't help but wonder if it was an omen for the future of the Conclave of Darkness. Not if he had anything to do with it, but then again he seemed to be surrounded by fools. Perhaps they would let him down again.

"What do you mean, they got away?" he demanded.

"They're very good, Great Guardian," she said. "They'd set up two perimeters of defence, with Mason in the cabinet room and Alicia inside the library door while Dr Hope retrieved the clue that they needed. The other one – the gumshoe I talked to on the flight to Aspen – had gone outside and arranged transportation."

"If they're very good then you need to be better!" His voice rising in rage. "Now, four absolute nobodies have got two-thirds of whatever it is the Fellowship of Light left behind. It is not good enough, Locusta. I can easily find myself another Number One if you're not up to the job and you know what that means."

"I am up to the job, Guardian. Please give me another chance."

"It's all very well begging for another chance, but I'm only interested in people who can get the job done right the first time. Where are they going now?"

"We have no idea, I'm afraid we lost them. We've got our people in the Conclave inside the Metropolitan Police scanning the entire city for them. It can't be long until we track them down and then we'll kill them all, just as you have ordered. Believe me, Guardian, I want to kill them more than anything else in the world."

"Want rarely gets anything. Need gets more. Why didn't our man inside the museum kill them before they found what they were looking for?"

"He attacked them with a sword, Guardian."

Snow could hardly believe what he was hearing. "He attacked them with a sword?"

"Handguns are not easy to come by in England, Guardian. Not even for Conclave members. They're not something that just gets carried around all over the place. He improvised. He did his best."

"His best isn't good enough," Snow said coldly. "You are to execute him immediately before moving on and finding Mason and his team. I don't want any of them to survive the week. Is that clear?"

"It is clear, Grand Guardian."

Snow ended the phone call without so much as a goodbye and tossed the mobile phone down onto the seat beside him. The storm was worsening outside his little aeroplane window, and so was the turmoil in his heart.

Only he had ever held this deep dark secret, at least for the past few thousand years. There had been others, long before him. Those others had been the architects of the Conclave of Darkness, a cabal of insiders privy to the great secret throughout the ancient centuries, but it had got lost in time until he had found it and breathed life into the ancient Conclave once again. The Freemasons knew nothing about it at all.

The modern history of the matter was simple. Around twenty years ago, his immediate superior in the Masons, Bernard Drake, an Englishman from York who claimed to be descended from Nathaniel Drake, an estranged cousin of the famous antiquary and surgeon Francis Drake, a prominent Freemason in York in the 18th Century. Through his keen interest in historical research, Francis Drake acquired many valuable historical documents, some of which, Bernard Drake believed, had ended up in Nathaniel's hands and then into his. Bernard Drake was also an accomplished and respected archaeologist who had approached Snow, knowing how much money he had, and asked if he would fund an excavation down in Iraq – using information passed down to him by his famous forebears. The site was in the vicinity of Babylon, and Leonardo Snow was immediately interested. He was excited by the prospect of funding a dig of the kind Drake had described to him and immediately agreed, almost writing him a blank cheque.

Drake had travelled down to the site and several weeks into the excavation he sent Snow an email telling him something had been discovered in the desert. Snow could hardly contain himself. He had always had an interest in antiquity and now he found himself at the very heart of possibly a great discovery. He immediately made plans to fly from New York – because he was working on Wall Street at that time – to Baghdad, which at the time was an extremely dangerous place because of the war. Snow was able to grease the same palms he had done to allow Drake into the country and get himself in without too much difficulty. Less than a day later he found himself standing in the desert sands of southern Iraq, with Dr Bernard Drake, staring at the work the Englishman had done over the past few weeks. When he asked him exactly what he had discovered – because the Englishman would not tell him on the phone – Drake took him by the elbow, shushing him, and wheeled him away from the team of junior archaeologists working busily down in the trench with their picks and brushes.

"It's something very important, Leo." Drake had muttered.

"What do you mean 'very important'? Tell me more!"

"I think we found evidence that the Tower of Babel was not just a myth but a real place."

Snow was deflated. "What are you talking about, you fool? The Tower of Babel has not only already been found, but it has been found twice! Some claim it is the site discovered south of the Babylon Palace, and others claim it is at the Babylonian site of Borsippa, discovered by Sir Henry Rawlinson in the 19th Century!"

"No, they're not right! Neither site is right, Leo! The sites are too new – the Ziggurat of Borsippa dates to 600 BC, and the Ziggurat of Babel, near the Palace – also known as Etemenanki – was a ziggurat dedicated to Marduk, the Mesopotamian god and it was constructed between the 14th and 9th Century BC."

"And that's not the correct one either?" Snow asked.

"No, absolutely not!" Drake said with a shake of his head, then lowered his voice after a glance over his shoulder. "No one knows when Etemenanki was originally built, but even if we take the oldest estimate of the 14th century BC, it still doesn't date older than the one I think I have found here. This is the original Tower of Babel, Leo! We're talking about the original Tower as referenced in the Bible, found by me here this week and I'm positive of it!"

"How can you be positive about it?" Snow asked sceptically.

"Because of its age! Can't you see? If my calculations are right, then this site we're only just beginning to get stuck into now is at least 3000 BC! That makes it several hundred years older than the oldest estimate of Etemenanki. And no one's ever been here before either, can you believe that? I don't think they bothered searching here because it's just too close to the other Ziggurat of Babel, but that is far too new. Trust me, Leo! You've trusted me so far. You've funded me and you've believed in me. Believe me, what I tell you now is that this is the site of the original Tower of Babel!"

"But there's no Tower here is there?" Snow said, glancing round the flat sands.

"Of course not, but what I have found is its foundations! I am absolutely sure of it. And according to this tablet that I have already found there's a treasure trove of knowledge buried deep in the foundations, some kind of ancient archive storage department, if you want to think of it that way. Just imagine what it could contain!"

Snow had felt his heart skip a beat. As the heat from the sands washed over him, he adjusted his hat to create more shade on his face. "You can't be serious?"

"I am serious, Leo."

"Tell me about this stone tablet."

"I found a stone tablet written in cuneiform, not just talking about the Tower as if it was a real place but talking about places inside the Tower, and giving directions on how to get there. Including the library."

"But it must be some kind of joke."

"It's not a joke, I've been in this business thirty years. It's a completely authentic relic, and I believe what's written on it is also completely authentic. This is the big one. The one we always dreamed of."

"If you say you have directions leading to the place, then why are you not digging it up already?"

Drake waved a fly away from his face. "First of all, we wouldn't be digging up the Tower, Leo. The Tower stretched high up into the air. As we have already discussed, the only thing left remaining today is its foundations. They're hidden under the surface of the desert. Second, the directions mentioned on the tablet, are vague. They simply talk about how someone travelled there one day. They don't give us a starting point, nowhere we can use to get going to find it."

"So where did you find this tablet? What is the trenchwork for?"

"It appears to be the home of some kind of junior official. I believe it was someone who worked for an architect who worked on the Tower – helped build it, perhaps."

Architects, builders, and stonemasons, all building a Tower to conceal the truth, to hide the secret.

Now Snow waved away the same fly. "So, what do you propose to do?"

Drake turned to him and began to wring his hands. "It might take more money."

"You're sure that you're on to something here?"

The question he had asked Drake all those years ago trailed into a kind of echo as Snow came out of his daydream and looked out across the American skies. Drake had been sure he was onto something and he was. Three weeks after that conversation they had discovered, deep under the Iraqi sands, the home of the senior official who had designed and built the Tower of Babel. There was not much left in the crumbling ruins of his old residence after so many thousands of years, but they had found definitive evidence of the Tower of Babel, including several artefacts from within it which for some reason the architect had taken to his home. They had also found something else in there that the architect had taken from the Tower, something that had frozen both men in place for a time that felt like forever before one of them had finally spoken.

"We must bring this to the world, Leo," Drake had said.

Snow knew that to do such a thing would be complete madness.

"What are you talking about, Bernard? There is no possible way we could bring this to the world. I can't even begin to contemplate what such a thing would entail. Neither can you. This knowledge can never be made available to the common man."

"What are you talking about?" Drake looked at him with a questioning expression on his face. "Of course, we have to bring it to the world! The entire site must be explored and excavated much more widely. This is earth-shattering. The world must know! We must continue to search for the Tower – there may be more evidence of what we have already found here."

Snow was back on his jet. He had come out of his daydream for the second time. He did not wish to continue down that path any further. He had genuinely enjoyed the company of Bernard Drake and stabbing him to death in the architect's house under the Iraqi sands had been a most unfortunate but completely necessary thing to do. He had to do it. He was compelled to do it, especially if he was to keep the terrible knowledge he had learned that day with his old friend secret from the world forever. It was then, holding that knowledge in his hands, and staring down at the cooling corpse of Dr Bernard Drake, brutally stabbed to death with an architect's shovel, that he knew he had to break away from the Freemasons and create his own Order – one named after that which Drake had uncovered in the desert – the Conclave of Darkness. Not only named after them but with their key belief system as well. As he had learnt, they were not named because they saw themselves as evil in any way, but named that way because they knew they had to keep what they knew in darkness forever.

Forever meant forever, and that meant extinguishing anyone else who ever learnt the truth outside the Conclave, even though only the top level of the Conclave knew, such as the Fellowship of Light and soon Wesley Baxter and his team of bungling misfits. What bothered him most of all, was that the knowledge he had learned that day he knew was only part of the truth and that there would be much more inside the Tower of Babel itself. The problem was, that he had murdered Drake in a fevered panic before the old man had been able to find the actual Tower of Babel's underground library, and despite several well-funded attempts after Drake's death, they had never been able to locate it.

His grave concern was that the Fellowship of Light had somehow located the library, and had left clues to its location for anyone intelligent enough to understand to find. He knew Dr Holly Hope was extraordinarily intelligent and the rest of her team provided other necessary skills to help her find the Tower. He could not let this happen under any circumstances, but unfortunately, he didn't know where the Tower was himself so he was unable to mount a defence of it.

He turned to Nocturnus who was sitting beside him and ordered him to go and ask the pilot when they would land. A few moments later Nocturnus returned,

"Two hours until Lyon, sir."

Two hours until Lyon, Snow thought. *Two hours until we speak to the Blacksmith. That should clear up a few things.*

Chapter 32

Mason was gratefully wrapping his hands around a large cup of hot milky coffee as he waited patiently for Baxter to return from the counter of the busy London café Reg had taken them to, and join the rest of them at the table. The foreboding London clouds had once again opened and were covering the ancient city in another non-stop deluge. He was grateful to be inside, out of the wind and rain.

Waiting for Baxter, Mason shot Alicia a glance and even tried a smile. He got something that probably would not be described as a smile by most people given back to him, but he knew the hardnosed woman from Chicago well enough to understand this was some attempt on her part to return his gesture, and definitely as good as he could hope for.

"How's life treating you?" He asked Alicia.

She shrugged.

Holly, who was sitting beside them, was ignoring them totally. Since she had collected the second clue from Marcus Beausire's secret entry into the Witherington book, also written in anagram form by the looks of it, she was busy at work, once again with a pencil and her notebook rather than her smartphone. Baxter was still standing at the counter, waiting longer than the rest of them as he had opted to try a traditional British café breakfast fry-up.

"Just a shrug, eh?" Mason said.

"It's not too bad," Alicia said at last. "My latest job was a pain in the ass though."

"What do you mean your latest job was a pain in the ass?"

"You really don't care."

"I do care or I wouldn't have asked," Mason said. This was true. Everyone at the table knew he was a man of few words.

"Fine," Alicia said, taking a second to sip some coffee and gather her thoughts. As she considered her reply, her eyes crossed out into the street and she followed a red double-decker bus as it chugged its way through the rain on the road outside. An army of people marched up and down both pavements, all carrying umbrellas and gave the scene outside a strange, almost comforting effect. Mason thought it looked like some kind of French impressionist painting, especially after having spent so long in the dry dusty hills of Portugal.

"I've just been – when I say 'I', I mean me and my team – babysitting Siren."

Holly's eyes flipped up from her notebook. "As in *the* Siren?"

"Yeah, *the* Siren," Alicia said.

Mason thought Alicia looked embarrassed by what she had just said, but even though Holly seemed to know what she was talking about, Mason was absolutely none the wiser.

"What do you mean you're looking after a siren?" Mason asked. "Like the kind of thing they put on top of police cars?"

Holly laughed and went back to her notes.

Alicia shook her head, and this time a smile almost broke out on her face. "No, Siren – it's not a thing it's a person, but she kind of behaves like a thing. She's literally the world's biggest pop star, Mason. Don't you read the news at all?"

"No," Mason said bluntly. "I do not read the news."

It was true. Mason had made the conscious decision not to read a newspaper the day he had arrived in Portugal, and he had religiously stuck to it. At first, it had been difficult. Like most people in the world, he was completely conditioned to need to know news at all times. He would wake up in the morning, open his phone or laptop and immediately scour several newspaper headlines and possibly some of the smaller stories until he felt he was entirely briefed on the world's events that day. Eventually, he realised that he was checking the newspapers throughout the day, sometimes whenever he was bored and very often it was the last thing he did at night. He worked out he had been baited and was being reeled in. The newspaper business was a business just like any other and needed its customers.

The Babylon Agenda

What took Mason a long time to realise, was that he was the product, not the newspaper. His constant daily reading of the newspapers, or watching it on TV or the internet, was what generated the ad revenue. When he moved to Portugal, he decided to step out of this little cycle of doom he had been trapped in, and he hadn't looked at one since. Unless someone mentioned something to him down in the local market or at the gym, or perhaps Benedita might mention something to him about local news, he had literally no idea what was going on in the world. He felt much better for it.

"Yeah, well… if you did read the news, you'd know she is just about as big as it gets right now," Alicia said. She did not say this with any sense of bragging or pride. She still looked embarrassed. "Just think of Beyoncé and Madonna and Pink all rolled up into one and then you have Siren. And if you're interested, she is a complete and total asshole. Me and my team were hired to give her close protection after she received an increasing number of death threats. It's not good work, Mason."

"I'm definitely not interested," Mason said. "I'm sorry to hear you're not enjoying it."

She shrugged again. "Hey, it brings in the dollars."

She disappeared into her coffee cup and Baxter arrived at the table. He was holding a cup of tea in one hand, and an enormous British greasy spoon fry-up in the other. He placed it down on the table beside Mason, and Mason genuinely felt a little disappointed he hadn't thought of ordering one for himself. There was a beautifully fried egg, a sausage, some baked beans, buttered toast, two rashers of bacon, a freshly grilled tomato, and the private investigator from Los Angeles had even opted for some blood pudding.

Alicia looked at it like it was roadkill. "You're actually gonna eat that thing?"

"I am gonna eat it and I can't wait to eat it," Baxter said, rubbing his hands together as he surveyed his imminent conquest, and then covered everything in salt and pepper and Daddies sauce from a big glass bottle in the middle of the table. "This is going to be one genuinely British experience I just cannot wait to have."

Holly did glance momentarily at the food but soon went back into her notes.

Mason saw this and spoke to her. "Sorry to interrupt, Holly, but have you managed to decipher Beausire's anagram yet?"

"Yes I have," Holly said. "I've gone beyond that now and I'm trying to work out what they're alluding to. The problem is it's pretty obvious to me that we only have two-thirds of a clue here. I mean what we have is some kind of a cryptic message that has been written in Latin and turned into an anagram – and by the way, it was not particularly well scrambled – so these guys might be guardians of some ancient secret, but none of them were cryptographers."

"Helpful," Baxter said, stuffing some sausage into his mouth and sighing with pleasure.

Holly continued. "As you know, the line of text I managed to decipher from Sullivan's clue was: *ad secretum discendum ire debes*, or in English 'you must go to learn the secret'. The line of nonsense in the Beausire book was simpler: 'Camille clouds'. I just deciphered and translated this as '*ad collem lucis*', or 'to the hill of light'. Together we have: '*Ad secretum discendum ire debes, ad collem lucis*,' which obviously means, 'You must go to learn the secret to the hill of light', or probably as we would say more naturally in English, 'to learn the secret, you must go to the hill of light',"

"But what exactly does that mean?" Alicia asked.

"It means we need to get some of these cooked breakfasts over in LA," Baxter said. "This thing is absolutely fantastic. Maybe if business stays bad, I might get the menu out of this place and set up my own greasy spoon café in Beverly Hills. Imagine what I could charge for a plate of this!"

"Yeah, just imagine," Alicia said sceptically. "Unless maybe you found a way to turn it into a smoothie."

Mason winced. "Is that as cryptic to you as it is to me, Holly?"

"The 'hill of light' is obviously the essential part of this statement," Holly said. "Especially considering a member of the self-styled Fellowship of Light penned it. But it could mean an awful lot of places, to be perfectly honest. It's suitably vague, but if you think about it for a moment and think carefully about the context that we're in, then I think this means we should look at this through the lens of Freemasonry. One of the most famous Masonic centres in Europe is Lyon in France, which just happens to mean Hill of Light. There are other etymological explanations for how the city got its name, but for our purposes, we'll use this one. Again, as I say, because of the context."

Baxter was cutting himself a nice thick triangle of buttered toast and had already squashed some sausage and beans up on his fork and was ready to create a kind of grease sandwich. Now he stopped and looked up at Holly. "You're saying that we need to go to Lyon in France?"

"No, I'm saying that the three members of the Fellowship of Light seem to be leading us to Lyon, but the problem is this is all we've got. Lyon is an enormous city and there are several sites of Masonic interest there. With only these two lines we have absolutely no way of knowing where to go once we get there."

"What do you recommend, Holly?" Alicia asked.

Mason answered first. "I think we need to find Philippe Laroche's amulet down in Paris. That's going to give us the final part of the riddle and that's going to lead us to the exact location in Lyon, where we'll find whatever these guys are all banging on about."

"In theory," Baxter said, mopping up some sauce.

"But what exactly do we know about Philippe Laroche?" Alicia asked.

"Not much," Baxter said, chewing some bacon. "And it gets worse. I researched Laroche's murder on the way to the café and it's not good. Remember, both Sullivan and Beausire hid the amulet near where they were murdered, but according to a news report on Philippe Laroche's murder, he was found floating in the River Seine. Where would he have hidden the amulet? We can't search the banks of the entire river looking for something as small as an amulet."

"Maybe we won't have to," Holly said.

Everyone looked at her but Mason asked the question. "Exactly what do you mean?"

She smiled, loving the attention. "Listen up, I've got an idea."

Chapter 33

Mason turned to face Holly, still envious of Baxter's breakfast after catching the aroma of the grilled bacon on his plate. "Exactly what have you got in mind, Holly?"

"It's nothing concrete, but I've just been trying to extrapolate Laroche's most likely course of action. We know from the notes left behind by Sullivan and Beausire in their amulets that Laroche was their leader. He was the man they called the Guardian of the Fellowship of Light. I also think that Beausire was asked to go down to the Masonic Initiation Well to discuss whatever they were talking about with someone from the Conclave. Why else would a man who lives in London and works in London fly down to the Quinta da Regaleira, unless it was on Conclave business? There's a Masonic Initiation Well right there and that's where his body was found. He didn't go there just to hide the amulet. He went down to talk to the Conclave."

"That's a hell of a jump," Alicia said.

"No, I really don't think so," Holly said. "I think it makes perfect sense. He wouldn't go there to be murdered, either. Sullivan was kidnapped from his home in Los Angeles and taken to Aspen by the Conclave. Baxter is convinced he was murdered while he was there at the White Fir Lodge, but why was he there? It seems to me that both Beausire and Sullivan had been asked to go to other locations where each of them was then consequently murdered, but Laroche was found floating down the Seine."

"I think you're onto something," Baxter said, finally mopping up the last of his sauce with a piece of toast, placing his knife and fork in a neat line on the plate and leaning back in his chair with a satisfied sigh. "Why not just do Sullivan in Los Angeles? Why take him all the way out to Aspen? They wanted to talk to him. Why did Beausire go to the Masonic Initiation Well? Presumably, Snow wanted him to talk to a senior figure based in Europe, and that figure probably lives in the region and they chose the Masonic Initiation Well for some bizarre symbolic reason. Who knows what these nutcases get up to or what they find important? With Snow being based in Aspen, it made perfect sense to have Sullivan brought to his place there."

"So, what does any of this mean?" Alicia asked.

"Laroche was the leader," Holly said. "So, they would definitely have wanted to have a conversation with him first, and then his body was found floating down the Seine. Witness reports show he was nervously looking at his watch while he waited for someone on a bridge. Then someone pulled up, there was an argument and he was shot and fell off the bridge into the water. A news report said it was an armed robber, but I think we all know it was a member of the Conclave."

"But what is your point?" Alicia asked, losing her temper.

"My point is that from what we know so far, the agreement that the Fellowship of Light made with each other was that they would hide the amulet very close to the location of their deaths if they had a chance to do so. It seems to me if Laroche was their leader and was standing on a bridge looking at his watch nervously, then he knew that there was a strong possibility of his being murdered. Sullivan was kidnapped so he had no chance to do anything about the amulet until the last moment, and we don't know why Beausire took the amulet with him to the Masonic Initiation Well yet. He may have not felt at that point that his life was under threat, but we don't know yet. I think we should assume Philippe Laroche knew his life was under threat so he hid the amulet before he went out to meet the Conclave on the bridge."

"I gotcha," Alicia said. "Makes perfect sense."

"It still doesn't get us very far though," Mason said. "Exactly where the hell do we start searching for something the size of a thimble in a city the size of Paris?"

Holly's eyes brightened. "Philippe Laroche wasn't trying to hide the amulet. He wanted someone to be able to find it. Just in the same way both Sullivan and Beausire hid their amulet near their bodies, so anyone who knew what was going on and had realised they had both been killed might be able to find them. I believe that Laroche would have left a perfectly obvious clue to anyone who can understand it, telling us where he hid the amulet."

Alicia straightened her jacket. "So where the hell do we start with that?"

Holly said, "We start where Laroche left off that day, before going to meet the Conclave on the bridge. Which must have been from his home because – "

"Because he met the killer on a Sunday morning and would not have been at work," Baxter said. "So now all we have to do is find out where Philippe Laroche lived in Paris and we go and search his apartment for some kind of a clue as to where he hid the amulet."

Alicia smiled and nodded her head. "I like it, but maybe he hid the actual amulet in his apartment?"

"I doubt that," Mason said. "If he knew the Conclave was on to him and wanted to meet with him down on the bridge, he is unlikely to have hidden it somewhere as obvious as his apartment."

"Absolutely," Holly said. "If you look at what Sullivan and Beausire did to hide their amulets, there is a certain amount of subterfuge involved. With Laroche being the leader, and presumably holding the key part of the riddle in his amulet, he was going to make whoever might be looking for it sing for their supper. I very much doubt we're going to find it in a simple wall safe in his apartment. For one thing, that's the first place the Conclave would have looked for it after realising he wasn't wearing it around his neck after the so-called robbery."

"But wouldn't the Conclave simply have gone to his apartment and then started searching for the clue you think he has left behind, all for themselves?" Alicia asked.

"Yes, they probably would have," Holly said. "And we don't know if they found it or not. For all we know, if he did leave a clue there they already found it and took it away. We have no way of knowing. On the other hand, I think Laroche was very clever. From reading about him in this newspaper article, I saw he was the Master of the Grand Lodge of Paris, and then there was his position as leader of the Fellowship of Light to consider. I think any clue he left behind would be both cryptic and not involve Masonry in any way. He wouldn't want to give anyone in the Conclave a clue on their own terms."

"In that case, we need to get going," Mason said. "Anyone know where Laroche lived?"

"I do," Baxter said waving his phone. "It's actually on the public telephone directory here in France."

"Great," Mason said, pushing away from the table. "Then let's head out there and get on with this thing before the Conclave kills us all."

Chapter 34

"Rayan, hi!"

Rayan Ibrahim Abu al-Rawi returned the cheery hello and told Wilde how pleased he was to hear from him. Wilde knew he would be; he was one of his best contacts in Baghdad in the relic-smuggling world and they had done a lot of lucrative business together.

"How can I help you today, old friend?" al-Rawi said. "Don't tell me you're bringing more business into my part of the world?"

"No, not today," Wilde said. He was talking on his wireless phone setup as he was cruising along the motorway in Iran. "I am actually driving between Ashgabat and Tehran at the moment. Something to do with a nice little collection of Bronze Age necklaces. Interested?"

Al-Rawi laughed. "No, not at all old friend. Not at the moment anyway. I'm snowed under with business at the moment. You wouldn't believe the demand for some of these beautiful ancient pieces among the wealthiest of Baghdad. Of course, much of it is their heritage and they don't see why these things should be hidden away in museums when they can have them in their private collections. But then look who I'm telling! The famous Mr Huxley-Wilde knows this better than anyone."

Wilde laughed. Al-Rawi was right. Wilde *did* know it better than anyone. He knew better than anyone the rank hypocrisy of the wealthiest people not just in the Middle East but all over the world, who pontificated publicly about all kinds of matters of ethics and morality, while secretly hoarding the world's greatest collection of ancient artworks and jewellery. He had been involved in several deals involving high-profile people including some world-famous names. Sometimes they took whatever he had, sometimes they specifically asked him to obtain very specific items. They demanded confidentiality, and he guaranteed it. They were still hypocrites.

"Well, not to worry," Wilde said. "As I said, I'm not here to talk business anyway, at least not our normal kind of business. I had a call from an old friend a little while ago, and he's getting himself involved in something to do with Babylon."

"Well, there is a place with a rich culture!"

"Indeed, old buddy. Problem is, he's also got himself wrangled up with a bunch of psychopaths called the Conclave of Darkness who claimed to have some kind of connection to the place. We don't know what they're up to, but what I'm calling about is to see if anyone you know has been poking their nose around down there."

There was silence for a few moments, which Wilde found to be slightly uncharacteristic of al-Rawi. Then his old friend spoke. "As a matter of fact, I think perhaps there might have been."

"Someone *has* been poking their nose around down there then?"

"Yes, someone unusual has been poking their nose around. Most of the people that come down to my neck of the woods in Babylon are professional in the sense that they represent archaeology departments from around the world, or perhaps television crews, and then we have tourists. What I don't find turns up on my door step very often are very serious-looking men and women in dark suits wearing dark glasses and sometimes wearing ear pieces, driving very expensive American SUVs."

"And you've seen this down where exactly?"

"I've not seen it personally, but several of my closest associates have reported it to me in the last few hours."

"The last few hours? That sounds about when all of this seems to have kicked off. What exactly did your associates say they saw then?"

"I've not got much more to tell you than I've already said. They told me that down in the Babylon area, there have been some very expensive American vehicles filled with the people that I just described, driving around the sites, going in and out of the desert, and asking questions of people. That sort of thing."

"That's very interesting," Wilde said. "It seems to me like our friends are a little bit further ahead in the chase than we thought they were."

Al-Rawi's voice grew thin. "The chase for what, old friend?"

"That's just it, Rayan. I have absolutely no idea. The friend who called me – the man who is fighting these people – couldn't really tell me what any of them were searching for. I think that they're just running blindly towards the light at the moment, hoping they're gonna get their hands on some kind of prize or treasure."

Al-Rawi laughed. "There's not much left down in the Babylon site that hasn't been found over the past few thousand years, I can tell you that."

Wilde chuckled too. "You don't need to tell me that, Rayan. But still, there must be something down there or in the vague vicinity because it seems to be attracting a lot of attention at the moment."

"And by the sounds of it very unwanted attention!"

"You can say that again, my old mucker."

"Are my people in danger, Guy?"

"I don't know. Listen, I think I'm gonna make a left turn at Tehran and drive down into Baghdad straightaway. You don't think you could put up an old friend for a couple of nights could you?"

"I would be absolutely delighted! I will tell my wife at once that you are coming. She will make up a bed for you in the spare room. There's a wonderful new restaurant here in the south of the city I would love for you to try."

"Let's hope that we've got time to go out and eat, Rayan, because if this business starts to heat up, then we might find we have too much on our hands to be thinking about enjoying a good meal."

"Very well," al-Rawi said. "I'll speak to you soon. Tell me when you get to Baghdad!"

Wilde bade farewell to his friend and cut the call. He was still cruising into Tehran where he was going to meet with an important client and deliver the necklaces. Before Mason's phone call, he was planning on spending a night or two there but now, and especially after his call with al-Rawi, he decided that he would turn south immediately after the delivery and head to Baghdad. As far as he was aware, Mason was still in Portugal and about to fly up to London to meet the rest of the team. He was pretty certain he could be arriving in Baghdad within the next twelve to fifteen hours if he made good time. He had no idea where the rest of his old team would be when he arrived, but he guessed he would be there before them and would be able to make some preparations for their arrival if it turned out they needed to go there. And after hearing what Rayan al-Rawi had told him about the mysterious black-suited figures driving around the desert in SUVs, he had a feeling he'd be seeing his friends before too long.

Chapter 35

Baxter didn't want to tell the rest of the team, but he was enjoying himself. His most recent cases in Los Angeles had been humdrum, to say the least. He'd been trailing a cheating spouse for a few days, and he was also involved in a fraud investigation. It was all very routine until Charlotte Sullivan had called him. Then everything changed all over again.

He walked up the steps to the front door of Philippe Laroche, who lived in one of the beautiful Haussmann Buildings on the Avenue de l'Opéra in central Paris. It was an attractive and imposing home built in an age when what buildings looked like mattered. With its sloping lead-tiled roof and its ornate balconies, it was a fine addition to the street. This morning, the front door was in a dappled shade produced by the canopy of a plane tree in the street. It made Baxter see why people said this city was so romantic.

The door was, of course, locked, but this presented little difficulty to Baxter who had packed in his bag back – as he always did – his lock-picking kit. It was an essential if slightly dubious and underhand part of a private investigator's equipment – but he had all the skills of a professional locksmith, having patiently learnt them when he decided to go into private practise and become a PI. As Mason and the others shielded his activities from the street, he got on his knees and went to work on the lock. It took around ten minutes, being slightly more challenging than he thought it would, but then they were inside. He quietly packed his kit away, picked his bag up and then stepped inside the hallway, where Mason, Holly and Alicia were all inside waiting for him. Alicia closed the door and the team of four were now all gathered in the hall of the late Philippe Laroche's impressive Parisian townhouse.

Except it had been comprehensively trashed.

"So, I'm guessing the Conclave has already been here then," Alicia said.

"Certainly looks like it," Mason said.

Baxter shook his head and whistled. "Either that or Laroche got into a real temper when he was looking for his car keys."

Mason looked down the hall. From the little of the house he could see, he knew what to expect from everywhere else. Pictures had been torn from walls, hall tables were kicked over. A plant pot was spilt on the floor with soil spilling over the floorboards and even the runner going up the middle of the stairs had been torn out and dumped in a heap by the front door.

"I think this is going to be harder than we thought," Baxter said. "Not only have these guys already been through the place, but they've made such a mess of it."

"That's not what's bothering me," Alicia said. "For all we know they already found it and took it and we're just wasting our time."

"That's no reason not to search for it," Mason said. "We have to presume whatever Laroche left behind is still here."

"And we need to get going," Holly said. "We don't know how far the Conclave is in this race, but we can't waste time standing around in this hallway chitchatting. Let's get going."

"If the other two amulets directed us to Masonic Libraries, why don't we just head to the nearest one of those?" Alicia said.

"I've already thought of that," Holly said, almost scowling at her. "Don't you think I've already thought of that?"

Alicia shrugged. "I don't know what you think."

"There are over two dozen Masonic buildings in Paris alone," Holly explained. "So we have no idea which one Laroche left his message in, and not only that but in each one of those buildings there are going to be hundreds if not thousands of books. And in each one of those books, there are going to be hundreds of pages. The chances of us managing to locate the correct page with the correct words within the next ten million years are pretty low if you ask me."

"I agree with Holly," Baxter said.

"Right," Holly said. "Thank you. First, we find the amulet then we find the location of the book. Think it through, please. I've already considered that the most likely place for the clue is going to be inside the Grand Lodge of France, in the centre of Paris. But what are we going to do when we get in there? The place has thousands and thousands of books. We're going to go through each individual one, scouring each individual page until we find more nonsense like we found inside the first two books? Not only that, who's to say that Laroche hid his anagram inside a book? We don't even know that much. We have to find the amulet first. Think it through."

That was that, Mason considered. He'd never heard Holly lecture anyone in this way before, but he guessed she was feeling the strain of the mission and everyone respected her too much to have a problem with it.

"Everybody let's get going," Mason said. "We need to search this place from top to bottom for the amulet. If we don't find it, I guess we're gonna have to think again."

They divided into teams and began searching the entire property, Mason opted for the small terrace garden out the back and the downstairs floor, while Alicia took the first floor, Holly took the second floor and Baxter went right up to the top and took the third floor which was smaller than the others but also included the attic.

The small terrace garden out the back was not unusual for this part of the city, and it did not take Mason very long to unpick the mess made by the Conclave and go through not only everything they had looked through but also things he thought they may have overlooked. This included apparently lifting the flagstones and looking underneath them, and also checking for any concealed walls inside the small potting shed that Laroche had at the end of the patio. When he came up empty-handed, he made a start on the downstairs floor of the house, starting with the kitchen at the back and working through the other rooms. It took him less than thirty minutes to be fully satisfied that there was nothing to be found in this part of the house. That was when he made his way along through the narrow corridor, going upstairs to find Alicia deeply engaged in her search of the first floor.

"Find anything?" he asked. It was a reasonable question, she'd already been hard at work for nearly half an hour.

She looked at him, exasperated and frustrated. "No, not a thing. I think maybe we're wasting our time. Maybe the Conclave already found the damn thing and they're long gone with it? Maybe I was right after all and we're just wasting our time."

As she spoke, Baxter came down the stairs from the top floor and could offer no more than a shoulder shrug. "There's nothing up there at all. The attic is almost completely empty and there's nowhere to hide anything. Below that, there are just two box rooms. One of them is completely empty and the other one has a spare bed in it and a nightstand. I went through everything, even looking inside the lining of the drapes. Nada."

"Then that just leaves Holly," Alicia said.

Mason led the three of them up the stairs to the second floor, where Holly was lying on Philippe Laroche's large king-size bed, stretched out long and thin with her arms folded behind her head and an enormous smile on her face.

"You guys didn't waste too much time, I hope!"

Mason felt a frisson of excitement as he saw the look on her face.

Alicia said, "As a matter of fact, yeah."

"Too bad," Holly said. "I think I might have found what we're looking for."

"Where?" Alicia asked. "Was I right about the Grand Lodge of Paris?"

"You were not right about the Grand Lodge of Paris," Holly said. "And I can't say how great that makes me feel. In fact, I think I want to lie here on the bed for a moment longer and just think about how you were wrong and I was right."

"Where's the amulet, Holly?" Baxter asked.

"Yes, I think you've had your moment in the sun," Alicia said. "Now it's time to tell the rest of us dullards what you found in here."

Holly raised her hand and pointed at a large oil painting flat on the floor beside the head of the bed. "That painting down there, it seems like the Conclave threw it down in one of their tempers, but I don't think they could have looked closely at it."

Mason walked around to the side of the bed, picked up the painting and hung it on the wall above Holly's head.

Then he stepped back and stood with the rest of the team, crossing his arms over his chest as he stared up at it. It was a large beautiful oil painting, mostly of creams and golds, featuring a man sitting at a terrace table at a café, in a typical Parisian scene.

"What am I looking at exactly?" Baxter asked.

"Look closer," Holly said. "At the name of the café."

Mason looked closer: ς.ƐΥՇ.Ɛll.μ :ləT ʇəbɒↃ ʇiʇəꟼ ə⅃. "It's just nonsense," he said. "Just squiggles in oil paint, like all those guys do."

"No, it's not nonsense," she said. "Because there was a mirror at the foot of the bed hanging on the wall on which the Conclave also threw to the floor presumably to see if there was a floor safe behind it. If you hang the mirror up at the foot of the bed where it originally was hanging and then look at the painting again…"

Mason now walked around to the foot of the bed and hung the large mirror up. Now the team walked forward and joined him. They stared in the mirror at the reflection of the painting hanging on the wall above the bed.

"Ah," said Mason. "Now I see it."

Now the nonsense was reversed, it read: Le Petit Cadet. Tel: 4.113.573.2

"So this guy got rid of his amulet when he knew they wanted to kill him and had this painting done?" Mason said. "Genius."

"And he hid a telephone number in the painting in reverse?" Baxter said.

"Think a little deeper," Holly said.

Alicia gasped and clicked her fingers. "That's not a telephone number, it's a reference number for a book."

"We're getting somewhere," Mason said.

"So, Laroche hid a book in a café?" Baxter said.

Holly and Alicia shared a glance. Holly said, "Do you want to tell him or shall I?"

"I think you should tell him," Alicia said. "You worked it all out."

"Come on, Holly," Mason said. "You're killing us."

Holly relented. "He didn't hide it in a café called Le Petty Cadet – there's a significance in the fact that the information on the painting is in reverse and it only becomes legible when you look at it in the mirror. He's telling us that we need to be looking whatever is opposite the café."

"And don't tell me," Mason said. "You've already looked this up, too."

"Yes I have," Holly said.

Mason grinned at her. "What's opposite the café?"

"Not the Grand Lodge of Paris presumably," Alicia said.

"Not the Grand Lodge of Paris, no," Holly said. "It's La Musée de la Franc-Maçonnerie. The Museum of French Freemasonry. It's on the Rue Cadet, about a mile and a half northeast of here. Twenty minutes by foot or ten in a cab."

"Let's walk," Mason said, already halfway out of the room. "It's going to take us probably half that time just to find a cab down here. We need to hurry up, and someone write down that reference number!"

Chapter 36

Mason and the team made good time walking through Paris's beautiful 2nd arrondissement. They left the small side street to the east of the Avenue de L'Opéra and made their way north past a series of townhouses and affluential apartment blocks before finally crossing the Boulevard des Italiens. Then, they made a right, crossing the Boulevard Montmartre and heading north, walking past a Ramen noodle bar before finally arriving at the Museum of French Freemasonry. Unlike the museum in London, this was an imposing glass and steel building in modernist architectural style, down an otherwise beautiful French street. Mason pointed opposite the museum at the tiny little Le Cadet Café, which Holly had used to derive the museum's location.

"That was some pretty good deductive reasoning back there, Holly," Mason said.

Holly couldn't help but smile and seemed very pleased with herself. "It was nothing really."

"I sometimes think you're wasted, toiling away deep inside Harvard University Library," Mason said.

Holly looked up at him, suddenly, her eyes full of hope. "What do you mean by that?"

"Nothing much," Mason said. "I just mean that with the way your mind works, gathering information from so many different levels and places and putting it all together to make a coherent truth, you could probably do something more useful than researching ancient documents."

Holly looked disappointed. Mason wasn't sure if this was because she had been hoping he was going to make an offer – something involving working with the team full-time – or because he had vaguely insulted her life's work by inferring it was not important. He knew he had to apologise.

"I'm sorry. I didn't mean to suggest that what you do isn't important. I know you love your work and I understand that academic research is very rewarding and can be very meaningful."

"Hey, that's okay. I know you meant nothing by it. The truth is, I've been thinking something similar myself, since the Vatican mission. I don't get out a lot, that's the truth behind it all and I really enjoyed myself on those few days. I'm not gonna say I wasn't scared when I was kidnapped by those maniacs the last time I was here in Paris, but I still enjoyed the second mission – at least I did after you rescued me."

Mason felt Holly's eyes all over him once again. He wasn't sure if he was misinterpreting anything, but he had a vague sense that she saw him as slightly more than a friend, at least potentially. That was not somewhere Mason wanted to go. He had enough difficulties as it was just looking after himself and if there ever was going to be any settling down with someone, then it would be back home in Portugal if he could persuade Benedita to go along with the idea.

"Okay, anyway. Here we are," he said, changing the subject and stepping up to the museum's large glass door. It was covered in posters advertising the good works of Freemasons and the treasure to be found within. He pushed the door open and gestured with his other arm for Holly and the team to step through.

He closed the door and followed the rest of them into the lobby area. It was an enormous modernist area with a high ceiling and rooms on the first floor either side of them, visible through windows flanking the enormous lobby area, creating a kind of enclosed mezzanine. There were soft backless seats situated around the lobby area offering rest to weary travellers, but Mason and the rest of the team headed up the steps towards an enclosed front desk, situated inside a kind of vestibule behind a glass screen. On the wall beside it was a painting of an enormous Masonic compass.

Mason's mother was from French-speaking Switzerland, Lausanne to be exact. Thanks to this, he was completely fluent in French, albeit with a Swiss accent. He now stepped up to the desk and spoke to a slim, brunette woman with horn-rimmed glasses.

"La bibliothèque est-elle accessible au public?" he asked.

She smiled. "Oui, monsieur. Bien sûr."

"Pouvons-nous visiter la bibliothèque aujourd'hui, s'il vous plaît?"

"Naturellement. Veuillez prendre l'ascenseur jusqu'au premier étage et suivre les indications sur la droite."

"Merci bien, Madame."

Mason turned to the others, who not being able to speak French were none the wiser. "She says it's accessible to the public and that we're allowed to visit it today. We need to use this lift to go up to the next floor and then it should be somewhere on the right. She says there are signs to follow."

"Does she say if there are psychopathic conclavists on the loose around here?" Holly asked.

"Conclavists?" Baxter asked with a smile. "Is that a real word?"

"These days it's mostly used to describe people involved with the Pope," Holly said. "But if these guys are in a Conclave of Darkness, then I guess that makes them conclavists."

"I'd rather stick with mercs," Alicia said. "That other thing there's got too many syllables for me."

Mason smiled as he walked from the reception area across the smooth polished floor to the lifts. He selected the first floor and then waited a few moments until they heard a gentle ping and the door swished open. After scanning one more time in the lobby for any unsavoury characters, Mason and the rest of the team stepped inside the lift and the doors closed behind them. A moment later they opened onto a long, bright corridor. Mason immediately saw the sign for 'La bibliothèque' halfway along the corridor and beneath it a white arrow pointing to the right.

"Looks like she was as good as her word," Mason said. "Let's make tracks."

The team walked down the corridor until they reached the far end and then turned right where they were immediately confronted by two large double doors. They were glass, which enabled them to see through into the Masonic Library. Mason pushed through the door and held it open for the others and when they were inside, Holly looked down at her phone and quickly navigated to her most recent photograph – the one she had taken in the mirror of the oil painting on Laroche's bedroom wall.

"Okay, we need 4.11 3.573.2," she said, looking up and squinting through her glasses at the ends of the shelves. "Looks like we need to go a little bit further down."

They continued walking through the large carpeted library. There was silence everywhere, although occasionally broken by the sound of a stifled cough or the shuffling of feet on the carpet. Light streamed into the room from a series of windows on the far wall, through which the jumbled rooftops of the 2nd arrondissement, complete with an endless tangle of TV aerials.

"I think I found the right section," Holly said, and turned away to her left, walking towards the windows.

Mason and Alicia glanced at one another and knew what to do.

"Baxter, stay with Holly," Mason said. "Alicia and I are going to patrol this part of the library and make sure we don't get a repeat performance of what happened back in London."

Mason and Alicia split up, the American woman going down to the end by the windows, her hand poised ready to pull her gun at a second's notice. Mason moved deeper into the library and pretended to browse some of the fiction bookshelves while he was really scanning over the top of the shelf for any sign of the characters he had seen back in London, or similar ones. He knew Alicia had managed to wound one fairly moderately, and the other had a flesh wound. He didn't personally think this would stop him from continuing on a mission and he doubted it would have stopped either of those guys. Still, it was perfectly likely that the Conclave – being as extensive a network as they presumed it was – would have other operatives in Paris, so no one at this point could be trusted.

Mason lingered at the action-adventure section, amazed to see a novel that seemed to be about a secret society based on something to do with Babylon, he almost considered reaching for it and taking it from the shelf to have a flick through, but he was at work. There was no time for reading today. And the truth was, Mason read very little even at the best of times. He rose early and worked on the farm as long and as hard as he could all day. Breaks were short and not often, and as long as he managed to fit in one good run or a good trip to the gym that day, he would retire in front of his fireplace in the sitting room, with a bowl of beef stew and a glass of local red wine and be more than happy with the day's progress. There was just never any time for reading novels.

He continued to scan the library. There were very few people in there as this was not a public library but a specialist area containing works relating to French Freemasonry, the exact same library they had visited back in London. Mason wondered who would be spending large amounts of time in a place like this, but when he thought of Holly, he had his answer. An elderly man came into the library and shuffled over to the far side, quickly disappearing out of sight behind one of the bookshelves. Mason paid him no mind. He looked too old and frail to be able to cause too much damage to a team of four, one of whom was armed with an automatic pistol.

Mason glanced across the library in the other direction and caught Alicia's eye. She nodded her head at him in some vague notion to demonstrate she had registered his appearance, and then she too disappeared behind a bookshelf. Mason felt like they were in a lifeboat on the lookout for circling sharks. Was that a fin he saw over there? He looked at the door and saw a much younger man in a leather jacket walk inside the library. Mason began to walk towards him, staying out of sight behind a bookshelf for as long as possible, but then the man walked immediately to a specific shelf on his left, reached for a book, pulled it down, turned around and walked back out of the library again towards a reading room.

The next thing he saw, Baxter and Holly were bustling out of the aisle they had been in with smiles on their faces. Holly walked over to him and waved her phone in his face.

"We have it," she said. "I think we should get out of here before anything unpleasant happens."

Alicia was now making her way to the entrance doors on the far side of the library, no more than a silhouette moving swiftly in front of the windows and the grey Parisian sky behind her. The four of them met at the entrance, pushed through the door and walked down the corridor to the left. Mason wished he had a gun, which was not a thought he had very often. These days, he spent nearly all his time praying never to see a firearm ever again. The thought unsettled him. He shook it from his mind and came back to the mission.

The lift doors opened and mercifully it was empty. Mason and the others stepped inside the lift, closed the door and pushed the button for the ground floor. Moments later it pinged open in the lobby. Mason was expecting an enormous firefight to erupt.

The place was in total silence, peace and tranquillity reigning supreme overall. Mason walked to the front desk, thanked the brunette woman very much and then the four of them stepped outside into the street where it had begun to rain.

"That was easier than I expected," Holly shrugged.

"These guys can't always be in exactly the same location that we are all the time," Alicia said. "That just defies belief."

"You're right," Mason said with an amused smile appearing on his face. "How about we go to Le Petit Cadet across the street and get some coffee while you work out exactly where we need to go next, Holly?"

"That sounds like a great idea," Alicia said. "I would absolutely kill for a cup of coffee."

Chapter 37

Thanks to his Swiss mother, Mason was keenly aware of the difference between a *café au lait* and a *café crème*. This was something he knew from conversations with many people back home in England that was lost on most people outside of the French-speaking world. *Lait* in French meant milk, but a *café au lait*, which literally translated meant a 'milky coffee', was not a cup of coffee with a dash of milk in it, as most people drank. A *café au lait* was half-coffee, half-warmed milk mixed together and taken at breakfast time. A *café crème* on the other hand, was what most English speakers thought of a coffee with milk – that is to say a black coffee with just enough milk in it to cool it down. It could be served with cream, but then a *café crème* in France was usually served with milk. Mason now walked the four *café crèmes* back to the table where Holly, Alicia and Baxter were sitting in keen anticipation of their drinks and also the four delicious, freshly-baked *pains au chocolat* he had also bought, just for the hell of it.

He placed the little silver tray down at the table and the team began to tear into their chocolate pastries. The place was table service, but Mason had offered to the woman behind the counter to take the goodies back to the table and she was perfectly happy with that arrangement. It was busy inside and outside on the terrace, it was bustling and full of activity and laughter. All around them people drank coffee and ate various items from the extensive and beautiful menu. The experience was further enhanced by a steady gentle rainfall outside on the Rue Cadet. In the background, some light 1950s jazz was playing, which Baxter had already identified as being one of his favourite Bill Evans tunes – 'Some Other Time'.

Mason sat down in his seat, and sipped his coffee, closing his eyes to savour it as much as he could because he knew soon they would be taking off into the next part of their adventure. Standing at the counter ordering the coffees, he had quietly prayed to himself that Holly had worked out what they needed to know and that the mission would be coming to a swift end with the discovery of whatever the Fellowship of Light was trying to bring to their attention – and whatever the Conclave of Darkness was trying to keep from the world.

When he opened his eyes, he saw Holly – now happily enjoying her delicious pastry – had clearly already deciphered the anagram hidden inside Laroche's book, but she did not look particularly happy.

"What's the problem, Holly?" he asked.

"The problem is I'm gonna need two of these," Alicia said, replying to the question instead. She gently tapped the last inch of her pastry with her forefinger. "Because they are too good."

"You can say that again," Baxter said. "I thought that breakfast back in Blighty was good, but this thing is on another level."

Alicia sighed and rolled her eyes. "Baxter, you're from California. Please don't call it Blighty. It just sounds weird."

Holly also sighed, but not because she wanted more *pain au chocolat* or because she was annoyed by Baxter's new habit of using words like Blighty and fortnight.

"Okay, as you've already guessed," Holly began, "the anagram was not difficult to work out. I've already deciphered it and like the other two clues found in Sullivan's book and Beausire's book, it was nonsense, reading: 'Laud four our beefier Quartermaster'."

"The best yet, I believe," Alicia said.

"Indeed," Holly agreed. "When rearranged, it makes the Latin sentence: *et loquere ad faber ferrarius mortuus,* which means: 'And speak to the dead blacksmith'."

Alicia shook her head in despair and stuffed the pastry in her mouth. As she was in the middle of chewing it, she opened her mouth and talked. "That's just great. Let's go and speak to the dead blacksmith. I don't know about you guys, but it's perfectly clear to me."

"Go through all the clues again, will you, Holly?" Mason asked. "I'd like to hear them again like altogether."

"Of course," Holly said.

She began, and Mason noticed she was speaking from memory and not referring to her phone.

"The full text together – by that I mean the three separate lines found in the three separate books of the three separate members of the Fellowship of Light – were this: *'ad secretum discendum ire debes, ad collem lucis, et loquere ad faber ferrarius mortuus'* This means, directly translated, that 'you must go to learn the secret to the hill of light and speak to the dead blacksmith'. But to be honest, the way Latin works, I would probably rearrange it in the English version, so our final completed clue would read something like – 'to learn the secret, you must go to the hill of light and speak to the dead blacksmith'."

"Yeah, but who the hell is the dead blacksmith?" Alicia said, with a smile of satisfaction as she sipped her milky coffee and sighed with delight.

"I'm not quite sure about that at the moment," Holly said, screwing up her face. "As I hope you'll appreciate, it is a rather cryptic clue. In fact, I wouldn't mind a bit of peace and quiet for twenty minutes or so while I work it out, hint, hint!"

Mason took the hint easily enough. So did the other two. Alicia got herself up from the chair, pulled a cigarette out of her pocket, strolled out onto the pavement, lit it up and disappeared down the road without a further word. Baxter looked at Mason and asked him if he wanted to go for a walk. Mason thought that was a good idea. He liked Baxter's company and had enjoyed the few chats they had shared.

They stepped outside into the light drizzle, and Mason pulled up his collar. Baxter did the same and then the two men strolled slowly down the Rue Cadet. Holly had asked for twenty minutes and that seemed just about enough time for the two of them to get to the end of the road and back and shoot the breeze.

"It's good to see you again, Baxter," Mason said.

"Yeah and you too, man," Baxter said. "I kinda missed the old days when we got together and defeated those weird societies."

Mason did not miss them, but he had picked up on many occasions, especially from Holly and Baxter that the missions seemed to have brought an extra dimension to their lives that they both enjoyed very much. Alicia didn't seem to care one way or the other, and he guessed Guy Wilde had enough excitement in his life with his relic-smuggling shenanigans not to give too much of a care either way.

"We nearly got killed on several occasions, Baxter," Mason said.

"But it made me feel alive again, Mason! It made me feel like I just came out of the cadets and I was out on the streets of LA for the first time. That was an exciting time in my life. I was so proud to serve. There was never a day that went by when something exciting didn't happen. I guess things slowed down a little bit when I became a plainclothes detective, I was a lieutenant."

"Yeah, I know. You already told me."

"There I go again, telling the same old stories over again. Over and over. But I can't help it. That was my life. I guess things went off the rails a bit with Debs and then when I started to realise that my PI business wasn't really gonna take off, I don't know... Things changed with Sally Wilton's case, of course. Do you remember that time you nearly shot me in the Vatican? Good times."

"I didn't nearly shoot you," Mason said. "You were lurking around the house and I thought you were there to attack Holly."

"Either way, I'm glad we met."

"Yeah, me too, Baxter. It's been fun meeting up with everybody all over again but between you and me, I'm pretty keen on it not happening a fourth time."

"What makes you say that?"

"It's not just these three missions I've been on with you, Alicia, and Holly. You remember I told you about my old boss in the British Secret Service – Rosalind Parker?"

"I remember," Baxter said, nodding his head in the rain. "But I didn't remember her exact name. She giving you trouble?"

"More or less. She called me out on another mission. It started in the Vatican and I ended up going out into the Croatian mountains. I nearly got killed then too, Baxter. I didn't move out to Portugal and leave all this behind to get constantly dragged back into it all. It's not something I want to do anymore."

"I can understand that," Baxter said with a chuckle. "I guess we're all different." He slid his shoe through a puddle and squirted a jet of water across the pavement in front of them. "Me and Holly enjoy ourselves so much on these missions, yet you would rather be anywhere else."

"It's not that I'd rather be anywhere else, Baxter. It's just that I've spent many years of my life in this game. Always in another city, either always on the run or always chasing someone. Being the hunter or the hunted. I hate guns, Baxter. I hate shooting. I just don't want to be part of it anymore. I'm starting to think I should have moved further away from England than Portugal."

"I'm sorry you don't seem to be able to escape your past, Mason. If there's any way I can help…"

Mason looked at him and gave him a low muttered thanks, then the two of them turned around and headed back in the opposite direction.

"I'll do anything I can to make this my last mission," Mason said.

"But you wouldn't leave Holly hanging in the lurch would you?"

Mason sighed and stared up into the rain, momentarily enjoying the feeling of the water running on his face. Then he wiped it off with his hands and shook his head.

"A better course of action would be if Dr Holly Hope just stuck to her business in Harvard and stopped getting embroiled in nightmares."

"But this time it was me who was getting embroiled in the nightmare!" Baxter said proudly. "It was me that had to call up Holly, then you and Alicia came next."

"Your fault eh?"

Baxter laughed.

They had reached Le Petit Cadet. When they stepped inside, Alicia was at the counter ordering another *pain au chocolat*. Mason noticed with amusement, but little surprise, when she turned around and saw there was only one on her plate. This time it looked like it had been dusted in cocoa powder. As the three of them gathered around Holly, still sitting at the table, Mason spoke up first.

"Any luck with our dead blacksmith, Holly?"

"I think so yes," Holly said looking up at them hopefully. "I think the problem was that the clue was originally in Latin, and then of course we translated it into English. But let's not forget that Laroche was French. So I had the idea to translate the clue from Latin into French. In French, it reads: 'pour apprendre le secret, vous devez vous rendre sur la colline de lumière et parler au forgeron mort'. Is that good French, Jed?"

He nodded. "Fine."

"But how does that help you anymore?" Alicia asked. She had already stuffed half the pastry into her mouth, making her words almost inaudible.

"At first not much," Holly said. "But then I started thinking about *forgeron* – the French version of the Latin *ferrarius*, or blacksmith. What occurred to me was they were obviously referring to an individual, but how many dead blacksmiths are there?"

"A question I have often asked myself," Alicia said, stuffing the final part of the pastry in her mouth and shaking her head. "Will we ever know?"

Holly ignored her "I realised that the French word *Forgeron*, meant blacksmith. And that got me thinking that in English the name blacksmith is also a name. In fact, the surname Smith originally came from blacksmith. So I asked myself what was the French surname for a blacksmith, and it came up with Ferrier. This took me nowhere, but then I did more research and found the old Occitan surname which means blacksmith is Fauré. As in the composer Fauré!"

Mason and the others stared at each other with blank faces.

"Never heard of him," Alicia said.

"Doesn't matter," Holly said. "What matters is the surname. As soon as I realised that the clue was telling us to speak not to just any old dead blacksmith, but to a specific dead man called Fauré, I was able to put that together with the information we already deduced from the clue about the hill of light being Lyon. What I found was a man called Jean-Michel Fauré, one of the most famous heads of the Freemasons in Lyon during the 19th century. He is buried in a tomb in the Basilica of Notre-Dame de Fourvière, a small basilica on a big hill in Lyon."

The others stared at each other still in silence. Mason spoke first.

"So you're saying this is telling us to go to Lyon and go to the grave of this Jean-Michel Fauré?"

"That is exactly what I'm saying. Maybe I'm the one that deserves a second *pain au chocolat*, huh?"

"I think maybe you are," Baxter said. "You want me to buy you one?"

"No, I'm only joking." Holly laughed.

"Okay, we need to book some flights down to Lyon," Mason said. "It can't be a long flight from here, can it?"

"No more than an hour or so, I guess," Alicia said. "Too bad we don't have Edmund Wilton's private jet to help us out. I like to travel in style."

Holly looked at her and smirked. "You have a little bit of chocolate on the side of your mouth, Style Queen."

Alicia looked embarrassed and turned to clean it off. "Thanks."

The four of them shared a laugh and Mason stepped over to the door and opened it, gesturing for them to walk out into the street. When he stepped out behind them in the rain, he turned and said to them: "How about that? That's the second place we've been now where the baddies didn't just jump out on us coincidentally! I think we're making progress."

Chapter 38

Baxter enjoyed the flight from Paris down to Lyon, especially the view across to the southeast where he could see the French and Swiss Alps rising majestically into the sky. The snowcapped peaks glistened under the bright sunshine that illuminated high up above the clouds and reminded him of some kind of paradise.

Life on the ground was a different story. The usual bright sun and piercing azure sky that the south of France was so famous for was today nowhere to be seen. The plane had descended roughly through a thick bank of cloud that was stretching over most of southwest Europe, and eventually jolted and tumbled beneath the cloud ceiling to deliver him and the rest of the team into a heavily overcast, dull and very rainy day.

The plane landed at Lyon-Saint Exupéry Airport and being an internal flight, official business at the airport was swift and minimal and they soon found themselves stepping outside and hailing a large family-sized SUV from the taxi rank. Baxter sat in the rear with Holly and Alicia, while Mason sat up front and chatted to the driver in French. They drove south for a short while before turning right on a main road which headed straight into the city.

The Babylon Agenda

After passing through Saint-Priest and Bron they turned into the city's 7th arrondissement and then headed north, driving for a time beside the River Rhône. They eventually crossed the road on the Pont Galliani and then drove northwest, this time crossing the River Saône, before turning north and driving past a beautiful hilltop park, called the Jardin des Curiosités. Then, after driving through a labyrinthine tumble of terracotta-roofed houses in an area called Antiquaille, they finally reached their destination on a hill above the west bank of the Saône – the Basilica of Notre-Dame de Fourvière.

Mason paid the cab driver and a small team of four climbed out and stood in the drab rainy day looking up at the impressive façade of the cathedral. On the short ride from the airport, Holly had given the three of them in the back seat a quick briefing about the place – a brief historical overview nearly all of which went right over Baxter's head apart from him now remembering something about it being at the top of eight hundred steps and incorporating Byzantine, Romanesque and Gothic architecture. He couldn't remember if that was right or not, but that wasn't unusual for him and he doubted he needed to know it anyway. Baxter did, from time to time, read action thrillers and was always amused when the author expended lengthy amounts of words describing intricate architectural details of buildings that sometimes lasted for pages. The cynic in him often thought this was merely a word padding technique, but then again he thought maybe other readers were genuinely interested in the difference between Gothic and Romanesque architecture. He was not. He just wanted to get to the action.

"When do we get to the action?" Baxter asked.

"There's not much action, sorry. We're looking for Fauré's grave, Baxter," Holly said. She was frowning and scratching her chin. She had no idea where to begin, Baxter could see that.

"Let's get in there first and see if they have some kind of map or floor plan or something," Mason said. "At least that's a start."

"Wasn't this information available online?" Alicia said with a yawn.

"As a matter of fact, Fauré is mentioned online and he even has a Wikipedia entry, and there's even a photograph of the grave," Holly said. "But it's not clear how to find it."

"But what if it's a fake photo?" Alicia asked, ever the cynic.

"What do you mean by that?"

Mason could see by the look of genuine confusion on Holly's face, that the innocent academic in her had not even considered such a thing.

"I mean," Alicia continued, "what if the Conclave got here first, took a photo of a fake grave, and then uploaded it to Wikipedia, just to send us on a wild goose chase?"

"Why would they do that?" Baxter asked, scratching his head.

"Just to make us waste time," Alicia said. "Every second counts in a race like this. If we can get straight to the grave, we might only be here five minutes, but if we go to a grave and discover it's the wrong one and then go into the cathedral and talk to someone and find out where the real one is, we might be here thirty minutes. That just gives them an advantage. And anyone can upload anything to Wikipedia."

"Either way, it doesn't really matter in our case," Holly said. "Because we can't see much from the photograph at all, other than the basic details, and we can only see the front of the headstone. All I can tell is it looks like a tomb. It doesn't tell us anything or we wouldn't be here in the first place. Let's get inside and ask some questions."

Baxter followed Holly, Mason and Alicia into the basilica and was genuinely awestruck when he stepped inside and looked up at the enormous interior. Born and bred in Los Angeles, he was a true Angeleno, and would always love the place. He knew every single square inch of the city through his police work or his private investigation work which had taken him to nearly every suburban district. But one thing LA couldn't compete with France on was a building like this. There was a strange epiphany to be had when you stepped inside a building like this, built over 800 years ago and dominating the Lyon skyline ever since. Its exterior was impressive enough, with its towers, but the interior seemed to be even more amazing. For a short while he stared up and tried to take in the breathtaking artwork painted on the vaulted ceiling, completely absorbed by the incredible atmosphere inside – one of silence and reverence and also that familiar musty smell to be found in all church buildings over 500 years old. He saw the rest of his team had been just as amazed as he was by the place and were also all standing and staring in silence.

"This isn't the first basilica I've been in," Mason said, "God knows that. But it is one of the most remarkable."

"I'll say," Holly said. "I've never been here before and I've made it my business to travel to religious buildings all over Europe. I really don't know why this one passed me by. Sometimes I think I should leave Boston and move to France. Although my last attempt at doing that wasn't exactly a success. I got kidnapped by a violent gunman and dragged out of my apartment!"

"I don't think that's a regular occurrence here in France," Mason said. "Anyway, shall we get on?"

Holly turned and walked towards a member of staff, a pleasant-looking woman with brown wavy hair. She was wearing an electric blue blazer with a symbol on the pocket and smart black trousers. She greeted them as she would any tourists, first in French and then in English.

Holly replied to her in English, saving Mason the task of conversing in French for the third time on this mission.

"We're trying to find a specific tomb," Holly said. "It's a figure I'm researching for some academic work I'm doing. I'm a theological historian based at Harvard University in the United States and I'm working on an academic text concerning the relationship between Freemasonry in France and the Catholic Church here. Is there some kind of map we could use?"

The woman nodded her head, clearly impressed by what she had just heard. "That sounds very interesting, Madame. If you follow me over here, I'll be able to get you a map. Let me just find a pen."

As they walked, the woman now rummaged around in her pockets but finding no pen, she stepped over to a desk which she leaned over and reached into a drawer on the far side, opening it and extracting a pen. She now completed her journey over to a circular rack filled with pamphlets, leaflets and other pieces of information relating to the basilica and various historical events in this part of France. After turning the rack nearly one full rotation, she smiled, having seen what she wanted, and pulled it from the slot. Then she opened it up to reveal a full map and took the lid off her pen, ringing an area on the crypt.

"I know this particular tomb," the woman said. "Jean-Michel Fauré was one of the most famous astronomers in France during the 19th Century and of course a leading figure in French Freemasonry. He was entombed down in the crypt, where many other important people lay in rest, mostly archbishops and clergymen and that sort of thing."

The tour guide directed Holly and the rest of the team along the nave and to a door on the left-hand side which was already open.

"You are in luck," she said. "You can visit anywhere in the Basilica or go down into the crypt now free of charge."

"That's fantastic," Holly said. Turning to Baxter, she had now a big smile on her face. "Shall we go and speak to the dead blacksmith?"

Chapter 39

Moving slowly from the bright, beautiful light in the Basilica, whose beautiful stained glass windows created a kaleidoscope of colours, they moved slowly down into the darkness of the crypt. After consulting the map, Holly immediately made her way over to the tomb of Jean-Michel Fauré. Her heels clicked on the polished marble floor, and for a while was the only sound anyone could hear. She turned to the rest of the team.

"All right," she said, scrunching up her face. "We finally found our dead blacksmith!"

"Doesn't seem to be a lot of information on there," Alicia said. "I hope we haven't wasted our time. There were a hell of a lot of places that looked great to buy something to eat that I saw in the cab on the way in here. I could be sitting in any one of them right now instead of hanging out with the dead."

"Unfortunately, that's not what you're being paid for, is it?" Holly said.

"I'm not being paid anything!" Alicia said.

"You're being paid in thanks," Holly said with a smile. "My thanks. I couldn't do any of this important research work without you. You are a very essential assistant on my journey."

"Assistant?" Alicia said, her voice rising and filling the crypt. "I'm not anyone's assistant! You called me up because someone nearly shot your ass off and here I am. Some respect might be nice."

"Ladies, ladies please," Baxter said. "Let's not go there. We all play an important part in the team when we go on our missions together. Right now we need Holly to work out why Sullivan Beausire and Laroche were so desperate to point us towards this tomb. If the Fellowship of Light were aware of some kind of secret and wanted it to get out to the rest of the world, and the Conclave of Darkness were so desperate to keep that secret to themselves that they have killed, then I'm imagining it's going to be pretty impressive. Seems to me that the only thing between us and that secret is some hidden message on this tomb, so let's just focus and Holly will work it out."

"With all due respect Baxter," Holly said, "It's really not as easy as that. As we saw from the clues left behind inside amulets, and then again inside the books that the Fellowship led us to in their various libraries, the clues were all either anagrams or Latin or cryptic in some way and needed to be translated or deciphered first. Not only that, sometimes you don't even know that you're looking at a clue."

As Holly said this, she stepped back and took in the entire tomb in one frame of vision, cocking her head from side to side, then disappeared into a deeper analysis of what she was looking at. It was at this point that Baxter knew it was best to take a step back and leave her to it. He was a gumshoe, a man on the ground in Beverly Hills who knew how to get things done out on the streets. Everyday things. His life was altogether more prosaic than the slightly anachronistic and abstract world that thinkers like Dr Holly Hope lived in. Right now he knew she was seeing something completely different than he was seeing when she looked at the tomb. Or at least, he hoped she did.

"You see anything yet?" Alicia said.

Baxter wanted to shush Alicia to help Holly in her quest to discover whatever had been hidden in the tomb, but Holly seemed happy enough to answer.

"No, not yet, but I don't even know what I'm looking for. I've already looked at it ten times. Just hasn't occurred to me yet what might be the clue that we need."

Holly returned her attention to the tomb, now looking at it from all angles and pausing once or twice to squint and look at it from a different angle, then she stepped back and repeated the process. Then she did something that gave Baxter and the others a little measure of hope; she pulled out her phone and started doing some research.

Baxter felt a frisson of excitement as he started to think Holly might have found what they were looking for.

"What is it, Holly?"

"It's the flowers."

"What do you mean 'the flowers'?" Alicia asked.

"The bas-relief carved flowers that are painted in silver, coming up on either side of the tomb. The ones bending in at the top and stretching towards each other just above his name, do you see?"

Baxter saw but didn't know why they were important.

"Okay, Holly – you're gonna have to let us into your world again," Mason said.

She frowned and slipped her phone away. "What's bothering me is why they're not even."

"I don't understand," Alicia said, taking a step back and now cocking her own head to take a look at the carvings of the flowers on the tomb.

"They're lilies and myosotis flowers," Holly said. "Lilies on one side and myosotis flowers on the other."

"I've heard of lilies, but never the other ones," Baxter said.

"Myosotis flowers are better known as forget-me-nots," Holly said, now sounding even more confident in what she was deducing from the information on the tomb. "Why they are significant to me is that lilies are closely associated with the ancient city of Babylon, and forget-me-nots are closely associated with Freemasons."

"We're getting somewhere," Mason said. "Well done, Holly."

She ignored the compliment. "The thing that was bothering me is why the leaves and petals are not even. Count them closely. On the left, we have the lilies, and there are 32 petals on the top side of the carving and 32 petals on the bottom side of the carving. Then on the righthand side with the forget-me-nots, there are 44 petals on the top-hand side then 25 petals on the bottom-hand side. This is wrong."

"So, this is some kind of numerical clue?" Mason said. "Coordinates?"

"Damn it, not more coordinates," Alicia said. "Why can't these guys ever just write anything plain and simple?"

"Because they don't want any old fools knowing our secrets!"

Mason spun around to see three silhouettes standing at the top of the crypt steps. He recognised the man on the left and the woman in the middle as the two Conclave members who had attacked them in the library back in London. The man on the left had a thin dressing on the wound on his temple, but the woman's injury was hidden beneath her jacket. Another man was standing on the other side of the woman, presumably recruited here in Lyon.

"Step away from the tomb please," the woman said.

"Just who the hell are you guys?" Alicia asked.

"I am Locusta, this is Scorpio and this here is Taurus."

"Tell me," Alicia called back. "With names like that, have you come to read our star charts?"

"This is no laughing matter," Locusta said. "You do realise that we cannot let you leave this place alive?"

Baxter took a step in front of Holly, acutely aware that right now she was the only one who understood what was carved into the tomb. He was also acutely aware that the team only had one handgun, and that was in a holster under Alicia's black leather jacket. They were trapped with nowhere to run and three dangerous armed assassins were closing in on them.

"What happened to the name Martha?" Baxter called out. "Decided you needed a new identity?"

"I have many identities," Locusta said with a smirk. "They enable me to stay undercover when being bored to tears by people like you and your sad little life stories."

"I don't care what your names are," Holly called back. "All I know is you represent something dark and evil."

"You don't know what we represent," Locusta said, slowly stepping off the steps into the crypt. She calmly pulled a pistol from a concealed holster under the lapel of her suit jacket and began casually screwing a suppressor on to the end of it. Baxter knew this was not a good sign.

"Look out, everyone," Mason said. "Get ready for trouble."

"If you knew who we were or what we were trying to do, you wouldn't be opposing us," Locusta said. "You've been given enough opportunities to break away from your search and go back to your lives, but still you persist and now here you are, down in the crypt of a basilica in Lyon, just feet away from one of our greatest leading lights, Jean-Michel Fauré, seconds away from your deaths. Not very clever."

"If what you are doing is so important and you're so intelligent and knowledgeable and reasonable," Holly called back, "then why not simply let us walk away? You know that we haven't got to the end of the clue trail yet."

"I know all about you Dr Hope, and I know you've been down in this crypt for at least ten minutes staring at that tomb. You've probably got a photograph of it on your phone. Even if you delete the photograph, you've already spent long enough looking at it to go away and use that great big brain of yours to work out what it means. So we let you go and the next thing we know, you're getting your little team together again and going on an expedition. I'm sorry to say that the secret we're guarding is far too important for anyone to discover, especially an academic keen to improve her profile in the community with what will inevitably be, of course, the greatest discovery ever made."

"So, that's it? You're just going to murder us down here in the crypt?" Holly asked.

"What do you think?" Locusta said. She was much closer now, almost halfway between them and the bottom of the steps. Baxter thought that coming so close was a tactical error, and he saw that Alicia did as well, because now with lightning speed the American woman from Chicago ripped the gun out from under her jacket and fired it. The sound of the gunfire was deafeningly loud in the marble-walled crypt and echoed and reverberated all around them for several seconds. Alicia had hit Taurus, and now his body was sprawled out dead on the marble floor.

Locusta turned to stare at her dead colleague in disbelief and now raised her silenced pistol to shoot Alicia, but it was already too late. In the second Locusta had turned to see if her colleague was dead or not, Mason had dived into a forward roll and now sprung up to his feet just inches away from her. When she turned to shoot Alicia, she instead saw Mason reaching out, grabbing Locusta's wrist and twisting until she dropped the gun. Mason fired a palm strike into her chin with a view of knocking her out there and then, but she was ready and immediately bent her head back and off to the left, missing the strike. Then she easily moved out of Mason's grip by bringing her left hand up and gripping Mason's windpipe, pushing him back until he was forced to release his grip on her so he could pull her wrist away from his throat.

Baxter was watching all of this with amazement, only half able to believe that it was happening and even less that he was still alive. Alicia scrambled over to pick up Locusta's gun, but Scorpio got there first and now he was standing in front of them with two guns, preparing to shoot both Holly and Baxter at the same time. Alicia, who had almost reached the gun, was closest to him and now as he aimed his weapons on Holly and Baxter, she piled into him, forcing both of the guns down to the ground. When he fired the weapon, the bullets hit the marble and ricocheted off noisily. Scorpio, angry with Alicia for making him miss his targets, now brought his left hand up, still holding a gun in it, and knocked her in the side of the head with it, knocking her back onto her backside on the floor where she looked like she was about to pass out.

Mason had Locusta subdued temporarily, although she was strong and he knew he wouldn't be able to hold her for long. Baxter now piled in to help Alicia, helping her up to her feet. Then, the two of them attacked Scorpio together and were able to overcome him and remove his weapons. Now Baxter and Alicia, both armed, took steps back until Scorpio was safely out of range and pointed their guns at him.

"You can let her go now, Mason!" Alicia said.

Mason looked relieved and released the powerful, angry, struggling Locusta.

She pushed him away with a red face spitting at him in rage. "So now you're going to kill us?"

"Sadly, that's not our style," Mason said.

"Holly, have you got everything you need?" Baxter called over.

"Yes definitely. I can't wait to tell you guys about it."

"And that will be your downfall!" Locusta said. "You pathetic fools."

Baxter watched Mason take Locusta's gun and armed with the three weapons, they now made their way to the steps, forcing Locusta and Scorpio to get down on the ground with their hands behind their head. When they reached the top of the steps, they closed the crypt door and Holly slid the bolt, locking it. She turned to the others.

"That's not going to hold them for long. They're going run up those steps and start banging on the door and then someone will let them out and they're going to come after us again. Who knows how many more Conclave members are in Lyon? We need to run."

Everyone agreed, and Baxter now followed the rest of the team through the nave, holding the gun he had taken inside his jacket while Alicia and Mason slotted theirs in shoulder rigs. Moments later they were stepping out into the cold rainy Lyon day, looking down the famous 800 steps staircase ahead of them.

"I'm not walking down that lot," Mason said. "Let's call a cab."

"Good idea," Baxter said, almost wheezing at the mere sight of them. "Then when we get somewhere safe, Holly, you can tell us what the dead blacksmith told you back in the crypt."

Holly smiled. "You're going to love it."

Chapter 40

Mason was not enjoying the coffee at Lyon Airport as much as he had the one at Le Petit Cadet. It was lukewarm and listless and tasted vaguely of damp cardboard. Still, it was better than being shot dead in a crypt, so he sipped joyfully as Holly explained what she had been able to deduce from Monsieur Fauré, erstwhile scion of French Freemasonry and very dead blacksmith.

"Right," Holly said, gathering the notes together that she had spread out all over the table. In doing so, she knocked her coffee cup over and the contents spilt all over her notes. "Oh, shoot!"

She desperately tried to wipe the coffee from them and save at least a fraction of what she'd spent the last hour writing down. Mason reached into the centre of the table and pulled a paper towel from the little pot filled with single-serve packets of sugar and toothpicks, and helped dab some of the coffee from the notes. He noticed while he was doing so Alicia sitting back in her chair rolling her eyes and shaking her head. Baxter was too preoccupied with the enormous croissant he was trying to squash some butter into.

"You realise those things are already just all butter?" Alicia said.

"I realise it and I love it."

"I hope you didn't lose anything important," Mason asked Holly.

"I don't think so," she said happily. "I can remember anything and all of the important stuff anyway. These notes were really how I got to the conclusion, what matters is the conclusion."

"Talking of which," Alicia said with vague sarcasm, "have we got to the conclusion yet?"

"Why? Wanna get back to your babysitting job?" Holly asked.

"No," Alicia said with emphasis. "I'm just thinking about how our nutcase friends back there aren't gonna give up on this, probably even if we find what we're looking for. They're going to want us dead even more."

"Unless we bring the secret into the light before they can kill us," Mason said. "After all, they can hardly kill the entire planet, can they?"

They all sat in silence for a while after that, all except Baxter who was now greedily savaging his way through the buttered croissant that he had just bought from one of the airport cafés.

"So," Mason asked. "What was written back on that tomb that was so important those guys tried to kill us there and then?"

The Babylon Agenda

"It wasn't exactly what was *written* on the tomb," Holly said. "It was to do with the flowers and the petals. I was bothered by the fact that they weren't numerically balanced. Not always, but normally on graves there is a certain aesthetic balance that is obtained by making things like flowers even on either side of the name, but these were very uneven and that bothered me. It made me start to ask questions, and the answer I got was obviously in the disparity between the two sets of numbers of petals or leaves. So not exactly written, but visually communicated through the carvings of the leaves and petals."

"There weren't any split hairs on there?" Alicia asked.

Holly gave her a look and then continued. "No, there were no split hairs on there, thank you very much, Agent Kane. But there were 32 petals on the top half of the lilies and 32 petals on the bottom half of the lilies, and 44 petals on the top half of the forget-me-nots and 25 petals on the bottom half of the forget-me-nots. So that means we have four numbers 32, 32, 44 and 25."

"So what does that mean?" Alicia asked. "Are we talking about some kind of a combination to a safe? What about a telephone number?"

"It's not any of those things," Baxter said. "These are geographical coordinates."

"How can they be geographical coordinates?" Alicia said. "Geographical coordinates are usually a series of four double-digit numbers. One for the north and one for the south, then for the east and one for the west. Then, two more to fine-tune. DMS. Degrees, minutes, seconds."

"That's true," Holly said, smirking that she finally had another one over Alicia. "But what if the exact geographical coordinates that the Fellowship of Light was trying to lead us to required only degrees and minutes? What if the seconds' value was blank?"

"Not getting it," Alicia said.

Holly said, "The Fellowship of Light was established long after Fauré died, so they must have paid to have his tomb changed to put this clue on it. You could see the carvings of the flowers were a new addition to the tomb because Fauré died back in 1876, but the Fellowship of Light wasn't formed until much more recently. They must have had the genius idea of carving the coordinates onto the tomb using lilies and forget-me-nots because they were flowers that represented both Babylon and the Masons. Absolute genius!"

Mason saw Holly was getting lost in her own world once again. "Holly, you haven't finished telling us what you were getting at with these coordinates not having enough numbers."

"Oh, yes. Sorry," Holly said, suddenly brought back to the table. "If the location of the place the Fellowship of Light wanted to lead us to happened to have only degrees and minutes with a numerical value, and then the rest of the coordinates were zeros, then these could indeed be geographical coordinates. So they would be 32 degrees, 32 minutes north, and 44 degrees, 25 minutes east."

"Question," Alicia said. "How do we know it's north and east? Why not west or south?"

"That's a good point," Holly said. "The thing is, we know anything to do with Babylon is going to be in the northern hemisphere and the eastern hemisphere, not only that if you type these coordinates into Google Earth, which I did a moment ago, you will see that they come up near the city of Babylon, not where the ruins are or the palace or the hanging gardens but much further south beyond even the Ziggurat of Babel, which many people believe is the Tower of Babel."

The team fell silent. "Wait, this is all about the Tower of Babel?" Baxter asked. "Wow."

"I've heard of that," Alicia said. "But what exactly was it?"

"It was the classic origin myth," Holly said. "A parable in the Book of Genesis which was created to explain why there are so many languages in the world. Why wouldn't everyone speak the same language if God created everyone? The myth says that once, everyone *did* speak the same language, and they came together and built a giant tower that reached into the sky. God saw this and decided to make them all speak different languages so they couldn't understand each other and then he scattered them all over the world."

"Kind of a 'divide and conquer' thing because their tower was too close to God?" Alicia asked.

"Maybe you could see it that way," Holly said. "There are a lot of myths about the Tower and several possible locations that could be the original site have been unearthed over the years."

"Earlier, Holly," Mason said. "You said many people believe the Ziggurat of Babel is the real Tower of Babel. You think that's wrong, don't you?"

"Yes, I think it's wrong. I think the real Tower of Babel is what these coordinates are leading us to. I think it's much further from the other site."

"And no one ever found it before?" Mason asked.

"Hey look," Holly said, navigating to the same location on her phone once again and this time laying it down in front of Mason. "If you look, you'll see that the ancient city of Babylon was built inside this meander of the Al-Hillah stream, a branch of the Euphrates. The city itself was built beside the palace which was built on a massive hill, just off to the southeast of what were once the Hanging Gardens of Babylon. This here…" She tapped her finger on the screen at a small square to the south of the palace, "is what is called the Ziggurat of Babel, which has been argued to be the Tower of Babylon. I dispute this. And this here… here is where the geographical locations carved into the flowers on Fauré's tomb point."

Mason watched her finger slide quite far south to an enormous expanse of undeveloped sands to the south of the city but still within the meander.

"And you think that this is where the real Tower of Babel was located?"

She looked up at him, her eyes full of the hope that he found so often there. "It's got to be, hasn't it?" she said with a goofy smile. "What the hell is all this about, if it's not leading us to the site of the Tower of Babel?"

"That's not what I'm worried about," Alicia said. "What's bothering me is what's the big secret that they've got hidden there."

"I don't think they've got anything hidden in the Tower of Babel," Baxter said. "Think about it, if they knew where it was, they'd already be there now, wouldn't they? I think they know their so-called secret from some other location, possibly quite close by to the Tower of Babel, and they fear more evidence of this secret being found inside the foundations of the Tower of Babel."

"I think that's a very reasonable deduction," Mason said. "I'd expect nothing less from a detective."

Baxter tipped his head and then began stuffing more of the croissant into his face.

"One way or the other, we have to get out there," Alicia said.

Mason looked over his shoulder at the departures board and saw the flights. Then, his phone rang, and he saw it was Guy Wilde.

"Who's that?" Alicia asked. "Not Rosalind yanking your chain again, is it?"

Mason gave her a look and held the phone up so she could see. He did the same thing, repeating the process so Holly and Baxter could see. "Looks like Guy wants a word with us."

"Answer it then!" Holly said. "It could be important."

"I'm betting it *is* important," Mason said. "We arranged that I would call him if we got down to Iraq and we needed him. It was not for him to call me. There must be something up."

Mason answered the call. "Hey, Guy! What's going on?"

"Jed! How are things?"

"Not bad at all," Mason said. "I was about to call you. It looks like we'll be coming down to Iraq after all."

Wilde sighed. "Good, but you're going to need an army if you do."

Chapter 41

"We're going to need an army?" Mason said.

"Yes, an army." Wilde was sitting in a noisy Tehran café and now he was forced to press his phone hard up against his ear and cup his hand around the outside of it so he could still hear Mason as he spoke. "I've been asking some questions about Babylon and it's not looking good."

"I don't like the sound of that," Mason said. "What exactly is going on, Guy?"

"I can't be sure exactly, but I got in touch with an old mate of mine called Rayan. He's ostensibly an antiques dealer in Baghdad, but he does a little bit of 'special' under-the-counter work from time to time if you get my drift."

"I get your drift," Mason said. "Where the hell are you? It's really noisy there!"

"I'm in Tehran, at a café. I'm sitting out on the pavement. To be honest, it's a little bit crazy here at the moment because I'm quite close to a market. Can you hear me alright now?"

"Much better."

"Good. I just moved inside for a bit. Anyway, as I was saying – me and Rayan were talking not long ago and he told me that he thinks there's a bit of trouble down in Babylon."

"What sort of trouble?"

"He said there's a bunch of people sniffing around out there who shouldn't be there. You know the drill, Jed. These guys are serious-looking individuals, many of them dressed inappropriately for tourists in a place like Babylon. They're swanning around in big black SUVS, and they also have a small party of what he thought looked like archaeologists with them. There's some ground-penetrating radar, or at least that's what he thought he saw them using. The point is, they're crawling like ants all over a bowl of ice cream."

"I see. You think this is the Conclave?"

"Who else can it be mate? Rayan knows that neck of the woods like the back of his hand, as you can imagine. He says he's never seen anything like this before in his entire life, and I'm thinking, hang on a minute – didn't I get a call from Jed Mason recently, telling me about a group called the Conclave who were interested in Babylon? It's all too much of a coincidence for a simple fellow like me."

"Yeah me too," Mason said. "I agree and I don't like it one little bit. Now I understand why you're talking about an army. The problem is we don't have an army."

"No, pity. What about you?" Wilde asked, sipping his coffee and hiding behind his battered baseball cap and dark glasses as he scanned outside for any sign of law enforcement. "Did you get any further on your clue trial? Is Holly singing for her supper?"

"As a matter of fact, she is and we did," Mason said. "I can't remember exactly how far we got when we spoke last, but Holly and Baxter worked together really well to get to the bottom of these clues left behind by this so-called Fellowship of Light. There were three of them in all, Kent Sullivan, Marcus Beausire and Philippe Laroche.

"Okay, sounds good."

"And these three blokes had all hidden a clue written in some weird Masonic alphabet which led to books they'd hidden in libraries by fictional authors. The clues led to specific passages in the books – I think Holly said it was a number for how many lines down, and then a number for how many words across – something along those lines, you know how it is with her. I think I'm wrong because she's shaking her head."

Wilde laughed. "Hey Holly! How's it going?"

Mason held the phone to her. "All good, Guy. Great to hear from you."

"You too. Put the Gaffer back on."

Mason continued. "Anyway, the clues led Holly to nonsense words which meant nothing, but then Holly realised they were probably anagrams, and when she started scrambling them around she found that they were still nonsense unless she put them into Latin. She could make Latin sentences out of them."

"What is it with these geezers and always writing in Latin?" Wilde asked, sipping his coffee and still carefully looking out for police or any sign of his business associate.

"She says it's because it is an important language to ancient secret societies and religions and it's more universal. I say it's because they're trying to sound clever."

"That's a good one, mate." Wilde chuckled, taking another sip of his sweetened coffee. He saw he had a call waiting and looked down to see it was from his Egyptian friend in Cairo. That would be a much more relaxed conversation than this one, especially as he knew what was probably at the end of this one. "I think it's because they're trying to sound clever too."

"Anyway, those clues revealed the location of a tomb in Lyon, France. It was at the top of 800 steps – I've never seen anything like it. They had been leading us to the tomb of a very famous French Freemason, whom they obviously respected very much even though they had joined the Conclave before forming the Fellowship. Holly's theory is that when they became a breakaway group within a breakaway group, forming the Fellowship, he was their inspiration and leading light because back in the 19th Century, he also formed a separate Freemasonry group called the Guild of Light."

"So, we're not gonna give them any prizes for originality then?"

Mason gave a low chortle. "No, we're not going to give them any prizes for originality. Anyway, when we got to this tomb, it was just a normal headstone built into the side of it with the usual details, but ..."

"But Holly found something that no one else saw?"

"Yes, Holly did find something that the rest of us didn't see. There were carved flowers on the tomb and she noticed something about the specific type of flower and how many petals they had. Anyway, they had significance to the Fellowship for one reason or another and it turned out that the carvings were geographical coordinates that pinpointed exactly to Babylon."

"I thought they might," Wilde said, he was still scanning the street for any sign of his contact who was coming to collect the necklaces. He thought he saw him walking along the pavement on the other side of the street and when he looked closer, he saw that it *was* him, walking furtively and scanning over his shoulder. He couldn't look any more obvious if he was dressed like Indiana Jones. Wilde rolled his eyes.

"So, I'm calling to say it would be good to meet up in Iraq, and I guess now to thank you for giving us this tip-off. That's really helpful, Guy."

"That's not a problem at all, mate. If you want me down there I'll be happy to meet you. Are you going straight to Babylon or to Baghdad first?"

"We don't know what we're doing yet. It looks like we're almost certainly heading to Iraq but we're just trying to get our thoughts together for now."

"You're in Lyon at the moment, aren't you?"

"That's right, we're sitting in the airport."

"Exactly, so if you decide to go, your flight's probably no more than seven or eight hours away, I can't remember right now. I'm not leaving my old Harley behind, so for me, it's a twelve-hour drive on the Persian Gulf Freeway. I think I'll head down to Baghdad after meeting my contact here in Tehran, whatever happens. I've got a lot of contacts down there including my mate Rayan who's gonna put me up for a few days. Just do some chillaxing. If it turns out you give me a call or need me then I'll already be down there. It might be that you arrive before me anyway, depending on when you fly. Either way, I'm completely chilled out."

"Thanks, Guy," Mason said. "I really appreciate it. We needed to know about the extra troops gathering down in the desert. The Conclave seem mighty desperate to get to the bottom of this before we do, that's for sure."

"They sure do," Wilde said. "Rayan said at least forty or fifty people are gathering down there. It looks like we're going to be heavily outnumbered."

"But I've got an idea about that," Mason said. "I've just had it since we've been talking and you've given me the numbers of the Conclave you're talking about."

"Well, I'm glad I could be of some help. I think I know what you're thinking, so if we are on the same page good luck with that."

"Thanks, I'll probably need it."

Wilde looked up. Indy was now crossing the street and walking towards the café. He looked a little bit lost, but that was because Wilde had moved inside to reduce the noise from the phone call, and his contact was expecting to find him outside. He wanted to get to him fast before he drew any more attention to himself than he already had done.

"Listen, Jed – I'm gonna have to go. Some business just turned my way."

"Your contact showed up at last?"

"Yes. I'll be in touch."

"Okay, take it easy,"

"All good?" Alicia asked.

Mason nodded. "He had to go. He's up for joining us."

"I knew he would be," Baxter said. "Helluva guy."

Holly looked at him quizzically. "What were you saying about there being an army down there, and you having an idea about that?"

"I'll explain on our way. We need to buy some tickets right now."

"Exciting," Baxter said. "I've never been to Baghdad before."

"We're not going to Baghdad," Mason said.

Chapter 42

When Mason stepped off the flight from Lyon and walked through the airport with the rest of his team, the information boards and posters around him were written not in Arabic but in Italian. This was not something he had expected to see when he had started on this mission, but he hoped it was a good twist of fate. If it went wrong, going to Babylon could easily turn into a one-way suicide mission, which was not something that appealed to him at all.

"And you say you had this idea when you were talking to Guy Wilde?" Holly asked.

"That's right," Mason said as they walked towards customs. "When he told me about the number of people the Conclave had managed to lay their hands on and gather together down at Babylon, he also told me that we needed an army. I knew he didn't have an army and I thought we were up shit creek without a paddle, if I'm being honest, but while we were talking I started thinking about our friends in the Vatican."

"Giancarlo Zabatino and Gabriel and his little Knights Templar force."

"Exactly," Mason said. "We worked with them twice before, and I thought there's no one else we can ask if we need a reasonable force to go up against someone like the Conclave. They owe us, even though they have a history of being somewhat reluctant with us."

"That's true," Holly said. "Certainly Gabriel and Zabatino are dead keen on keeping control and stability in the world of religious beliefs. At this time, we have absolutely no idea what it is the Conclave are trying to keep from the world, but if we can persuade Zabatino that it could have serious repercussions on either world stability or at least on the Catholic Church, then he might be able to scare up a small force of warriors to help us out in the desert."

"My thinking exactly," Mason said.

"I hope you're right," Baxter said, butting into their conversation.

Mason looked across at him and saw the much older man had broken out in a sweat as he waddled along next to them with his paunch, trying to keep up with them as they walked through Rome Fiumicino Airport.

"If there's one thing that wasn't on my mind when Charlotte Sullivan walked into my office, it was getting involved in warfare against a secret breakaway Masonic group called the Conclave of Darkness and then asking a splinter group of the Knights Templar to help us out, but right now, I'll take any help I can get."

"I'll second that," Alicia said. "These guys even make Siren look human."

Mason smiled at the easy banter among his team as they walked. As it happened, he was in full agreement with them. The last thing he had expected to be doing this week was chasing around Europe in a race against the Conclave of Darkness in a bid to finish the work of this so-called Fellowship of Light and find whatever it was they were trying to tell the world.

He had described Zabatino and Gabriel and their Order just now as reluctant, but that word was also perfect for him. No man on Earth was a more reluctant hero than Jed Mason. He wanted to turn his back on these people and go back to his life so much that he even began to feel guilty about it when they shared a laugh or a relaxing cup of coffee. He felt a little bit like a traitor to them. On the other hand, they needed him. Alicia was more than capable enough when it came to handling a weapon, but he knew she wasn't enough.

They needed his experience, strategic vision and street smarts equally as much, if not more. He was in no doubt that without him, at least Holly and Baxter would both be dead by now and perhaps all three of them. Then again, that just made things even. Alicia had saved his life on at least two occasions, and in their own way, Holly and Baxter had also helped him come back to life. He admired Holly's enthusiasm and optimism and she had inspired a little of that in his own broken soul. As for Baxter, he had been impressed by the way the older man had pulled himself together after a devastating divorce and was doggedly determined to create his own private investigations business and start a new life for himself, even at a much older age than Mason was. He owed them more than they owed him.

After they had made their way through customs and were walking out of the airport towards the taxi rank, Holly was already deep in conversation with the office of Giancarlo Zabatino. There were some difficulties with language and Holly looked uncharacteristically frustrated and even annoyed at times, leaving Mason with a bad feeling this entire journey had been wasted. They had called ahead from Lyon in the airport, but there had been no response from Zabatino or his office in the police. There was of course no way to get in contact with Gabriel. As Rome was on the way to Baghdad from Lyon, they decided there was no harm in stopping off for a few hours and trying to talk to Zabatino personally. It was a gamble they were willing to take, knowing they would not lose that much time. It would be more important for them to arrive in the desert with a proper fighting force. Thanks to Guy Wilde, they knew the Conclave was already out in the desert anyway.

Holly switched off her phone and dropped it in her bag as Baxter walked out to the edge of the pavement and hailed a taxi.

"You got through to them this time?" Mason asked.

"I got through to someone," Holly said. "I don't think she was very senior in the police. They told me to stop wasting police time. They told me if I had a crime to report then I should do it in the usual way."

Alicia laughed. "That sounds helpful."

"She got more helpful. She told me that Zabatino wasn't at work anyway because he was at a family wedding. I explained to her that I was one of Giancarlo's American cousins, and I was lost and didn't know how to get to the wedding. She gave me directions."

As she was talking, Baxter and Alicia were climbing into the back of a taxicab. Mason now climbed in behind them and looked up at Holly standing on the pavement. "You had better get around to the front of this cab and give the driver those directions, and I hope you packed a nice hat because we're going to a wedding."

Chapter 43

Mason had never been to an Italian wedding before. He had also never been to Castello Brancaccio, an enormous sprawling castle built on the side of a hill in the Sabine Hills to the east of Rome. The beautiful baronial castle was one of the most famous landmarks in Italy, imposing mightily out of the hillside in an enormous jumble of sandstone and honey-coloured stone walls and terracotta roofs.

Originally built upon the ancient ruins of a former castle owned by the Colonna family, the enormous structure dominating the hills today was built over 1000 years ago and was the subject of many struggles for ownership and control in the intervening centuries. At the centre of it all was the enormous fortified borgo of San Gregorio da Sassola, a giant rectangular building, its enormous high walls adorned with merlons. The building had its own drawbridge and its centrepiece was a quadrangular tower. In the centre was an enormous courtyard, where Mason and the rest of the team were now climbing out of a taxi.

"Ah, my house," Alicia said looking up at the beautiful building looming all around her.

"Imagine the heating bill," Mason said.

Alicia winked at him. "But imagine the parties."

Mason stared up at the chapel's bell tower and saw that it had been converted at some point in history into a turret. "It's certainly giving off some serious fortress vibes."

"The problem is, I'm not seeing any signs of a wedding," Holly said.

Baxter shrugged in his usual relaxed matter-of-fact way. "Then let's go ask someone."

Mason followed the team inside the borgo, where they walked through an impressive hallway whose walls were covered with frescoes and oil paintings showing the various historical periods of the castle. They made their way to a reception desk.

Holly spoke to a woman there and explained that she was a cousin of the wedding but she had lost her ticket.

The woman seemed patient and genuinely concerned, clearly believing her story. When she looked at the other three members of the team she seemed less certain. She asked them to wait where they were and disappeared through a door behind the reception desk.

Mason wandered back through the lobby area and stood in the doorway, hearing the unmistakable cry of a peacock echoing out across the hills beyond the castle. He heard Holly and the woman engaged in a tense conversation and at that point, his mind started turning to less pleasant ways of locating the wedding party. Then he saw a woman in a floral dress and large hat speed-walking across the courtyard. He turned and got Baxter's attention, pointing out what he had just seen. Baxter in turn fetched Alicia and

Holly and then the four of them were walking across the courtyard in the direction of the woman who now disappeared through a doorway.

Mason followed her inside the doorway, up several flights of stone steps and through a series of corridors before coming out in a large dining area set with tables full of untouched polished glasses and plates and silver candles. On the other side of the room were large open French doors, leading out onto a stone terrace, high above the hills. There were hundreds of people out there, smartly dressed and sipping champagne.

Mason now made his way across the room onto the beautiful rooftop terrace outside, which had been dressed with candles and lanterns and yet more tables covered in white linen and bottles of champagne. It didn't take him long to find Giancarlo Zabatino, who was leaning up against a wall in an Armani suit and shielding his eyes with a pair of expensive designer sunglasses as he chatted amiably with a woman in a cream dress. He was gesturing with his hand in the time-honoured Italian way and then the two of them laughed loudly. There was no sign of the bride.

Mason walked over to him and when he was around ten feet away, Zabatino caught sight of him and his face changed immediately. The warm, relaxed smile fell away like a dead leaf and a look of sombre misery and anger appeared in its place. He said something quietly to the woman and she turned and walked away and then Zabatino pushed off the wall and stood up to his full height in front of Mason and the others.

"Just what the hell are you doing here?"

As he spoke two large men in black suits appeared as if from nowhere and began walking towards them, but Zabatino waved them away.

"We're not here to cause any trouble, Giancarlo," Mason said. "We're here to ask for your help."

"Help? This is a family wedding! My sister is getting married today!"

"There's not going to be any trouble here today," Mason said. "I promise you it will be an entirely peaceful meeting between us. We just need your help."

"If this is business concerning the Order of Jedediah, then I suggest you speak to me on Monday morning."

"It's more urgent than that," Holly said. "We're really up against it this time. We're fighting a group called the Conclave of Darkness – they're a breakaway group from the Freemasons and they seem to be in control of some kind of secret, something about the Tower of Babel. We're not sure. We're still just trying to find our way through. What we know from a contact down in the desert in Iraq – at the Babylon site – is that the Conclave is gathering a large number of forces down there in search of something and there's only five of us!"

"There's only four of you!" Zabatino said. "You can't even count."

"Guy Wilde is down in the desert," Mason said. "He's already promised to give us some backup if we go down there."

In the background, the volume of the music increased and everyone cheered. Mason heard the sound of a wine bottle being uncorked.

"And how many people are in this Conclave?" Zabatino asked, nervously scanning the crowd for any sign of trouble.

Mason now heard a bottle of champagne pop behind him and a roar of joyous laughter. "We don't know exactly how many are in the Conclave, but Guy told us there are forty or fifty people down there near Babylon. If we go down on our own we'll probably be slaughtered."

"Slaughtered?" Baxter said. "I'm not sure I'm up for that."

"This is impossible," Zabatino said, shaking his head. "You ought to leave here immediately. I cannot believe you came here today with this. I don't even know who this Conclave of Darkness are and this is not how the Order does business. This Conclave will need to be looked into and researched. You don't understand how these things work. Who are they connected to? Who are their ruling elite? There may be an overlap with the Order – there may be members of them inside the Catholic Church. We have to be careful not to tread on any toes. We don't just go in there guns blazing because of some secret that you know nothing about."

The joyous laughter Mason heard now turned to screams. Down far below on the cobblestone street, below the rooftop patio they were standing on, they heard several gunshots – Mason recognised them immediately as nine-millimetre handguns. There was more screaming and shouting and then the sound of doors slamming. Mason and Zabatino shared a look of mutual suspicion and nervousness as they both ran to the low stone wall running around the rooftop terrace. Mason got there just in time to see a group of men pushing a woman in a white wedding dress into a car far below. Then the car revved, spun its wheels, producing a cloud of thick burnt rubber smoke, and skidded off down the cobblestone street out of view below the castle.

"My sister! Maria!" Zabatino cried out. "You stupid bastards have brought your problems here to my wedding and now they've taken my sister!"

"That doesn't sound right," Alicia said. "That's not how the Conclave has been doing business."

"It doesn't matter who it is at the moment," Mason said. "But I think we all know the Order of Jedediah has plenty of its own enemies."

Zabatino glanced at him, removing his sunglasses to reveal eyes full of burning hate. "Si, the Order has plenty of its own enemies but who would dare strike us here today, like this?"

"I'm not interested in any of that," Mason said. "Alicia you are with me. Everyone else is to stay up here!"

Chapter 44

Mason descended the stairs three at a time and raced across to the exit. It was already frenetic with terrified activity as staff hurried to respond, making telephone calls and trying to pacify guests. Mason sprinted outside into the bright Italian sunshine and could still smell the burnt rubber smoke from when Zabatino's sister had been snatched. Directly across the cobblestone entrance to the castle was a sign pointing to the 'Carabinieri', the Italian police, and Mason guessed the reception staff inside were already busy telling them about what had happened. He had no idea how quickly they would respond, but something made him doubt they would be able to deal with the problem effectively anyway.

Searching around him, he found a thirty-year-old Renault 5 and ran over to it. There was a black steel rubbish bin positioned on the corner of the castle and now he picked it up and put it through the driver's window, pulling up the small lock on the door. He swung open the door and pulling his leather jacket up over his hand, he brushed the shards off the seat. He climbed into the car and smashed the plastic housing off the bottom of the steering column, finding the correct wires he needed to hot wire the vehicle in a matter of seconds. Alicia climbed in and then they were moving.

The vehicle that had snatched Maria Zabatino had raced down a narrow cobblestone street to the south of the castle called the Via Vittorio Emanuele, and now Mason raced the Renault 5 down the cobblestone alley as fast as he could, shifting up from first to second gear. The sound of the small one-litre engine roared angrily in response and echoed and reverberated off the high castle walls on either side of them. The tiny roadway, originally built back in the days of horses and carts, was barely wide enough to accommodate the Renault and certainly would not have allowed a wider, newer vehicle to pass. As it was, Mason and Alicia were driving at such high speed that more than once he scraped the side of the car up against the castle wall on his right or the wall of the other building off to his left, producing an insane shower of sparks that flew up into the air.

The Renault blew out of the narrow cobblestone street to reveal itself in a tiny little square, also cobblestoned and decorated with a beautiful white eagle, inlaid in the cobblestones. Mason slammed on his brakes and brought the car to a juddering halt.

"Why are you stopping?" Alicia asked.

"Because there are two ways they could have gone," Mason said.

He was right. Up ahead, the road they were on continued bending around to the right, but to the left, obscured from Alicia's angle by a low stone wall, there was another road leading around backing up behind them.

"Well, I can't see which way they went! Alicia said. "You have to make a decision."

Mason switched off the car, a trick he had done more than once in his life and used his ears. Then switched the engine back on and floored the throttle.

"They went that way!" he said, pointing straight ahead. "I can hear their engine somewhere off to the right."

Mason and Alicia continued speeding along the Via Vittorio Emanuele, with the castle high on their right and off to their left a solid line of townhouses, five storeys high. Their engine reverberated again off the walls, noisily and loudly through the window forever opened because Mason had smashed it. They tore through another small square, this time off to the right, Mason saw the only other exit was a set of pedestrianised steps, which meant they must have continued on the road ahead. Mason continued in the same direction.

"What are we going to do if we catch up with them?" Alicia said.

"We're gonna get Maria Zabatino back, that's what."

Mason wondered exactly how messy that might be. Alicia still had her handgun, thanks to her contact at the CIA. They had been allowed to fly into Italy with the weapons so long as they were in the hold below and did not have live ammunition inside the firearm. When they landed in Italy, a series of extensive forms had to be filled out and telephone calls made. Only Alicia was allowed to bring hers in, as Mason did not want to contact Rosalind Parker unless he absolutely had to, although she could have pulled the same strings for him.

They got to another square, and Mason now saw the vehicle that had snatched Maria Zabatino had been abandoned. It was parked in the middle of a mosaic compass in the centre of the square, with all of its doors wide open and there was no one to be seen. He also saw there was nowhere for a vehicle to continue from this point.

"Out of the car!" he yelled. "They're on foot!"

Mason and Alicia now listened for any sign of Zabatino or her kidnappers and quickly heard a woman screaming ahead of them down an alleyway. They each took flight together, sprinting as fast as they could down the alleyway past a tobacconist and a small café. Mason almost tripped over an ancient terracotta pot filled with a dwarf rose and cursed as he saved himself from falling over. High above them, a bright blue sky stretched for acres, but the terror on the ground was brought back to them in vivid form when they reached the end of the alley and saw a helicopter parked high above on top of a round tower at the south end of the rocky outcrop on which the little village was built. Alicia took out her gun but there was no way to get a clean shot – they could really only see the tail boom of the chopper and hear its rotors going around.

"They must have got up there somehow!" Alicia said.

The Babylon Agenda

Mason searched for the way up, then he followed the curve of the tower wall around and saw a fire door that had been smashed open. Inside he saw a circular staircase leading up.

"This way!" he cried out.

Alicia ran past him with her gun into the aim and sprinted up the steps. Mason, unarmed followed behind her. Moments later they reached the top of the tower and Mason, still standing a few feet behind Alicia heard her open fire. There was a return of fire, and Alicia slammed inside the doorway, moving from bright sunshine into shadow and holding the gun down at her side.

"There's three of them, plus a pilot," she said. "And Maria."

Without saying another word, she turned and fired more shots from her gun. Mason heard two men cry out in pain and then their bodies hit the deck. Then she fired more shots and spun around to face him as the surviving members of the kidnap crew returned fire.

"I think I hit the tail boom so they're not going anywhere. I'm gonna try and hit the pilot."

"Where the hell is Maria Zabatino?" Mason asked urgently. "That is someone you really don't want to hit."

"Yeah, thanks Sherlock," Alicia said, leaning back around into the sunshine and firing another three rounds. She then ran forward, and Mason followed her up onto the tower roof into the sunshine. He saw the devastation she had caused but never doubted this would be the result. She was one of the most expert marksmen he had ever worked with. All four of the men who had kidnapped Maria Zabatino were now dead, three of them on the roof of the castle sprawled out in pools of blood, and one hunched down dead over the controls of the helicopter with several bullet holes smashed in the aircraft's window right in front of him.

Staggering around in a circle in the middle of the roof was an Italian woman in her thirties with dark brown hair and wearing a wedding dress. Her veil was pushed up over her head and her hands were on her temples. She was muttering to herself. Mason had never seen anyone look quite so distraught. Alicia ran over to her and began to comfort her, putting her arm around her shoulder and wheeling her around to the tower doorway. Mason made his way over to one of the dead men and searched him. He found what he was looking for.

"Very interesting," he said.

Alicia looked down at him as Maria sobbed. "What's very interesting?"

"Something I found on this guy's body. And I think Zabatino is going to be even more interested than us."

Chapter 45

When Mason and Alicia returned to the Costello Brancaccio with Maria Zabatino, the place was crawling with cops. A woman in a Carabinieri uniform immediately walked over to them and took Maria away, while two uniformed male officers cornered Mason and Alicia and began firing questions at them. Mason was losing his patience, but luckily they were called off by Giancarlo Zabatino, who only had to utter a few discreet words to make both of the police officers disappear into thin air.

"She'll be alright, Giancarlo," Alicia said. "We got to her before they could do anything."

Zabatino turned and looked at his sister over his shoulder. She was still sobbing and was now being comforted by her groom-to-be, a tall, slim man in an expensively cut suit wearing a single rose in his buttonhole.

"I hope so, but now that you have brought this Conclave of Darkness into our lives, how can we ever be sure? I do not even know who these people are. Not even I, Grand Master of the Order of Jedediah have even heard of them. Can you imagine the kind of resources and effort it takes to stay secret from me?"

Mason reached into his pocket and pulled out the wallet of the man he had searched back on top of the tower roof. "They're not the Conclave of Darkness Giancarlo. Take a look at this."

Mason opened the wallet and handed it to Zabatino. He watched the Italian man's face as he studied the information that he had just supplied him with.

"But this cannot be true," Zabatino muttered, almost incoherently. "Voluntas Dei has been dead for centuries!"

"Volunteers *what* now?" Alicia asked.

"Voluntas Dei," Zabatino repeated grimly. "It's Latin."

Alicia stuffed her hands into her pockets. "Isn't it always?"

"It means the Will of God," Zabatino said. "May I keep this?" He waved the wallet at Mason.

"Be my guest," Mason said.

"Who is this Will of God?" Alicia asked.

Zabatino sighed. "They are an ancient group. Some say they stretch back to the 12th Century, but I have my doubts about that. I think they were formed during the Reformation in the 16th Century. But it matters not…" Zabatino pocketed the wallet in his suit and replaced his sunglasses as he stepped out onto the stone terrace. "All that matters is that they have made an attack on the Order of Jedediah today, and they struck at the very heart of the organisation by trying to kidnap my sister. Today, a terrible war has broken out between the Order and the Will of

God. I fear much blood will be spilt before there is a victor."

"But why?" Mason asked.

"The Will of God is an extreme, radical Catholic group, who believes the Catholic Church has through most of its existence been far too liberal and not interpreted the – *Will of God* – literally enough. In the past, they created great resistance movements against the Church and fought desperately against any form of modernization. I'm not interested in politics and I never have been, I'm only interested in threats to stability. As I say, today a war has started. They have declared war against the Order of Jedediah and a good part of the Vatican."

"But they're not the Conclave, Giancarlo," Mason said. "And today we're already in the middle of a war against the Conclave."

Zabatino looked across to his sister, now beginning to calm down. The female Carabinieri officer was wiping her streaked mascara from her cheeks, and her fiancé was walking back over to her with a glass of champagne.

"It looks like I owe you for saving my sister's life, Mason," Zabatino said.

"And me," Alicia said.

"And you."

Mason said, "I know how difficult that is for you to say, Giancarlo."

"Then you also know what I'm going to say next."

"You'll help us?" Alicia asked.

Zabatino gave one curt nod of his head and pulled his telephone from his pocket. "I'm going to call Gabriel. He will assemble a force of Knights from the Order of Jedediah and they will accompany you to Babylon. I hope you win your war, Mason."

Mason gave him a genuine, grateful smile. "And I hope you win yours, Giancarlo."

Chapter 46

Mason gazed at the large sweeping black domes high above his head in Baghdad International Airport and was surprised to find himself back in the Middle East so soon. The architecture of the airport was designed to blend modern with traditional Islamic styles, and it worked; there was no misunderstanding about where you were standing when you were waiting in line at the customs desk in the airport. Originally built as RAF Hinaidi, it was used as a strategic base by British and American aircraft during World War Two, and then much later became renamed Saddam International Airport until 2003, when the dictator was removed from power by Western forces.

There was some difficulty at the airport when Alicia and Gabriel went to collect their sidearms from baggage reclaim, but the paperwork of each – the CIA in Alicia's case, and Giancarlo Zabatino and his slightly more shadowy Order in Gabriel's case – checked out eventually and soon they joined the rest of the team and stepped out into the Iraqi heat. They hailed two large eight-seater SUVs to accommodate Mason, Alicia, Holly and Baxter, and Gabriel and his half dozen Jedediah Knights Templar.

Baghdad International Airport was around sixteen kilometres west of downtown Baghdad, and the journey was similar to other trips Mason had made through Middle Eastern desert regions, with crumbling, poorly maintained roads lined with decrepit brown plaster houses and date palms everywhere he looked. This morning the sky was heavily overcast and the atmosphere was thick and humid, which was unusual for this part of the world but happened from time to time when a heavy storm was making itself known. As a consequence, the driver up front had already cranked the air conditioning up to full and Mason, who was sitting beside him in the front repositioned the vent so the cold air was blowing directly on his face. In the back, Holly was buried in her phone as usual. Alicia was sleeping and Baxter was staring out of the window in wonder.

After getting caught up in heavy traffic southwest of downtown, the taxi made its way east along Airport Street before turning north and driving down into the Kindi area of the city where Wilde's friend Rayan al-Rawi had a large townhouse. It was opposite the Al-Zawraa, a small recreational area in the centre of the city filled with various attractions and play equipment for children, and Mason observed hundreds more date palms. When the taxi pulled up, everyone climbed out and Mason paid with a wad of dinars that he had got out of the *Bureau de Change* at the airport while Alicia and Gabriel were arguing about their weapons with the customs staff. There was still some confusion about how the team was going to get from the city down to Babylon, so the SUV drivers were both paid and drove away, leaving the team time to discuss the issue in al-Rawi's townhouse.

Mason walked across the pavement and up the path to the gate which was embedded in a high wall running around the front of al-Rawi's house. There was a buzzer on the side of it which he now pressed and a second later it crackled to life with the sound of someone speaking Arabic. Mason asked if Guy Wilde was staying at the property and then he heard his old friend's voice, not loud and clear but still crackly and distorted.

"Jed! You made it! I'll buzz you in."

They all heard the sound of an electronic buzz, and then the gate clicked open. Mason pushed it open and the team walked through into al-Rawi's garden, before closing the gate firmly behind them. They walked up to the house and by the time they reached it, the front door was wide open and they were greeted by the sight of Guy Wilde standing in front of them with a cold bottle of lager in his hand and a massive smile on his face.

"The Groovy Gang regroups at last!" he said. "This is better than when Zeppelin got back together at the O2 Arena!"

Mason was always vaguely surprised by how much Guy Wilde looked like James May from Top Gear. Seeing him today, standing in al-Rawi's doorway with a beer bottle in his hand, his old heavy metal T-shirt hanging limply from him, his scuffed boots and jeans with a slight tear in them and the enormous mop of shaggy grey hair on his head, did nothing to change that image of him in his mind.

"Do not ever call us that again," Alicia said. "We are not the Groovy Gang. We don't have a name, because we're not a team. We are a loose collection of affiliated specialists who from time to time get together to help someone when they are in need."

"Yeah," Wilde said, his smile widening as he nodded his head up and down, "but how groovy is that?"

Alicia rolled her eyes and pushed past him, followed by Holly who gave him a big hug and a kiss on the cheek. Baxter fronted up to him and presented his hand for a strong, meaty handshake. Mason had somehow graduated to a matey pat on the back and then the five of them stepped inside al-Rawi's townhouse and Wilde closed the door.

Inside was very similar to other Middle Eastern houses Mason had spent time in; it was impeccably clean and tidy with a polished stone floor, and smooth, painted plaster walls. There were not too many windows to minimise the light, which in this part of the world always meant heat, and the lights, at least in the hallway, were embedded in the ceiling. There were two photographs on the wall – classy black and white affairs of al-Rawi's family sitting in some kind of ornate courtyard, but by the time Mason had got round to viewing the second one, he was the only one in the corridor and Wilde was calling for him from down the other end.

"Are you coming or not, Jed? We've got a bit of a groovy party going on down here and it would be great if you could join us!"

Mason shook his head and couldn't help smiling. It was Wilde who knew better than anyone exactly how many of the Conclave's forces were gathering down in Babylon, and yet here he was with a cold beer, having a party in downtown Baghdad with not a care in the world.

He'll outlive us all, Mason thought.

Chapter 47

Wilde saw his old friend step into the main living area from the corridor where he had lingered to look at the photographs and then waved him over with a big smile. Holly, Alicia, and Baxter were already sitting down with al-Rawi and his wife and eldest son in a more brightly lit space on soft chairs, in the middle of which was an enormous table laden with food. Gabriel, and the other men from the Order who had joined him, had already moved through into the back garden and were standing around chatting under the shade of a large sun cloth stretched over part of the patio. Mason was not surprised that Gabriel had chosen to absent himself from the activity.

Wilde now leapt up, as did al-Rawi and his family. The English aristocratic dropout now made the introductions for the fourth time.

"Jed, this is Rayan al-Rawi and his wife Nazik and his eldest son Najem. Rayan is a very good friend of mine and an even closer business associate!"

Al-Rawi found this funnier than Mason and laughed loudly.

"Rayan, Nazik and Najem, this is Jed Mason, a friend of mine who I have travelled the world with over the past year, getting up to all kinds of jolly japes and hijinks."

Wilde watched Mason shake everybody's hands and then asked him, "How did the business go in Tehran – with the necklaces?"

"Good, got rid of all of them except one. He tried to tell me it wasn't authentic, but it definitely is. His loss. You're not in the market for one are you?"

"No, sorry," Mason said with a smile.

"Too bad," Wilde said with a click of his fingers, then directed him over to the table and the enormous serving of food that awaited him.

"This is *quzi*," Wilde began. "Nazik is absolutely first class at making this – it's some roasted lamb on a bed of rice and it's dressed up with almonds, cashews and raisins and that sort of thing. The trick is that the lamb is roasted over almost an entire day and that slow roasting process makes it the best lamb you've ever tasted."

Nazik waved the compliment away. "Please, Guy…"

Wilde winked at her. "It's also stuffed with spices and vegetables and I can't tell you how nice it is. You *are* going to have some. This here is *masgouf*, basically grilled carp. It's one of the oldest recipes in the entire country and goes right back to the…" Here Wilde paused and smiled and pointed his finger almost right into Mason's face. "For ten points?"

"It goes back to the Babylonians," Holly said for Mason. "They used to catch the carp from the Tigris River. It usually involves a simple recipe of olive oil, salt, pepper, turmeric and some tamarind and is grilled traditionally over a special charcoal oven until it's crispy and then it's served with vegetables and dressed up with lemon and rice. Am I right?"

Wilde was impressed and gave her a round of applause. "That is exactly right! I forget that I'm dealing with one of Harvard's biggest brains whenever I'm talking to you."

He continued his tour of the table, pointing out lamb and rice wrapped in vine leaves which he called *dolma* which Mason recognised from the Greek word *dolmades*. Wilde was particularly enthused by a broad bean and egg salad which was described as *bagila bil dihin*. After pointing out some meatballs bound together with rice that looked a little like Italian arancini but which Wilde called *kubba halab*, the tour finally ended with something he called *balah el-sham*, a deep-fried dough sweetened with sugar syrup which Mason guessed was some kind of ancient Middle Eastern doughnut. It all looked great.

"Please," Nazik said, gesturing with her hand as she stood beside Wilde. "Please, help yourself. I have offered this food to those other men but they chose only water."

Wilde turned to see she was now pointing at Gabriel and his force outside in the back garden, beside the fountain.

"Yeah, they are a crazy bunch that sure know how to party," Wilde said. "That's absolutely for sure. You can take it to the bank."

Mason was actually quite hungry and picked up one of the clean plates in a stack on the side of the table and helped himself to various bits and pieces that had been laid out for the guests. Wilde had been correct when he had told him how amazing the slow-roasted lamb was and Mason decided to give it a try when he got back to Portugal. He would either try this recipe exactly, or maybe ask Benedita if there was some sort of Portuguese equivalent. He was sure there would be. The small group chatted as the sun slowly made its way across the sky until late afternoon. Al-Rawi left for a brief time to take a phone call, after which he returned and was able to update Wilde and the others on what was unfolding south of the city in Babylon. It did not sound promising.

"My business associate who works for me down in Babylon says this Conclave seem not only to be there in very large numbers but also seems to be very heavily armed. He has associates all over the area, and he knows that they have been delivering large numbers of guns, and other weapons such as grenades. The word was written in French on the side of some crates. And he also saw explosives – lots and lots of explosives. I think you are absolutely insane to go down and try to fight these men with just the twelve of you."

"We have no choice," Holly said. "They've already murdered the three members of the Fellowship of Light, and many other men and women on this mission. There is no way we can walk away now. The Fellowship wanted us to bring this secret to the world, and we cannot allow the Conclave to win and keep it hidden from humanity any longer."

"Yes, but what is this secret?" Najem asked, giving his father a concerned look.

"We have absolutely no idea," Mason said. "I know that's frustrating, but there it is. I happen to agree with Holly though – there's no way this group would go to this amount of effort if it wasn't a very significant knowledge that they were trying to suppress."

"I still think you're completely insane, especially you Guy! But then again, I have always thought you were completely insane, so perhaps it all makes sense now."

There was some subdued laughter and then Gabriel stepped back into the room. He was holding his phone in his hand and had clearly just made a telephone call.

"There is a safe house belonging to the Order not far from here. We will go there shortly to arm ourselves and then we are to go immediately to Babylon."

"Hold on a minute, I'll decide when we go to Babylon," Mason said.

"Actually, I'm the reason we're doing any of this," Baxter said. "Maybe I should be the one to decide?"

"And I'm the one who knows Babylon better than any of you," Wilde said jovially. "Maybe I should be the one to decide. Just kidding – don't leave any important decision up to me. Ever!"

"None of you are deciding because you're not in charge anymore," Gabriel said. "When you went to the Grand Master and asked him for help, you also gave him authority over this mission. If you want to be in charge, then me and my force will leave immediately and go back to the Vatican. If you do not want that to happen, then I decide when we go, and we go now."

Wilde was as easy-going as they came. He could see that Gabriel had irritated Mason a lot, and the rest of the team didn't look too pleased either, so he decided to try and mellow things out a bit.

"Hey, listen – that's cool! Everyone c'mon! We need to get down there as soon as possible anyway because like you know, man, these guys are already down there with their explosives. They're probably trying to blow up the Tower of Babel as we speak. I say we get down there and get this whole thing sorted out and then come back up here as quickly as possible and carry on with our party."

Gabriel spied him with scepticism. "There will be no party after we have concluded this mission. We are to go to the safe house and arm ourselves at once."

"But we got rid of the cab drivers," Holly said. "Is there some way we can get hold of a new company to send a couple of cars out, Guy?"

"That will not be necessary," Gabriel said, already moving towards the front door. "There are two of our vehicles parked out the front of this house, idling. We go now."

Mason looked at Wilde.

"Looks like we're going to Babylon."

Chapter 48

Mason had not appreciated the tone in which Gabriel had spoken to them back in al-Rawi's home but had little option other than to do as he said and move out at once. He would have preferred to wait until nightfall to make his move on the Conclave who had gathered, as far as they were still aware, south of the Babylonian ruins, presumably in their search for the Tower of Babel. As it was, he was now sitting in the back of one of two Chevrolet Suburbans, as they made their way northeast through Baghdad. They drove on Yafa Street until they crossed the River Tigris and then moved directly into an obviously poorer district, cruising past very poorly maintained residential properties. He watched the Iraqi Ministry of Oil pass on their right before they turned left at the al-Madina International Stadium and drove into Habibiya. From here, they drove northeast again until arriving in Sadr City, an area of Baghdad that would be advisably out of bounds to tourists.

"This place looks pretty rough," Alicia said.

"The Order has had a presence in Sadr City for hundreds of years," Gabriel said, turning from his seat up front beside the driver. "We generally prefer our safe houses to be out in regions away from general interest."

Well, that answered that Mason thought.

The suburban turned left onto a street full of ramshackle, broken-down brick properties, with billboards on their roofs and their facades littered with air conditioning extraction fans. Old 1980s sedans and tuk-tuks were everywhere he looked, and the shop fronts were worn and faded with posters peeling off them. Some of the more beautiful mosaic facades were crumbling to almost total disrepair. A handful of men lingered here and there on the broad, crumbling pavements, and litter gathered in drifts in the gutters like snow back at home in England. The Suburban now turned right and disappeared into a labyrinthine residential area before pulling up outside what looked like an almost totally decrepit hovel.

Gabriel turned as he unbuckled his belt. "If you please, everyone will follow me."

Mason led the team as he followed Gabriel up the path to the wreck of a property, and when they reached the door Gabriel pushed a button and a voice spoke back to him in Latin. Gabriel responded in Latin – too fast even for Holly to follow by the look on her face – and the door opened. Mason followed Gabriel inside and stepped inside the house. The interior looked like it had been partially destroyed by a tornado, with plaster and wallpaper hanging off the walls, chipped tiles on the floor, ceiling plaster stained and peeling, and threadbare curtains half hanging across the windows.

"Looks like this place had one hell of a rave in it," Wilde said, nodding with approval.

"Follow me please," Gabriel said, leading them to a door in the hall on the way to the kitchen. He pushed another button and a similar conversation took place, once again in Latin, and then the door opened and they stepped inside. Mason was amazed to see that they seemed to be standing inside the most modern of high-tech 21st Century rooms. There was a polished concrete floor and smooth plastered walls. No windows. The shelves were black-painted metal and sitting over on the far side at a desk in front of a bank of plasma screens – some sort of security system covering the front of the property and the two parked Suburbans out front – was what Mason had now come to realise another Order man. He was wearing black jeans and a black T-shirt but had that look about him and when he turned and muttered something in Latin to Gabriel it was confirmed. On all of the shelves surrounding this man were more weapons than Mason had seen since he left the army.

"This place is a veritable arsenal!" Alicia said. "I've never seen so many weapons in my life."

"Yeah, it's great isn't it?" Wilde said, turning to Gabriel. "If ever you're in the market for any kind of vintage weapons or anything like that, you know who to call, right?"

Gabriel looked at him as if he had been speaking in a foreign language. "We have no need of vintage weapons. Everything you see here is considered by the Order to be a tool, each one designed and used for a specific purpose, and each purpose building towards the defence of the Order of Jedediah. We have no need for illegally trafficked weapons Mr Wilde."

Wilde waved his hands in a gesture of surrender. "No problem, man. Absolutely no problem. I was just saying if you needed my help, I am definitely the man to ask. By the way, if you're in the market for some beautiful necklaces, I might be able to help you out there, too."

"I have no need for necklaces or any other kind of jewellery," Gabriel said, clearly losing his patience with the Englishman. "I am only interested in serving the Order and obeying the instructions of our Grand Master. He has led the Order through some very dark times and kept us safe over many years, and if he says we should now join you in this fight against the Conclave then so be it."

"Talking of fights," Mason said, fixing his eyes on Gabriel. "Did Zabatino tell you about Voluntas Dei?"

"As a matter of fact he did," Gabriel said, clearly stiffening at the mention of the word. "But I don't see that this is the time or place to be discussing private Order of Jedediah business, especially with someone who is not inside the Order."

"I was good enough to save Maria Zabatino's life," Mason said. "But not good enough for you to talk to me about it?"

"I understand you were very brave. It has been noted in Order records. But you must understand that we can deal with Voluntas Dei, Mr Mason. All you need to do is concentrate on winning your own war against the Conclave."

"What do you think we've been doing for the last day or two?" Holly said. "Twiddling our thumbs?"

"Yeah buddy," Alicia said, raising her hand and jabbing Gabriel in his lapel. "We've been working our tails off running all over America and Europe trying to nail these guys. If it had been up to me, I would have gone down there into the desert and kicked their asses without your help, rather than going on bended knee begging Zabatino."

"No one begged Zabatino," Mason said angrily. "Guy told us they have an army of forty or fifty people down in the desert. Holly and Baxter phoned me up and asked me for my help and my experience, and my experience says five people, including two who don't even have special forces or secret service training, do not beat a force of fifty heavily armed personnel, especially if they've been dug in for a day or two in a defensive position. Asking Zabatino was our only play."

Alicia looked surprised by the tone Mason had taken with her and immediately backed down. "Alright, I'm sorry, Mason. Maybe I shouldn't have said that."

"I don't think you should have said it either," Holly said. "Jed is doing his best to keep us safe and make sure we beat the Conclave. I happen to agree with him, for what it's worth. I wouldn't want to go down there and fight that many conclavists with just the five of us."

Holly now turned to Gabriel. "I'm really glad that you're here, Gabriel. I'm really glad that Zabatino agreed to send you down with us."

Gabriel softened slightly. "For what it's worth, I think the Grand Master made the right decision. You would have been slaughtered down there in the desert, and for all we know the Conclave of Darkness may be rising to challenge the Order of Jedediah. Once again, his wisdom allowed him to make the right decision for us all."

"What, are you sucking up to him all the time so you can be Grand Master one day?" Alicia said.

"The Grand Master of the Order of Jedediah occupies the post for life," Gabriel said. "And as I wish the Grand Master a long and healthy life and I am not that much younger than him, I have never considered the position as one to which I could realistically aspire. Does that answer your very rude question?"

Suitably chastened for the second time in as many minutes, Alicia raised her hands and apologised all over again. "Alright, alright! Let's just get the guns and get the hell out of here!"

"Quite," Gabriel said. "We will take what we need from here and load up the cars. I think you will find we will want for nothing. We have handguns, compact machine pistols, grenades, rocket-propelled grenades, explosives and even anti-personnel mines. I don't think we'll need the anti-personnel mines, but we'll take some anyway just for good measure."

Wilde was once again nodding enthusiastically, his face beaming with joy. "Yeah, just for good measure, man."

Mason was genuinely dumbstruck by the quantity and quality of materiel in this most strange of locations but was determined not to show Gabriel how impressed he was. "Okay, well then let's load up and move out."

"I recommend we do exactly that," Gabriel said.

He opened the door and the six men from the Order were now forming a human chain leading from the weapons room down the corridor, down the front path to the Suburbans.

"Mason," Gabriel said. "You are first in the chain. I understand you know weapons better than most. Start passing what we will need down the line. It is quicker this way than each going in and out of the house."

"Fine." Mason looked over at the shelf and immediately saw a box of Glock handguns and beside them a metal crate full of nine-millimetre ammunition. With an amused shrug, he turned and handed the guns to Wilde who was standing beside him. "Let's get this party rolling, Guy."

Chapter 49

Gabriel was unnerved. He had worked hard to ensure no one in Mason's team was aware of how disconcerted he was about this mission and how nervous the Conclave of Darkness made him. His briefing from the Grand Master of the Order of Jedediah, the splinter group of the Knights Templar of which he was a proud part, Giancarlo Zabatino, who was also a senior officer in the Rome police force, had briefed him fully after Mason's unexpected intervention at his sister's wedding in the Sabine Hills. Zabatino had also been gravely concerned.

Their chief concern was that the Order of Jedediah prided itself on knowing everything that was going on within their sphere of influence, which meant anything connected with religion, belief, the advancement of science and technology and the general wellbeing of mankind. It was a wide remit. Any other secret order or society, or their secrets, no matter how well kept, were generally well known by the Order and kept in their archives.

The fact that this Conclave of Darkness existed at all was of severe concern to the Grand Master and Gabriel, as was the idea they seemed to be the holders of some kind of secret of which they had never heard. That simply would not be able to pass. Gabriel had his orders from the Grand Master, and they were to seize the secret, if at all possible before Mason and his team ever learnt it and return it to the Vatican for analysis and safekeeping under their own stewardship. He was also to destroy the Conclave of Darkness if they were able.

Sitting now in an Order of Jedediah transport helicopter flying out across the rooftops of Baghdad on their way south to Babylon, he found a little time to sit back and reflect on his position in the Order, and his life. How had a man from his relatively impoverished background ended up sitting here, working for the most elite society in the world on board a helicopter racing out of Baghdad and across the sands of the Iraqi desert? How had he become a part of all this? It was a question he had never been able to answer, except if he thought of how devout his belief and commitment were to the organisation. This was why he could never respect a man like Mason, a man who had been part of something important to him – and continually walked away leaving colleagues and friends behind him in his wake, like so much litter. Gabriel never understood how anyone could do this. He would live and serve the Order of Jedediah for the rest of his life, and die doing so, surrounded by its loving embrace. He would be given a warm and loving burial in the special, sacred place where only those in the Order of Jedediah were buried, hidden in a quiet and beautiful grove outside of Rome. His name would be immortalised forever on one of the sacred Order of Jedediah headstones. The Order of Jedediah was his life, he had no other.

Now he would go into battle for the Order against the Conclave of Darkness, but they were now fighting a war on two fronts. Voluntas Dei had made an egregious mistake when they attacked the Grand Master's sisters at the wedding and tried to kidnap her. Preliminary research had revealed little. The ancient group, formed at least four or five hundred years ago, had disagreed with the way the Order of Jedediah was working alongside the Catholic Church, and they also disagreed strongly with the liberalisation of the Catholic Church. Gabriel was slightly sympathetic to some of their views, not that he would ever tell the Grand Master. The Catholic Church, in his opinion, had slid to the point where it was almost ceasing to be a religious organisation and instead was some kind of social organisation. This did not impress Gabriel. However, he strongly disagreed with the way Voluntas Dei did business, and would of course loyally serve the Grand Master and the Order of Jedediah in their total destruction.

It was important that no other group rose to prominence until they became powerful enough to challenge the Order's dominance in the world. This was simple power politics. Voluntas Dei or the Conclave of Darkness made no difference to Gabriel, the Grand Master or anyone else in the Order. Archbishop Vesco, a senior member of the Order of Jedediah who worked closely alongside Giancarlo Zabatino, had already given his full support to the Order's quest against Voluntas Dei, and Gabriel would happily fight them until the last man in their ranks bled out on the ground and died. He now thought exactly the same thing about the Conclave of Darkness. They knew just as little about the Conclave as they did about Voluntas Dei. As far as the Grand Master had briefed him, they were a splinter group who had broken away from the Freemasons some time ago, after one of their leading members had discovered a terrible world-shattering secret under the sands of Babylon.

Gabriel was sceptical. He was always a sceptical man. But this is what had unsettled him so much. If there were earth-shattering secrets to be found in the world, then the Order of Jedediah knew those secrets and guarded them possessively. Could it be possible that another group in the world had known something as serious and important as was being claimed, and managed somehow to keep it from the Order?

He looked across at Mason and the others. How simple and little their lives were, amazed him. Men and women like that woke up in the morning, got their coffee, went off to work, spoke with some friends here and there, came home from work, watched television, ate some food and slept. This was rinsed and repeated throughout the year. Throughout their lives. Most of them never asked questions, at least not the questions that he had asked. Questions that the Order of Jedediah had been able to answer for him. The entire world was one giant lie, and that was the brutal truth. As he had slowly ascended the rank structure of the Order, each year getting closer and closer to the Grand Master, various secrets and truths about the world – totally obscured and kept from the everyday person – had gradually and carefully been revealed to him. At first, he had been shocked, but eventually, he had grown used to the process of revelation.

Most of these secrets concerned history. Nearly everything the people of the world were taught in their history classes was a total lie. He understood that – or at least he thought he understood it. Until today and his briefing from Zabatino about the Conclave of Darkness. He knew things about the history of the world that would amaze or even terrify other people. Now he was being confronted with the harsh possibility, that there was something that had been kept even from the Order.

He looked out across the desert sands and checked his watch. Off to the far right the sun was slowly sinking over the desert, still slightly visible, but still burning bright and hot as it did in this part of the world throughout the year. There were no stars visible yet but they would be visible soon enough. The sand itself was turning from yellow through amber to almost a purple colour. It wasn't as uniform as people thought. When you saw it up close, as he was able to when the chopper descended to less than two hundred feet in anticipation of their imminent landing, he was able to see scraggly bits of plant life, dried-up river beds, and even gnarly bushes and rocks. It was an ugly and foreboding landscape. It was a harsh and hateful world. Not like his beloved Tuscan home, with its olive trees, fruit groves and beautiful hidden valleys. Thinking of these things was enough for him to focus his mind on the task at hand and impress upon him how important it was to be victorious and return home.

And when he came home it would be after having destroyed the Conclave of Darkness and taking possession of their most guarded secret. He turned to his men, who were sitting on his side of the transport helicopter and speaking through the communication system, he solemnly said: *"Victoriam habebimus!"*

We will have victory!

Chapter 50

"We must be victorious, Locusta."

Leonardo Snow had spent the last few hours avoiding the Iraqi desert heat beneath a temporary shade cloth that had been assembled by junior conclavists. Now, as he watched the sun sinking into the western horizon, the temperature had dropped enough for him to step out under the bare sky, but he still cursed at the insane number of flies that were attacking him from all directions. Ahead of him, twenty or thirty feet or so, were the ruins of the archaeologist's house Professor Bernard Drake had found all those years ago. Exactly the same place where he had murdered Drake in cold blood. They were here looking for more rooms, but further out there was another team, the team which had used the coordinates on Fauré's tomb, as returned to the Conclave by Locusta and Scorpio. That team had found something very interesting indeed beneath the shifting sands of Babylon.

Strolling with Lacosta, with his hands in his pockets, and his face partially obscured by a Panama hat, Snow was taking one last look at the original site before wandering over to the new one. The exciting one. He had stayed clear up till now because of the use of explosives and the vague possibility of collapsing through the sand into freshly opened tunnels. Now, standing over the original dig, staring down at the exact place where he had so brutally stabbed Bernard Drake to death, he tried not to recall the details. The archaeologist's corpse was long gone and instead, a team of new archaeologists he had hired from the University of Baghdad, were busy at work trying to find anything Bernard Drake might have missed before Snow killed him.

At least there was no sign of the idiot private investigator, and the Harvard academic, not to mention the one they called Mason – he seemed to be some kind of ex-army man who thought an awful lot of himself. Then there was a former CIA agent called Kane. He didn't know too much about her, the Conclave had more reach than most organisations but there was a limit to its powers. There was a senior Conclave member embedded at the CIA, but he had not yet got back to him with Kane's full details – it hardly mattered, Snow thought with an inward shrug. None of them were here anyway and he had to presume that their attempt to use the Fellowship of Light's treacherous clues had failed to lead them to Babylon. He was certain they would be here by now, had they done so.

Walking past the trench he now strolled over to the new location – the one his chief archaeologist had been able to find after a senior conclavist cryptographer had deciphered critical clues from the tomb of Jean-Michel Fauré in the Lyon Cathedral. Snow was a trader – a corporate raider – a money man, a sharp suit obsessed with power who couldn't care less about codes and clues. He certainly wouldn't waste any of his precious time dithering around trying to solve them. But the cryptographer had told him that there was some kind of code embedded in the tomb in a carving of leaves and flowers. He told him that when it was analysed properly, it yielded a series of geographical coordinates pointing to the exact location where they were standing now – just three hundred metres away from the original dig discovered by Bernard Drake. The actual location was in the middle of nowhere, some distance away from the main Babylonian ruins which he could see now to the north, their sandy sides lit amber by the setting sun, but slowly fading to grey with the dying light.

"How much longer until we're ready?" he snapped.

Scorpio, who was down in the trench with the archaeologists, looked back up. "We're ready to go now, Grand Guardian."

Locusta looked at Snow with hope and greed in her eyes. Snow did not like the greed he saw in those eyes but was of two minds whether to have her neutralised or make her his wife.

"Are they sure?" Snow called down.

"They say that they're ready to pack the explosives, sir," Scorpio called up. "We need to get back some distance because they're going to have to use a lot to blow through a substantial quantity of rock blocking the entrance to the foundations."

The archaeologist Dr Iqbal Basri now crawled up out of the trench using a trench ladder, dusted his hands off and then wiped them on his old well-worn field jacket and fixed Snow in the eyes. "There is a large stone tablet that has been positioned over the top of what we believe is the entrance to a subterranean tunnel leading to the foundations of the Tower of Babel."

"And?" Snow had never felt his destiny so near and so far at the same time.

"We will require nearly all of the explosives to break it up and get it away, so we can gain entrance to the tunnel."

"Well, get on with it then!" Snow said. "We haven't got all day. We've nearly lost all our daylight!"

"That's no problem," Basri said. "We brought lanterns and torches. As soon as that stone tablet is out of the way, we can get down into the tunnel and make our way to the Tower's foundations. But, what is it exactly you hope to find there, though?"

Snow said nothing, but he knew what he hoped to find there. The small carved tablet Bernard Drake had found all those years ago, not only alluded to Babel but to the original creators of the Tower of Babel. It said that much more evidence of them was buried by them in a library deep in the foundations to be found in the far future. Snow thought with amusement that this was, at least from their perspective, the far future. He was the one who was going to find that evidence and keep it for the Conclave. No one else in the world could be trusted with such a desperate and terrifying truth.

"Never mind what I hope to find in there," he snapped. "Everybody get back while these explosives are being put into position! Clear the trenches!"

Another man climbed out of the trench, Dr Emile Liesch. He was in his sixties, with a crumpled cream suit and wore a straw trilby hat. "This is all very impressive, Mr Snow, but I am still unsure why you need an astronomer at the site!"

"All in good time, Dr Liesch."

"As you wish," the Luxembourger said with a smile and a cheery wave before clearing away from the explosion site.

Snow strolled back with Locusta to at least fifty metres away from the new site. The rest of the team had moved to a similar distance in a sort of horseshoe shape around the new trench system. He saw Scorpio and two or three of the other conclavists – all former special forces men – now climb up the ladder and over the top of the trench before walking over to them. When they were beside Snow, Scorpio asked if he had permission to detonate.

"Do it now," Snow said.

Scorpio nodded at one of the special forces men who pushed a button on a tiny remote, less than one second later an enormous explosion roared and echoed out across the desert in every direction. A giant fireball blew up into the sky then quickly turned to smoke and formed the shape of a mini-mushroom cloud. All around it, jets of stone and sand and other detritus sprayed out all over the desert. The earth almost seemed to shake beneath their feet, but then as the smoke slowly disappeared into the sky, Snow had already begun marching forward, gripping a torch in his right hand and a look of steely determination on his face.

He turned to face Locusta. "This evening we take control of the true secret history of the world. And there is no one here to stop us."

Chapter 51

Mason didn't think much of Gabriel or the way he did business. He was secretive and suspicious and he never seemed to either give or accept trust from the people he was working with. The former boxer and soldier from London was having these thoughts as the transport helicopter carrying his team and the Order of Jedediah force was about to land in the desert at the coordinates Holly had deduced from Jean-Michel Fauré's tomb. Mason had no idea how the Fellowship of Light had managed to locate the original Tower of Babel, or why they had done nothing with it – he could only deduce that their discovery of the location had been very recent and they had not had time to gather the manpower or financial resources to make a successful and covert excavation of the site. All he knew was, that it had come down to him and his small team once again, only this time they had no idea what they were about to find down there.

Holly's best deductive reasoning had been able to come up with nothing, and like Alicia and Baxter, Mason himself had no chance if the religious historian from Harvard had come up short. Weirdly enough, Wilde had been full of talk about what might be underneath the desert sands beneath them, although he was more of a layman on the subject and his ideas quite often turned to rambling speculation. Yet, as Mason knew only too well given his line of work, he spent an awful lot of time in the region and spent a lot of time talking to people whose entire lives were centred on the ancient world, including the site of Babylon.

Wilde had explained to them when they had boarded the chopper back in Baghdad, that there had always been a lot of talk linking Babylon to ancient mysteries, specifically about the original provenance of mankind, but Wilde had been a little reluctant to say too much in front of either Holly or Gabriel or both. Mason wasn't sure why but he had noticed Wilde seemed to pull back from his more radical speculation when catching the eye of either of these two people. Mason himself was a blank slate on the subject. He had an ordinary upbringing, as far as he was concerned; he joined the army where he took to boxing – a more pragmatic sport could not be found, in his opinion, and then he'd done retrieval and rescue specialist jobs and espionage work before finding himself sitting on this helicopter. He was not one to have far flung and fanciful ideas about ancient aliens, or whatever the hell it was Wilde was alluding to.

His thoughts were rudely interrupted by the helicopter jerking hard to the left. It nearly knocked everyone out of their seats and had they not been buckled in, they would have been on the floor now. It woke Mason from his daydream in a heartbeat. Suddenly alert and filled with adrenaline, he looked at the faces of the others and was horrified to see through the window opposite him, just over Amy's shoulder, the sight of a surface-to-air missile racing past the helicopter. It was no more than a blinding flash as the missile itself reflected the sunlight outside, and then an enormous billowing column of bubbling smoke behind it. The helicopter jerked again and Mason looked over his shoulder through his window to see a second missile blowing past them, faster than the speed of sound.

"We're under attack!" the pilot said through the headsets. "We're under attack! Ensure you are buckled in properly and brace for impact."

"Where the hell did those arseholes get missiles from?" Mason said.

"I told you, man," Wilde said through the headsets. "Remember?"

Mason noticed Wilde looked unusually relaxed as ever.

"Remember what?" Mason asked.

"Rayan said that they were seriously armed down there – don't you remember? Big boxes of kit? It was more than just guns and grenades – he said there was all kinds of stuff down there. Seems to me the Conclave isn't taking any chances."

On the flight, Gabriel's face had been as inscrutable as ever, but now Mason saw a flash of anger in his eyes. "That is because they want the secret! Whatever it is, it must have the power to control all of the other secret societies in the world!"

"You seem to want it pretty badly too," Mason said.

"We are the Order," Gabriel said. "We control all histories of this world, especially the hidden histories."

"Not unless you brought some missiles with you," Mason said. "And being as I helped you load up the kit from the safe house, I know that we didn't."

The helicopter jerked violently again, this time once more to the left and Mason also felt it rapidly ascending through the air at the same time. His stomach turned over and he felt like a cork being thrown around on a wild ocean during the storm. The truth was, Mason was not a big fan of flying, particularly not in helicopters. He had gradually turned against the practice since buying his farm and realising he preferred his feet very much firmly planted on the earth. Now he was holding onto his seat for dear life and felt like throwing up. He saw a third missile scorching past the window behind Amy's head. The pilot was damn good, but even Mason knew they had been very lucky not to have been killed in the air before even landing at the site.

Holly looked terrified. She was clasping her hands on her face and reminded Mason of the Munch painting The Scream. She was beside herself with fear, absolutely certain that the helicopter was about to be struck by a fourth missile and blown into a thousand pieces. Mason was moving to comfort her when he saw Baxter step in and get to work. He was a good guy, Baxter, and he really appreciated him being on the team. As Baxter put his arm around Holly and told her that everything was going to be okay, Mason felt the helicopter now sinking in the air rapidly. At this point, Gabriel climbed out of his seat and staggered to the back of the helicopter towards the rear door. He pushed a button on the hull of the helicopter and the rear cargo door began to lower. Mason watched Gabriel tear the cloth off of what he had thought had been no more than crates of ammunition to reveal a menacing and substantial general-purpose machine gun bolted into the floor at the back of the helicopter.

Gabriel slammed down behind it as another Order of Jedediah agent, got up and began to feed an ammunition belt into the gun. Gabriel turned over his shoulder and looked at Mason.

"You were saying something about us not being armed properly?"

Mason had no time to reply before the Order of Jedediah man squeezed the trigger and opened fire on what he could now see through the rear door was a small party of conclavists and what looked like an archaeological team standing around a surface-to-air missile battery. Gabriel strafed them with fifty mil rounds, sweeping the machine gun's muzzle from left to right. Mason watched the bullets fly with a certain degree of guilty satisfaction. The bullets chewed into the desert, pocking its surface and spitting up small clouds of sand all over the place, and Mason watched with interest as the rounds gradually snaked their way to the missile battery and hit their target, ripping into several conclavists and a couple of the civilians and killing them on the spot. The helicopter now swung wildly to the port side, pushing Mason forward in his seat. He was only held in place by the belt. A renewed wave of terror came over Holly and she once again turned to Baxter for support. Alicia and Wilde gave each other a high five. The four Order of Jedediah men remained in their seats and looked calm and satisfied with the mission so far.

The helicopter was now turning hard to port, and Mason knew they were coming around for another strike on the missile battery. At that point, someone down on the ground got a fourth missile off and this time Mason was able to see it screeching up towards them through the open rear cargo door. For a moment he honestly thought it was going to come right inside the helicopter and explode but at the very last minute, the pilot pushed the helicopter down even lower and the missile screeched over the top of them. Mason had broken out into a sweat and was working hard to control his nerves. This was as close a situation as he had known to meeting an early demise.

The pilot explained to everyone that they were going lower to reduce the amount of time the missile had before hitting its target. Mason wasn't exactly sure he followed the logic of that, but his former army experience could make sense of it – a missile had to lock onto its target and this needed a certain amount of time, but if the helicopter was really low it would be outside of the most efficient envelope that a surface-to-air missile worked with. As they raced back towards the battery, Mason saw nothing but empty sand through the cargo door then, all of a sudden as they flew over the top of the missile battery, Gabriel opened fire once again, peppering the entire crew with rounds and finishing off any survivors.

"They're out of business," Gabriel said, climbing out from behind the machine gun. "The rest of them have been driven underground into the foundations. We need to get down there immediately."

"Roger that," the pilot said.

Mason looked at Holly, Baxter, Alicia and Wilde as the helicopter yanked them hard to the right then made a hard turn to starboard before coming about, levelling up and descending down into the sands. The rotor wash blew sand up into the air and the back of the chopper, making Holly cough and splutter and cover her eyes. Everyone else was doing the same thing as they unbuckled their belts and walked to the back of the chopper.

"Okay, everyone! We're going in," Gabriel said.

Slightly put out by Gabriel once again taking the leadership position, Mason turned to his own small team and asked them if they were ready to go underground. A round of keen and eager nods, even from Holly, made him feel slightly more satisfied with leading them down into battle against the conclavists.

"Okay then, let's get going," Mason said. "And remember – we have two objectives here today. One, we are to take out the Conclave to the last man. Two, we are to secure whatever secret they have been trying to keep from the world. We can't let them take that away today."

"No, we can't," Gabriel said sternly.

Chapter 52

Leonardo Snow was dimly aware of some kind of firefight playing out on the surface above his head. He heard thuds and bangs and explosions and, from time to time, screams. These things were of concern to him only so far as they might impede his destiny – which meant following Dr Basri down through the tunnel leading to what the dithering Iraqi archaeologist had described as the 'True Heart of Babel'.

Babel.

The very word sent a shiver up Snow's spine. The Tower of Babel held a special significance for many Freemasons, and there were many legends within the organisation about why the Tower was constructed. It was the largest construction to be found anywhere in the many books of the Bible and many believed it was built by the descendants of Noah in the generations following the Great Flood. No one was sure so many thousands of years later why there was a connection between the Freemasons and the Tower of Babel, not least because the very beginnings of Freemasonry have been completely lost in antiquity, but one theory Snow enjoyed was that Freemasonry began as a society when stonemasons thousands of years ago built wonderful constructions such as the Temple of Solomon and the Tower of Babel.

Other explanations about why the Tower of Babel was built were slightly more prosaic, such as the Babylonians building it simply to get closer to their gods in the act of worship. History recorded how the Jews went into exile in Babylon way back in the 6th Century BC and witnessed people from all over the area gathered at the Tower of Babel speaking in multiple languages, and were amazed by how high the tower reached up into the heavens. Snow was clear that this story was describing the Ziggurat of Babel, not what he was about to discover today. Over time, this building and the original account of it from back in the 6th Century BC, enjoyed a process almost like Chinese whispers, until it took on a much greater significance and size than was really true.

But Snow believed the tower, whose foundations he was going to find today, really was as enormous as some of the artwork from the intervening centuries portrayed – especially the wonderful paintings by Pieter Bruegel created back in 1563. The first was a miniature painted on ivory, which many believed was lost to history but was in fact in a safe in the White Fir Lodge, the other two were more famous. They were entitled The Great Tower of Babel and The Little Tower of Babel, each featuring a tower with many stories, stretching up above the clouds and teeming with people all over them. Snow liked to believe in his more fanciful moments that this was what he was about to discover now. The foundation of something that once resembled those immense towers painted by Bruegel, and it was easy for him to imagine them stretching up thousands of feet high above the clouds.

It was also easy for Snow to see why the Tower of Babel had become so important to Freemasons, particularly to the English masons. The Tower was real, he was absolutely certain of that, so had to be built by someone. The architect's house that Bernard Drake had discovered all those years ago belonged to the chief architect of the Tower – Snow was also certain of that – and that chief architect may well have been the very first Mason. How the true purpose of the Tower of Babel never became more commonly known among Freemasons was explained by the first incarnation of the Conclave of Darkness. A splinter group who broke away from the very earliest Freemasons to protect the secret of which he already knew a part and would soon know everything. Emulating those great early men who broke away from the original Conclave of Darkness, Snow had done the right thing by reforming the Conclave today and rededicating their purpose to preserving the secret and keeping it out of the hands of the Masons and anyone else who might want it but did not deserve it.

Many Masons rejected these theories, legends and secrets and in his view, this meant they were simply unworthy of possessing them and guarding them for future generations. That was a job that only the Conclave of

The Babylon Agenda

Darkness could be trusted with. Most Masons today believe that Masonry began with the Temple of Jerusalem and that Solomon was the first Grand Master, but Snow believed that the first Grand Master was the architect of the Tower of Babel, the man whose home Drake discovered and that Masonry began there and not in Jerusalem. Snow had heard some American Masons still talking about what they described as 'anti-diluvian masonry', but most dismissed his latest theories on the subject of their provenance. None of it mattered to Snow; all that mattered to him was that the Conclave of Darkness could trace their provenance to the Tower of Babel's construction, and the secrets they had protected – far older than even they were – were still to be found deep down within its hallowed walls, the same hallowed walls he was now hurrying past. He was flanked by Locusta on one side and Scorpio on the other. Basri was a few steps ahead of them, shining his torch along the corridor and had to be constantly prevented from stopping and marvelling at some strange cuneiform lettering written here or there on various peeling wall paintings.

"Get a move on, Basri!" Snow said. "We haven't got all day for your dawdling."

"You would dawdle too if you knew the significance of these works," Basri said. "For thousands of years, we have searched for the Tower of Babel and now after so many false alarms we finally have the foundations of the real thing! And look at some of this work! Look at this strange mosaic work! This is artistry of a kind even greater than that seen in Egypt thousands of years later. To think that such a place existed for real is enough to strike the breath from one's body, but to see how advanced they were in their art and their poetry is a holy experience!"

"I told you to keep moving," Snow said.

"Yes, I think we need to move along," Emile Liesch said, licking his lips from fear. "If I had known guns would be involved, I would never have agreed to be involved in this venture!"

"You're being paid very handsomely, Dr Liesch," Snow said. "So please remain calm."

Locusta stepped forward, drew her a handgun and put it in between Basri's shoulder blades.

"You heard him," she said. "We want to get to the library as fast as possible. This place is like a maze and we need you to take us there because you're the only one who can read this crazy writing."

Basri surprised Snow by turning and knocking the gun away from his body.

"Don't you dare point that thing at me again!" he said. "I'm helping you, and you need my help. Not only that, but I happen to believe in what we are doing here today. If what you say is true and the ancient Babylonians held some dangerous secret, which they hid down here at the bottom of the Tower of Babel, that this so-called Conclave of Darkness somehow found out about in some way, some kind of secret that will bring terror and devastation to the world. That is no good for anyone."

"That's a very impressive speech," Snow said coldly. "But I'm not interested in your views or whether you endorse my mission or not. Take us to the library immediately or my colleague here will put a bullet in the back of your head."

Basri was defiant. "What will you do then? How will you find the location without me?"

Snow, a hardnosed corporate raider of decades of experience was not one to be bluffed at the poker table. His face was now as cold as steel as he fixed his eyes on the short Iraqi archaeologist. "Don't push your luck, Basri. I've got billions of dollars in my bank account at my disposal, I'll find another version of you in less than a day."

Basri folded his hand, he gave Snow and Locusta a respectful dip of his head. "Very well then, let's just get there."

Snow watched the diminutive academic shuffle away down the corridor, stopping now and again to shine his torch on the walls and read some ancient cunciform. He took them off to the left and then to the right, each one a T junction which Snow had no idea how to navigate, and then they reached some stone steps.

"This goes to the library, to the heart," Basri said.

Snow's heartbeat quickened as he followed Basri down the steps, but when they reached the bottom there was an enormous stone wall.

"What is this, some kind of joke?" Snow said.

Emile Liesch sighed. "It's just a wall!"

Basri was sweating, shining his torch from corner to corner, with no idea what had gone wrong. "I don't understand, my reading of the cuneiform is correct. This is the library down here!"

Locusta stepped forward and pointed the gun at the man's head. "I want to kill you so much."

"Shut up, all of you!" Snow snapped. "Basri, you've made some kind of mistake. Correct it at once."

"Look!" Scorpio said.

Scorpio shone his torch down to the floor where they saw footprints slightly ahead of theirs leading to the stone wall in the dust.

"Then it must be a door!" Snow said.

Basri mopped sweat from his brow with a filthy handkerchief. "I knew I was right!"

Behind him, he heard not the low thud of explosions on the surface, but the crisper, treble chatter of submachine gunfire somewhere inside the foundations. "We have to hurry up, someone's already attacking our men. It must be Mason!"

Basri fell to his hands and knees and started scratching at the dust where Scorpio saw the footprints. He laid his head flat down to the floor with his cheek and temple touching the cold stone and then he blew under the stone blocking the entranceway. Then he got to his feet and dusted himself off. "It is a door! There is a small crack at the bottom of it. But how do we get it open?"

"That's for you to work out," Snow said. "And you've got less than a minute to do so before we are under fire in this corridor and we'll be cut down dead where we stand. You won't need to worry about Locusta shooting you if Mason gets down here."

Basri seemed to understand the urgency and shone his torch over the stone slab impeding the entranceway one more time. This time he put his hand on the surface of the stone and noticed that it began to peel away as he scratched at it with his fingers.

"It is a fake surface! It has been made to look like the same stone on the tunnel walls when in fact it's some kind of strangely painted plaster."

Snow looked more closely and saw the Iraqi archaeologist was right. The door, which had looked no different to the walls on either side of them, was in fact painted to look that way. As Basri scratched away at the surface plaster they were able to see underneath and saw four haut-relief panels of stone, each one containing cuneiform script. Not only that but now they saw the door was made from a circular piece of stone.

"What does it mean?" Snow asked. "Can you read it?"

"It's cuneiform," Basri said. "But it's been altered slightly so it's harder to read."

Snow towered over him. "But you can still read, right?"

Basri nodded enthusiastically. "Yes, I can still read it, but only because I have the benefit of thousands of years of research after cuneiform existed as a language! I think perhaps it would have been harder to crack at the time. There are four panels here and written on them are the cuneiform words for Take, Field and Enemy."

"None of that makes any sense to me," Snow said. Behind him, the machine guns grew louder. "You need to get this door open at once and then you better hope to God you can close it again."

"It is an ancient Babylonian proverb, regarding stealing other people's things and what you can expect if you do that. The proverb is – 'If you take the field of an enemy, the enemy will take your field'. I think they want me to push the panels in the order of the proverb."

"Then get on with it!"

Basri now pushed the six panels in order – Take, Field, Enemy, then Enemy, Take, Field.

Something behind the door clicked with a deep heavy thud, and then the strange circular doorway seemed to drop down, closing the gap Basri had spied through at the bottom. Basri now took hold of the circular door, pushing his fingers in the carved panels for purchase and rolled the enormous stone circle out of the way, to reveal an entirely black space behind it.

Snow looked at Basri and shone the torch in his face. "Well? What's stopping you? Get in there and report back what you see!"

Basri was nervous, but his thirst for archaeological knowledge overcame any fear he might be harbouring, and now he shone his torch inside the circular entranceway and stepped inside. Seeing that he had survived at least a few feet inside the room, and hearing the increasing volume of the gunfire behind him, Snow now ordered Locusta and Scorpio into the blackness. Ordering Scorpio to roll the stone door back into place and wedge it shut, Snow now shone his torch around an enormous stone cavern carved out of the bedrock deep under the Iraqi desert, at the very heart of the foundations of the Tower of Babel. Recesses had been carved in the walls to produce shelves in the rock that contained thousands and thousands of rolled-up papyri, as well as other smaller boxes, and stacks of silver and golden tablets.

"My God," he said. "What have we found?"

Basri swept his hand forward. "The Library of Babel!"

High above their heads, painted in beautiful blues, indigos and blacks, were two murals divided by a simple white line. They were the most intricate, perfect images of the night sky Snow had ever seen. It took his breath away. When Liesch followed Snow's gaze up to the ceiling and saw the breathtaking murals, he gasped. "No, this is wrong."

Snow stared at him with wide, terrified saucer eyes. "What do you see?"

"I see something that is impossible."

Chapter 53

Mason was sick of guns. The thought grew stronger in his mind and heavier in his heart every time he squeezed the trigger and killed another human being. Luckily, thanks to Gabriel taking out the missile battery up on the surface, they had much less work to do to breach the foundations and had now fought their way through two waves of conclavists before finally reaching their first fully underground level.

Gabriel and the Order of Jedediah men, as well as Alicia, seemed to harbour no such doubts about the efficacy of the firearm in this situation and were savagely cutting their way through another defensive line of conclavists who were trying to hold an entranceway to a set of steps. Mason was standing further back beside Holly, Baxter and Wilde. The three of them were also armed but none of them had fired their weapons yet. When Gabriel and his team cried out that they'd killed the last man defending the stairs, Mason watched as the Order of Jedediah force disappeared down into the shadows and turned to Holly and the others.

"Looks like we're going down again."

"I'd be excited, but..." Holly looked at the corpses strewn all over the tunnels and mezzanines of the complex foundations. "But there's just so much killing, Jed!"

Mason couldn't disagree with her there, but reverted to his training and led the three of them down along the corridor and then descended the steps where Gabriel and his men had disappeared a few moments ago. They found themselves in a long corridor which they followed along to the end turning left at a T junction and then following footprints in the sand. Not sure which way to go at another T junction, he followed the voices of Gabriel and his men who were up ahead on the right. They turned right and followed them and found themselves at the bottom of another flight of stairs where Gabriel and his men were standing in front of a strange circular door.

Gabriel turned, a look of anguished frustration on his face. "We need Dr Hope!"

Mason couldn't help but gloat. "You need us?"

"Not *you*, Dr Hope! And now is not the time for this, Mason," Gabriel said. "I can hear them! They are in there now, talking. We need Dr Hope to get through this damn door!"

Everyone made the way clear for Holly to walk down the steps and along the short passageway to the circular door. She stared at the six strange panels for a few moments and then turned not to Gabriel but to Mason.

"It's written in cuneiform," she said. "They're the words for Take, Enemy and Field. I don't know what it means beyond that. Sorry!"

"What do you mean?" Gabriel said. "Some expert!"

Holly frowned at him. "I am an expert in religious theological history, primarily Christianity. I do have some knowledge of cuneiform, which is why I have been able to translate this for you. On the other hand, I have no idea what these words symbolise. They are clearly requiring that we press them in some kind of order to open the door."

"You must be able to do better than that!" Gabriel snapped.

"Watch your mouth!" Mason said.

Gabriel backed down. "I just mean we must be able to do better as a team!"

"We *can* do better," Mason said. He reached into his pack and pulled out some C4 plastic explosives. "Everybody get back to the top of those stairs!"

"Jed, wait!" Holly said. "We don't know what's on the other side of this door – you could be destroying ancient Babylonian treasures!"

"There's no time for that, Holly!" Mason said. "If we destroy anything like that we'll just have to live with it. Get to the top of the stairs right now!"

Mason listened to the footsteps of his small team as they clattered up the stone steps behind him and only took a few moments to position the C4 in the most vulnerable locations around the circular doorway. Then he joined his team at the top of the stairs and hit the detonator switch. An enormous explosion roared through the corridor, almost deafening them, but the C4 explosives had blown the door inwards so they were largely unaffected by the explosive detritus created by the detonation.

Mason reacted quicker than Gabriel after the explosion, raising his handgun into the aim and ordering everyone forward. At the head of the small unit now, he skipped down the steps and ran along the corridor through the dust and smoke, screaming at anyone inside the chamber to drop their weapons. He heard the sound of Gabriel and his men and his own small team running up behind him and fanning out on either side of him, making a lethal horseshoe of people with guns raised. As the dust began to clear, he saw Leonardo Snow standing at the end of the room, with Locusta, Scorpio, Dr Liesch and Dr Basri around him. Liesch was staring up at the ceiling, muttering to himself and Snow was holding a golden tablet in his hands, looking very much like he had seen the very face of God.

"Put it down, Snow!" Mason yelled. "The game is very much up."

Snow was silent, still staring back at Mason with a dreamy, unnerving look on his face as if he had not heard a word he said, nor even the explosion.

"I said put the tablet down and get your hands in the air like the others!"

Mason was holding his Glock in a two-handed grip, and looking down the sights which were pointing directly at the space in between Snow's eyes. His grip was steady and his trigger finger was calm.

"It's true!" Snow said softly. "But it's true. What Bernard Drake found all those years ago, the small tablet we found, telling us about the secret. Why we resurrected the Conclave. Here on this golden tablet… it confirms it's all completely true."

Mason made to shoot snow when Holly brushed his arm with her hand and stopped him.

"What's true, Mr Snow?" she asked.

"The secret," Snow replied as if he was still dreaming. "The original Conclave's secret that we got a brief description of when we found the other tablet in the architect's house, it's true and there's much, much more! There's so much more to it that we could never have dreamed of. It's all completely true. Everything we know is a lie. This whole world is a lie."

Mason followed Liesch's gaze to the ceiling. The murals of the stars were beautiful and instantly captivating but had not much significance for him. He saw that it had made a very different impression on Emile Liesch.

"This cannot be true," the Luxembourger kept muttering, almost to himself.

"What cannot be true?" Holly asked.

"The paintings of the stars," Liesch said. "Their position is all wrong."

The Babylon Agenda

"I'm sorry?" Mason asked.

"It's called celestial navigation, or astronavigation," Liesch said, marvelling and pointing upwards with a trembling finger. "We're talking about precession, the process by which the gradual change in the orientation of the Earth's rotational axis over long periods causes the position of the stars from our view to shift. It's established science today but it was not discovered until somewhere around 150 BC by Hipparchus of Nicaea, in ancient Greece. Not eighteen-thousand years before!"

"But what *exactly* is the problem?" Alicia asked, staring up at the astonishing work of art.

"The problem is," Liesch said, pointing at the mural on the left, "the stars have not been in this position for twenty-thousand years. At least fifteen-thousand years before Babylon was founded. And over here," he now pointed his shaking finger at the mural on the right, "this mural depicts how the stars will look in several thousand years. This knowledge demonstrates a profound understanding of astronomy and artistry that predates our oldest concept of human civilisation by fifteen thousand years."

"If true," Holly said, "this will upturn the world. Science, history, anthropology, religion. Everything will change."

Liesch shook his head. "No. No way. The implications are simply too great. This must be some kind of practical joke. Someone has been down here, into this place, and painted this in the last few years. Only modern computers could predict this mural on the right. The stars won't look like this for something like another twenty-thousand years. It's impossible. The artwork is too precise, too beautiful. Whoever painted it simply could not have known this position of the stars in the first mural unless they had stood here twenty thousand years ago and they could not know the position of the stars in the second mural at all. Not ever. It would be totally impossible. Even fifteen thousand years later when Babylon and Egypt started to rise, our knowledge was nowhere near this level, and neither was our capacity to paint it on murals like this. I feel like I have been punched in the gut. This changes everything we have ever known."

"More than that," Snow mumbled. "It changes all human history. It changes everything. It is the greatest secret in the history of mankind."

Gabriel stepped forward, walking halfway between Mason and Snow. "Give me the tablet."

Snow turned away, shielding the tablet with his body. "Oh, I can't do that." He was clutching it to his chest now and cuddling it, almost as if it were a newborn baby. "I can't give you the secret. You are in the Order of Jedediah. You are a Knight Templar. The Conclave can know the secret, but you cannot know the secret."

Mason had had enough and wanted to take Snow down. He was a dangerous psychotic megalomaniac and the world would be better off without him. On the other hand, he was unarmed and at this exact moment, he assessed him as no threat to human life. He decided to maintain his aim on Snow and let Holly and Gabriel do the talking.

Holly went next. "What does the tablet say, Mr Snow?"

"What I always suspected – just what the much smaller silver tablet told Bernard Drake and me all those years ago – the tablet that belonged to the original architect who designed and built the Tower of Babel! But the silver tablet only told me a tiny fraction of the truth, but now I know the whole truth. The *whole* truth about the world. The whole truth about the people. Humanity. The truth about humanity. The architect was a Mason, but they wanted to share the truth, so he formed the original Conclave of Darkness, who then constructed the Tower to hide the truth. All this got lost in time, but the Conclave existed in pockets here and there across the centuries. Hiding the truth from the light, concealing it whenever it neared the surface. Today it is my job, my most solemn duty to do this. Now you must see. I must continue their legacy. There was one master civilisation, one language, who then designed and built everything we know, from *our* civilisations to *our* languages. I know the truth. I am the Great Guardian."

Mason was concerned at the way Snow's mind seemed to be breaking down and the weird way he was talking, the soft rambling repetition of his sentences. "Holly we need to wrap this up."

Gabriel stepped in once again. He was slowly walking towards Snow. Mason watched Locusta and Scorpio getting anxious as the Order of Jedediah man neared their boss, but they had dropped their weapons after the chaos of the explosion. Their hands were also still raised and the Order of Jedediah men were covering them as were Wilde and Baxter. There was no way they could reach their weapons without being killed.

Gabriel was now immediately in front of Snow, the ageing British stockbroker billionaire, his eyes had now glazed over almost completely and Mason noticed that he was rocking backwards and forwards ever so gently on his heels, trying to comfort himself. He was so out of it, that he didn't notice now as Gabriel slowly prised the tablet from his fingers and took some steps back until he was once again in the middle of the library. Gabriel looked down at the tablet but was none the wiser.

"Only Holly has a chance at reading that," Mason said. "Hand it over to her."

"We have people who can read cuneiform, Mason!" Gabriel said defiantly. "I'll give it to whoever I want."

Holly walked over to Gabriel and put her hand on his shoulder. "It's okay, Gabriel."

Mason watched Gabriel closely. The inscrutable Order of Jedediah man seemed to be breaking. The problem was that he had to know what the tablet said and he had to know it now. Not even the cool and calm Gabriel was prepared to wait for the days it would take to get the tablet back to the Vatican and locate a specialist with the suitable Order of Jedediah security clearance to translate the tablet.

"Go on, man!" Wilde said cheerily. "You know you want to! Give me to Hol!"

Gabriel paused in silence, thinking it through. Then he nodded his head slightly up and down and let Holly pluck it from his hands.

Mason watched as the Harvard academic's eyes crawled over the tablet. Her mouth fell slightly open as she read it and then she began to shake her head from side to side. "This can't be right. None of this can be right."

"It is all completely correct," Snow said, as if to himself and still staring into the middle distance. "It is all true. It is written by the same ones who painted the murals."

"What does it say, Holly?" Mason asked. "Just what the hell is all of this about?"

"It seems to be some kind of a master plan for the world," Holly said, not quite understanding what she was reading or even what she had just said. "It seems to be some kind of blueprint. It talks about creating a master religion, which explains why nearly all the main religions are almost identical in nature, including many of their stories and proverbs. It says that there was one civilisation and all others were based on it."

"Who created this master plan, this blueprint?" Gabriel said.

"They're not named," Holly said. "I think that there was some other civilization here long before Babylon, long before Sumer, long before everything we've ever been told."

"My God, this is dynamite!" Alicia said. "We might finally have found something that's actually worth more than the gold it's written on."

Mason wasn't really understanding what Holly was saying.

"I still don't get it," Baxter said.

Mason was relieved someone else on board the team was also in the dark.

"Keep talking, Hol," Wilde said. "This seems to confirm some of the more insane theories I've come up with."

"Whoever wrote this tablet simply refer to themselves as 'we' and 'us', but the way it's written is odd. It's in cuneiform, which is the language of Babylon, but they talk about creating Babylon in a way that distances them from it. They say they have this blueprint for the whole world and they talk about seeding civilizations around the world, and… oh, my god…"

"What is it, Holly?" Mason asked, genuinely surprised by the vague horror in Holly's voice.

"This can't be right. It talks about Babylon, the civilization of Babylon, but there's talk about the Mayan Pyramids – how they should be constructed. It's about architecture and building. Masons. They talk about civilizations all around the world, but this tablet predates all of them. This is written by some higher civilisation, whose name we don't know. This is their blueprint for creating human civilization, our past, present and future."

The Babylon Agenda

The gravity of what Holly had just said had no time to sink into Mason, because at that moment Locusta dived for the floor and snatched her gun. In one smooth forward roll, she leapt to her feet and fired shots into the Order of Jedediah force, killing three of them immediately. The others fired back, but at that exact same moment, Scorpio dropped to the ground, reached for his gun and fired at them. It was a brutal and savage exchange of gunfire in which Scorpio and Locusta were both killed, as well as every Order of Jedediah man except for Gabriel and one other, a man named Castiel. Even Emile Liesch was cut down, raked with rounds that tore through his cream suit and exploded into his body, killing him where he stood.

Time seemed to slow down. Mason saw Castiel take a bullet in the shoulder and fall to the floor, crying out in agony. Snow raced forward and punched Gabriel in the side of the head, having been woken from his daydream and made the decision to take the secret back into the Conclave's possession. Gabriel was a strong man but had been taken by surprise. He was knocked out and fell to the floor, then Snow grabbed the tablet in the chaos and sprinted for the circular doorway. Alicia spun around and fired a bullet at him, but Snow used the golden tablet as a shield and the bullet ricocheted off of it and smashed into the ceiling. Snow had almost made the door, when Mason fired three shots into his back and killed him, sending him tumbling to the floor, just outside the chamber. He died right in front of them still clasping the golden tablet.

Mason and the other survivors, stood in the gun smoke and said nothing for a long time.

Chapter 54

Night in the desert was cold. When they finally reached the surface and climbed out onto the sands, the surrounding landscape was no longer a burning bright yellow in the burning sun, but a strange dull grey silver in the light of a rising moon in the east. Mason was last out of the foundations, climbing up one of Snow's trench ladders feeling exhausted and disgusted with himself. When he reached the top, he threw his gun off into the sand and joined the rest of the small group who had gathered in front of the bonnet of one of Snow's Land Rovers.

Gabriel had taken possession of the golden tablet back in the library and was now gripping it tightly to his body as he spoke on the phone, presumably checking in with Giancarlo Zabatino and reporting the success of the mission. A major success, Mason thought. The entire top brass of the Conclave of Darkness had been executed and a strange golden tablet talking about the entire future of mankind had been secured for the Order. *Yes, some success*, Mason thought. The world would never know and no matter how much he and the rest of his team talked about it, no one would ever believe them. Holly Hope would certainly never dare publish anything on the subject for fear of being subjected to such utter ridicule it would permanently destroy her career.

Holly, Alicia, Baxter and Wilde were leaning up against the bonnet of the other Land Rover, more than happy to segregate themselves from Gabriel and the one other surviving Order of Jedediah man. Mason walked slowly over to them with his hands in his pocket and a tired smile on his face. His friends looked strange in the moonlight, the desert breeze stirring their hair. They looked tired but they looked strangely energised at the same time. There was a light sparkling in their eyes because they knew something that the other eight billion people in the world did not know. Mason felt the same.

"What do you think Zabatino's telling him?" Baxter asked.

"How do you know he's talking to Zabatino?" Alicia said. "Maybe the dude's ordering a pizza."

"I don't think they deliver out here," Wilde said with a smile.

"He's talking to Zabatino, all right," Mason said.

"Yeah, but I really wish it was a pizza, man," Wilde said. "What I would do right now for a massive pepperoni pizza – a huge twelve-inch job, just glistening with greasy fat and with a big fat crunchy crust! Damn it, I'm hungry. I haven't eaten since Rayan's buffet."

Mason laughed and nodded his head. "I'm pretty hungry too. I guess we'll eat when we get back to Rayan's place in Baghdad."

"Yeah, I'm gonna call ahead and sort something out," Wilde said, pulling his phone from his pocket. "Bugger, the signals really crap. Hang on – I think we're just close enough to the Babylon site to pick something up. Pizza, pizza… I'm gonna have pizza tonight!"

Mason watched Wilde wander off with his phone and then leant up against the bonnet of the car in between Holly and Alicia. "I'm glad that's over."

"Me too," Holly said. "I just can't stand all the killing."

"You two are talking like a couple of big girls," Alicia said. "They were a bunch of Psychopaths! They had it coming. It was a good result."

"And now the Order of Jedediah have the tablet," Mason said. "Even better."

"Look," Alicia said. "Say what you like about Zabatino, but at least he can be reasoned with. At least we know that he keeps his word. He helped us today, didn't he?"

"He helped himself today," Holly said. "Jed saved his sister's life, and then he decided to make it look like he was doing a favour, when in reality, as soon as he found out about the existence of the Conclave of Darkness he was tripping over himself to get involved. He just had to *look* reluctant."

"That's even more cynical than me," Alicia said.

Mason pushed away from the car and kicked some sand up into the air. He looked out across the dunes and watched the moon rising higher in the east.

"For what it's worth," he said. "I'm glad Giancarlo has got it. The Conclave of Darkness was definitely not the right place for information like that, and let's face it – what the hell are we gonna do with it? We're not at that level. This is way above our pay grade. We don't know what to do with information like that. Just let Gabriel take it back to Zabatino, and they can all sit around and talk about it in the Vatican for a few months and then lock it away in their little safe. If they decide it's the right thing to come out with it, then they'll come out with it."

"Why don't you just roll over so I can tickle your tummy?" Holly said.

"Eh?" Mason asked, shocked at her tone.

"The world needs to know about this stuff, Jed!"

"I'm not so sure," Mason said. "I don't even know what it means and I've been involved in crazy stuff like this since I met you guys. Who wrote that tablet? Other humans? I mean it must be, right? Was there another human civilization long before anything we've been told about? Is that what it means? That they planned everything out so we're just like rats in their little maze, and they already know our future? Does it really mean they planned all our civilizations and put them in those places? I don't know. I want to forget about all of that as soon as possible and get back to my olives. The world cannot handle any of this."

"You really like working on your farm, don't you?" Holly asked.

"Yes, I do."

The Babylon Agenda

"Will I ever get an invite to come visit?"

Mason had dreaded the question but had been waiting for it since he'd told them about the farm all those months ago. It wasn't that he didn't enjoy their company, in fact, he very much enjoyed spending time with them, especially when they weren't getting shot at like today. The problem was the way Mason had compartmentalised his life to try to get over the trauma of some of his past experiences. The farm was somewhere that was not connected with anyone else in any way, least of all those he went on violent and aggressive and dangerous missions with. That was one of the reasons why he hated receiving telephone calls from Rosalind Parker there – she was part of the other world, his other world, she was part of the world of espionage and lies and subterfuge and murder. When she telephoned him it felt as if she was reaching into his world through the sky and breaking the peace he had created there. The only person who belonged in that compartment of his life was Benedita and no one else.

Imagining Holly or any of the others at the farm seemed somehow incongruous to him, as weird and unsettling as it would be to imagine Benedita running alongside him with a firearm in some Russian backstreet, taking pot shots at a gangster or fleeing in a stolen car from a member of some deranged secret society intent on world domination. Neither picture worked for him. Neither of them was right. Now he had a real dilemma because he would never want to upset Holly or hurt her feelings in any way or any of the others either. He had to be careful with how he replied, but before he made his response he was saved by the bell.

Gabriel was wandering over to them now, as was Wilde from the other direction. Wilde reached them first, slipped his phone into his pocket and gave them a massive double thumbs up and a beaming smile.

"Good news, shipmates! I managed to convince Rayan to get a pile of pizzas in. They're gonna be there in an hour all ready for us and there's cold beers in the fridge as well. Oh yeah, man, it's party time.

Alicia gave Wilde a high five and communicated her sincere pleasure at the prospect of beers and pizzas. Holly also looked happy and Mason was too. He was hungry and the idea of kicking back in a comfortable, safe garden, looking up at the stars, drinking beer and eating pizza after such a horrible few days was more than a little appealing.

"That sounds like a good time to me," he said.

"Talking of good times," Alicia said. "Here comes Gabriel."

Gabriel was upon them now, but no longer holding the tablet. The other Order of Jedediah man, Castiel, had already taken it back to the transport chopper which was now firing up its rotors in the desert night.

"We're going back to Baghdad," he said. "Like a ride?"

Mason and the team looked at the transport chopper and then at the Land Rovers and then before anyone spoke, Wilde opted for the chopper. Everyone else fell on board with that.

The Babylon Agenda

"And before we go," Gabriel said, "I don't have to tell any of you that you are sworn to secrecy about what you heard down there and everything contained on the tablet."

"Of course," Holly said, without consulting the rest of the team. "I would never discuss anything like that with anyone."

"I believe you and I trust you, Dr Hope," Gabriel said. "What about the four of you?"

If Mason had his way he wouldn't talk to another soul apart from Benedita for the rest of his life anyway. As for Wilde, he had a lot of tall tales and this one would just fall in among the rest of them and get lost. Mason doubted that anyone in the Los Angeles area wanting a private investigator would take anything like this too seriously, and Alicia didn't seem to care less either way. Mason guessed that Gabriel's secret was safe for now.

"We're good, Gabe," Alicia said, giving him a wink.

Gabriel eyed her suspiciously "Good because you have now sworn to the Order of Jedediah to keep a secret. That means if you break it you will be killed."

Wilde laughed but stopped quickly when he realised Gabriel wasn't joking.

"This will be taken back to the Vatican where it will be handled properly and given to the correct people," Gabriel said.

"But what about the site?" Holly asked. "We just discovered the Tower of Babel! The real thing! I know the

Tower no longer exists, but that library is just a treasure trove of ancient information!"

"The Tower of Babel will be secured by Order of Jedediah forces who are already on their way in great numbers. They will examine the site thoroughly for any other evidence relating to what was on the tablet. When we are satisfied that all traces of that have been removed, including all tablets, papyri, and the murals which will be carefully transported back to the Vatican, the Grandmaster has decided very kindly to allow it to be revealed to the world."

"How very generous of him," Alicia said, her voice dripping with sarcasm.

Gabriel looked at her then turned in the sand and walked back to the helicopter. "If you want a ride then hurry up!"

Mason and Holly exchanged a glance.

"Looks like that's our last call to get the hell out of here," Mason said.

Chapter 55

Mason had wandered up to the top of Rayan's house and climbed out onto his rooftop terrace, which his Iraqi host had told him about a few moments ago. The house was in a tidy, prosperous part of Baghdad, although that was a relative term if you were used to rich parts of Western cities. Mason had heard enough of the talk downstairs but had been quietly impressed by his team's maintenance of their vow of Order of Jedediah silence, with none of them, including even Wilde, mentioning even the slightest hint of what had gone on this evening to al-Rawi or his family. Mason wasn't sure if Gabriel had been bluffing or not with the threat of execution, but he didn't want to push his luck and try it out. The Order of Jedediah was an ancient and bloodthirsty organisation as far as he was concerned. He knew they held some pretty dark secrets and he guessed they could keep those secrets only if they played a pretty tough game. Mason would tell absolutely nobody, including Benedita.

He leaned his elbows on the rail running around the patio, sipped some beer and stared up into the night sky. Stars were hard to come by here, even though it was a clear night, thanks to the terrible light pollution burning up from all corners of Baghdad. He thought about what Liesch had told them all before being killed in the crossfire down inside the foundations of the Tower of Babel, what he had said about the positions of the stars, about how it was impossible, how it changed everything. Mason was not a man of science, but he had no reason to doubt the astronomy professor from Luxembourg City.

The implications were profound: the Tower of Bable had been built twenty-thousand years ago by an advanced civilisation, fifteen thousand years before Babylon. Even more unnerving, Liesch seemed to think whoever painted the murals knew how to predict astronomical precession almost eighteen thousand years before we believed had been the case when the Ancient Greeks discovered it. If made public, it would shake up global history in a way never before known. Mason began to see why Snow wanted to keep it secret. He understood why Gabriel and the Order of Jedediah back in the Vatican would almost certainly do the same thing.

So now he turned and leaned his back against the rail and looked out across the patio instead. It was a beautiful space that al-Rawi had made, with a large Persian rug stretched out on the concrete floor, and large potted fan palms at each corner. There were two long three-seater sofas on either side of the rug and a table in the middle with some bowls of nuts and fruit on it. Mason now wandered over to one of the sofas and stretched his long frame out on it, taking one final sip of beer before reaching out and setting it on the table behind a large bowl of pomegranates.

He closed his eyes and was beginning to drift off when he heard footsteps. He knew they were Holly's and now he opened his eyes and craned his neck around to see her walk into view, from his point of view upside down, but she was smiling and she said 'hi'. Then she walked around and sat down on the sofa opposite him. She was holding a bottle of beer half-finished and looked relaxed but tired.

"Well, none of that was on my bingo card for this week!" she said at last.

"Mine neither," Mason said. "And I hope it doesn't happen anytime soon, as well."

"I kind of enjoyed it," Holly said. "I know they were bad people, but just seeing that many people die tonight… I didn't like that at all. Men like Basri and Liesch were totally innocent."

"Maybe not totally innocent," Mason said.

"What do you mean?" Holly asked.

"They took Snow's shilling. They must have known what sort of man he was. Who secretly excavates a desert site with armed men carrying machine pistols? I don't want to speak ill of the dead, but they must have seen that and asked themselves some questions. They answered those questions by turning a blind eye. They allowed their greed for knowledge to go against their better judgement and they paid a price."

"The price was too high," Holly said. "They didn't deserve to die and I don't believe you think that either."

"No, I don't think that. I'm just trying to make the point that you have to be careful not to allow curiosity or greed to force you into making the wrong decision. At the end of the day, all we have is our integrity and the respect of our friends and family. If we do the wrong thing to get something, to make some kind of a gain – lying, stealing, thieving, defrauding someone, turning a blind eye to the insane dreams of men like Leonardo Snow – then we lose more than we gain, because we lose the respect of those who mean the most to us."

"I know that, Jed," Holly said, sipping her beer. "I was brought up to believe in all that and I still do. Ethics are very important to me, in work and life. I'm just saying death seems like a pretty steep price to pay for indulging the crazy aspirations of a man like Snow."

"I guess you're right." Mason took some more beer. The cold, refreshing liquid felt good after the dry, dusty desert sand and air. He didn't really believe Basri or Liesch deserved to die, but his conscience was a little clearer when it came to people like Locusta and Scorpio. They were the cogs that allowed Snow's machine to turn. Had he succeeded and used what he had learnt to inflict harm on the world, they would have been directly responsible for the ensuing misery and chaos. No one would ever know if Basri and Liesch would have continued serving Snow if he had taken control of the Tower's foundations and its contents, or done the right thing and turned on him. The reality of the situation was had they not served Snow, he would have probably had someone like Locusta or Scorpion execute them. In a way, their fates were sealed the moment they agreed to work for him.

Holly stretched back on the sofa, reclining like a princess, bringing her long legs up and stretching them out and crossing them. She was sitting up with her arm draped over the back of the sofa and her other arm on the arm of the chair.

"If it means anything," Mason said, "I feel exactly the same way. I couldn't even count how many people I've taken out of the game with guns. It's been going on for so long now it just feels like it's who I am, but it's not who I am, Holly."

"I know, Jed," she said. "You can see it when we're out there and everyone's shooting and screaming. Your heart's just not in it, but you're very good at what you do. We couldn't have secured the tablet without your help today."

"We didn't secure the tablet. Gabriel secured the tablet."

"C'mon! Don't split hairs. You know what I mean."

She looked off in the direction of her legs and saw someone coming out of the house. She smiled and said hello. The next thing Mason knew, Baxter, Alicia and Guy Wilde had joined the two of them up on the roof. Wilde was ruddy-faced and had clearly been enjoying himself, but Alicia and Baxter seemed a little more with it.

"So, you two have been hiding up here, huh?" Alicia said. "Should we have anything to worry about?"

Holly laughed and glanced at Mason, but Mason shook his head and said no.

"Jeez, I was just making a joke, Mason," Alicia said. "No need to sound so funereal."

Wilde sidled up to Alicia, trying to change the subject. "You're not in the market for a necklace, are you?"

"I might be," she said, eyeing him suspiciously. "But I'm a fashionable girl so I don't want anything too old."

"Ah, that *could* be a problem."

"How old is it – eighties?"

He waved his hand. "A little older than that, Alicia."

"Then count me out."

After the atmosphere cleared again, Holly in her usual optimistic and upbeat tone asked everyone what their plans were for the next few days. "Because I'm gonna stay in Baghdad and take a look around some of the sites and museums! Anyone wanna stay with me?"

"I will, man," Wilde said. "I've got nothing going on for a little while."

"Anyone else?" Holly asked, looking at Mason.

"Not me," Baxter said. "I hate to say it, but I gotta get back to LA. I have some terrible news to break to Mrs Sullivan. Not only am I gonna have to report that back to her, but I'm also gonna have to tell my friends in the LAPD so they can start a formal investigation. So I'm gonna get straight back – back to business! Who would have thought I could ever say that? I finally cracked another great case!"

"That's too bad," Holly said, "but I understand why you have to go back, Baxter. What about you Alicia?"

"No, forget about me."

"Still babysitting that little tyrant, Siren?"

"You've gotta be kidding, right?" Alicia said. "No, I'm not gonna do any more of that. One of my guys got killed on the job protecting her, and I know his funeral's gonna be happening next week, so I'm gonna want some time to be part of that. And then I'm gonna take some time out and go visit some family. They have a fishing cabin up in Minnesota. I'm gonna go up there and have a think about things for a few days. So count me out."

Holly looked at Mason. "I suppose I don't need to ask what you're doing?"

Mason now swung his legs around to make room on the sofa for the others and shook his head at Holly. "No, you don't have to ask, Holly. I'm touched you thought about inviting me, all the same. I'm going back to Portugal first thing in the morning and trying once again to dedicate myself to the grand, old cultivation of olives. Life seems to have other plans for me, but I'm determined to have it my way, no matter what fate throws at me."

"Good luck all the same," Holly said.

Mason thought he might need some luck as well, especially after what happened since his so-called 'retirement' started. He thought the first thing he might do when he got back was bury his phone, then after that he'd see how life panned out. He had some hope at last, having looked at his phone before Holly had joined him on the patio and seen three missed calls from Benedita, each one asking him if he was okay. This was an encouraging sign. This made him happy, but one way or the other, he knew deep in his heart that it was time for the killing to stop. He needed to save his soul. He had to redeem himself and if redemption could be found anywhere, it was in the dry dusty hills of olive-growing country.

Author's Note

Thanks for reading this latest instalment in the Mason series and as always I really hope you enjoyed reading it. I originally created Mason, the ex-British Army boxer and assassin back in 2017 when I wrote *The Raiders* and he was always one of my favourite characters to write, so it's always a pleasure to give him another mission. With that in mind, the next stories will most likely be two more Mason novellas: *The Inferno Sanction* and *The Labyrinth Key*.

About the Author

Rob Jones has published thirty-seven in the genres of action-adventure, action-thriller and crime. Many of his chart-topping titles have enjoyed number-one rankings and all of his Joe Hawke, Hunter Files and Jed Mason books have been international bestsellers.